P9-DEK-805

Tempting Fate

ALSO BY JANE GREEN

Family Pictures

Another Piece of My Heart

Promises to Keep

Dune Road

Straight Talking

Jemima J

Mr. Maybe

Bookends

Babyville

Spellbound

The Other Woman

Swapping Lives

Second Chance

The Beach House

Tempting Fate

JANE GREEN

St. Martin's Press
New York

This is a work of fiction. All of the characters, organizations, and events portrayed in this novel are either products of the author's imagination or are used fictitiously.

www.stmartins.com

Library of Congress Cataloging-in-Publication Data

Green, Jane, 1968-

Tempting fate / Jane Green.—1st ed.

p. cm.

ISBN 978-0-312-59184-7 (hardcover)

ISBN 978-1-4668-4203-8 (e-book)

1. Middle-aged women—Fiction. 2. Empty nesters—Fiction. 3. Family secrets—Fiction. 4. Domestic fiction. I. Title.

PR6057.R3443T46 2014

823'.914—dc23 2013031011

St. Martin's Press books may be purchased for educational, business, or promotional use. For information on bulk purchases, please contact Macmillan Corporate and Premium Sales Department at 1-800-221-7945, extension 5442, or write specialmarkets@macmillan.com.

First Edition: March 2014

10 9 8 7 6 5 4 3 2 1

Acknowledgments

As always, my extraordinary publishing team and home at St. Martin's Press, and my family at Penguin in the UK. Louise Moore for so much love and support over all these years together, and Jen Enderlin, who has swept into my life and dusted out all the corners, with so much wisdom, brilliance, and talent.

My agents—Anthony Goff, who has blessed me with sage advice and true friendship for such a very long time, and the incomparable Jennifer Rudolph Walsh, for whom I am truly grateful.

My friends—you know who you are.

Michael Palmer, who so graciously and kindly offered up his wonderful old farm in New Hampshire for me to use as a writing retreat. Without Michael, this book would not have been written, and that's no exaggeration.

The people who helped enormously in coming up with the story, aided with research, and supported me throughout.

Glenn Ferrari, Alberto Hamonet, Dr. Adam Rosen, Dusty Thomason, and Randy Zuckerman.

To the many people who were open and honest enough to share their heartbreak and their stories with me.

Finally, my husband, Ian, who is truly the only man I want to walk with, side by side, as we continue the journey.

Part One

One

It's just a night out with girlfriends, not the Academy Awards, thinks Gabby, frowning at her wardrobe as she endlessly pushes hangers back and forth, hoping something compelling, something worthy, will suddenly appear and jump out at her: the perfect shirt, the perfect dress.

It shouldn't matter, this being a girls' night out, but of course it matters far more than a night out with Elliott. She is dressing for the other women, not to attract the attention of men, although she has heard that on these girls' nights out, it is not unusual for men to gather round the girls, not seeing, or ignoring, the wedding rings on all their fingers; ignoring the wedding rings so often on their own.

Gabby doesn't care about these men, but she wants to fit in, wants to at least look like she has made something of an effort, that she too can scrub up into something of a glamourpuss, that she deserves her place at the bar, just like the rest of this particular group of friends.

She settles on black pants, all the better to hide her thighs with, and knee-high boots, the only pair in her wardrobe that have something of a heel. These boots are almost ten years old, old enough for them to have gone completely out of fashion, then revolve full circle to be not dissimilar to all the boots she passes in the store windows in town.

She bought them when it seemed important to look good, before life, children, pots, and pans got in the way, before it was easier to slip her feet into furry Merrells and be done with it.

In their thirties, all her friends wore the same dull uniforms, but suddenly, in their forties, these same girls are reemerging from their self-imposed cocoons, eschewing the dull blanket of motherhood and grind, emerging in a flurry of bright chiffons and silks as their children no longer needed babysitters, tripping out on girls' nights out in impossibly high heels and blown-out silky hair they flick flirtatiously, wanting to be *seen*.

Gabby does not have bright chiffons and silks, *would* not have bright chiffons and silks for that is not her style, but she does find a black floaty blouse that no one needs to know was $15.95 from Marshalls. As long as you didn't look too closely, you might think it was silk organza rather than the eminently more practical polyester.

There. A shake of her hair, a brush of mascara, a slick of gloss. She looks good, she thinks, without looking as if she is trying too hard. Unlike some of the others, in their plunging blouses and glittery jewelry, Gabby looks as if she is out to have fun with the girls, men be damned.

Gabby orders a second martini, knowing she won't be able to leave anytime soon, wishing she had turned down the invitation to go out, was tucked up warmly in bed, watching a movie, her husband by her side.

When Ella invited her to a girls' dinner, Gabby had looked forward to a large table of fun women in the corner of the Grey Goose, but when she and Claire arrived, the women had already established themselves at the bar, and were lapping up the attentions of a swarm of eager, older lotharios, flicking their hair back as they gave the men flirtatious smiles, punctuating every sentence with loud and, to Gabby's ears, slightly forced laughter.

The energy these women are giving off, their overt flirting, is making Gabby uncomfortable. Used to seeing them with their husbands, or occasionally during the day by herself for walks around the beach or lunch, she is unused to this transformation. It is discomfiting to see these women, who she had assumed were just like herself, turn into the seductive, provocative creatures who are here tonight. Married to Elliott for eighteen years, Gabby no longer has the desire or inclination to flirt. Even if she did, she's pretty sure she's forgotten how to do it.

Although, she thinks, examining herself in the mirror lining the back wall of the bar, it would be nice if someone, anyone, looked at her these days. Lately she has felt more and more invisible. Last week she went into New York, and noticed that as she walked up Park Avenue, during what was clearly lunch hour, all the men passing her flicked their eyes to the two younger women flanking her, in miniskirts and high-heeled boots. She didn't blame them particularly, but surely one would catch her eye, look her up and down. Even an old one. Someone. Anyone.

Her growing handful of grey hairs was subsequently banished this week with a chestnut brown dye, and she has made an uncharacteristic effort tonight, but it is nothing compared to the effort her friends have made. It is because I am English, she often thinks.

I may have lived here for years and years, but I simply can't pull off high maintenance. It's just not me. Look at Ella, with her springy curls, her chiffon blouse that displays more than a hint of cleavage, her high-heeled sandals bouncing prettily at the end of a tanned leg.

Look at the tanned older man—attractive if you like a touch of lechery—now whispering in her ear as she laughs, her body tilted toward him, looking up at him through thick lashes.

What are all these women *doing*? wonders Gabby. Why are they behaving like this? I know these women, know their families; my children go to school with their children. How have I not seen this side of them before, and what does it say about them? About me?

"Is this as much of a scene as I think it is?" murmurs a voice next to her. Gabby turns, finding herself facing a young man. He gestures at her friends with a shake of his head. "I feel like I'm in a cattle market."

"I know," Gabby says with a polite smile. "I haven't been here before. It's pretty . . . intense."

"That it is. And not my scene. I'm Matt." He offers his hand as Gabby shakes it, noting his rolled-up blue sleeves, his strong arms, remembering for a moment how it felt to have the bloom of youth, for he must be in his late twenties. At forty-three she is almost . . . almost old enough to be his mother, and it is this that causes her to relax, smile as she introduces herself.

"I'm Gabby." She settles into her chair, relieved to have someone to talk to, someone who has no ulterior motive, who has not come here to pick up women. Even if he had, he would definitely not be interested in her.

She looks at him curiously. He is, by any definition, gorgeous. Dark hair, blue eyes, a twinkle and a kindness in his eyes that were she twenty years younger and single, she would find utterly disarming.

"So why are you here, Matt? Particularly if it's not your scene."

"Good question." He grins, showing straight white teeth, raising his glass and toasting her. "I'm here on business. One night only. I'm staying across the street, but I thought I'd grab a drink here before I check in."

"Business?"

"I have a social media website."

"Like Facebook?"

He laughs. "I wish. Maybe one day."

"Would I know it?"

"I don't know," he says, naming a website that Gabby knows well; that everyone knows well.

"That's you?" She looks at him again, reassessing, for she has read about this company, knows it was started by two young men, the heirs apparent to the Facebook throne. She was mistaken in thinking he was just some kid. He is an accomplished businessman—she recalls articles about him, how they built the company, and she is impressed. And excited.

"You're huge!"

He cocks an eyebrow, as Gabby blushes and starts to laugh. "Sorry. I mean, I know exactly who you are. I've read about you."

"It's such a weird thing, that I have this strange kind of celebrity that isn't. No one would have any idea who I am, but as soon as I mention the company, everyone knows."

"At least you're able to sit anonymously at bars. And I bet you have an amazing house." She peers at him with a teasing smile.

He snorts with laughter. "It's true. I do have an amazing house."

"Is it in LA?"

"Better. Malibu."

"Oh, God." She groans. "Do you step outside your living room onto a beach?"

He grins as Gabby prods him for a description of the kind of house she has always dreamed about.

They keep talking, Matt telling her about some of the more glamorous parties he's been to, including providing her with celebrity gossip that is better than any issue of *People* magazine. Gabby hangs on to every word, everyone and everything in the room dropping away as she notices nothing other than the fun she is having.

"And it was Lil Wayne," he says, finishing his story. "Sorry. You probably don't—"

"Know who Lil Wayne is?" Gabby scowls. "Believe it or not, despite being a middle-aged mom, I know exactly who he is."

She stops, midsentence, as Matt lays a hand on her arm.

"You're hardly middle-aged," he says, frowning. "You're, what? In your thirties?"

Gabby looks down at his hand on her arm, noting how beautiful his hands are, how smooth and strong. Briefly she wonders why he has not removed it, before looking back up at him with a burst of laughter, enjoying herself.

"Right," she says. "Ten years ago, perhaps. I'm forty-three, and yes, that definitely classifies me as middle-aged."

Matt shakes his head in genuine bemusement. "I swear I'm not just saying this, but you really don't look it. I thought you were around thirty-four."

"I think I may love you." Gabby grins. "Although your point of reference probably stops at thirty-five. At your age you can't imagine there *is* anyone older."

"Bullshit." He grins. "And I'm not that young. There's hardly anything between us."

"Let me guess." Her eyes run over his face, taking in the

smoothness of his skin, the lack of lines around his eyes. She thinks of Elliott, his hair now more grey than brown, the deep lines around his eyes when he smiles, his physique, once so toned, now soft and cuddly; comfortable.

Everything about Matt shouts youth. His jeans, his scuffed-up brown boots. His blue shirt tucked into his jeans, with hints of intensive working-out rather than the paunch she is used to seeing in Elliott, in most of the men she knows.

"I think you're twenty-seven," she says.

"I knew you thought I was younger. For your information, I'm thirty-three. See, we're not so far apart."

"You may think that now, but wait until you're forty-three and you look back at how much you changed over that ten years."

He gazes at her over his glass. "How have *you* changed over ten years?"

"Seriously?"

He nods, calling the bartender over and ordering another martini for her, giving her pause to think.

For the truth is, not much has changed in the last ten years. Ten years ago she was married to Elliott, as she is now, only with smaller children. They lived in a different neighborhood. She drove an old Cherokee. Her life was preschool and playdates, coffees with women she hardly sees anymore. She had less lines, less grey hair, was fifteen pounds lighter.

Ten years ago she cared about dressing up and going out. Ten years ago she made an effort, wanting to be popular, pretty, invited to people's houses for dinner. She and Elliott would go camping, up in Vermont. They hiked, and skied. Now it is all she can do to take the dog for a walk.

What has happened in the last ten years? she thinks. When did life become so . . . she won't use the word "dull," chooses instead to use "pots and pans." How did she and Elliott drift so seamlessly into middle age, and where did all that energy go?

She can't tell all that to this stranger, choosing instead to share the positive.

"I am more comfortable in my skin. Turning forty was a turning point. I stopped needing to prove myself to anyone. I probably ought to make more of an effort"—she gestures to her friends, all of whom now make more of an effort, at the other end of the bar with a new group of men—"but I love that it doesn't matter to me anymore."

"I think you look great," Matt says evenly. There is not a hint of flirtation in his voice, and yet, as he says it, he holds her gaze until she blushes and looks away, feeling something inside her give a slight jolt.

Don't be ridiculous, she tells herself. *There is no way in hell this lovely young boy is flirting with you. I have no idea what just happened, other than that it is in my imagination.*

Gabby covers her embarrassment with a forced bark of laughter. "My friends over there?" She gestures toward them. "*They* look great."

He glances over before turning back to Gabby with a dismissive shake of his head. "No. To me they all look overdone. Too much makeup, too much hair, too much flounce. I prefer my women natural. Like you." There it is. That gaze again.

Grateful for the darkness, Gabby flushes as she says thank you, jumping as the phone in her back pocket starts to vibrate. She pulls it out to see Elliott's name on the screen.

"I have to get this," she says, hopping off the stool. "I'll be right back."

Threading through the crowd, she breathes a sigh of relief. Even if she was imagining it, she has not led him on. She told him she is married. That should put him off, if, indeed, there is anything to put off. Which there couldn't possibly be.

"Hi honey!" She sits down on a low stone wall outside, aware suddenly that she is not as sober as she had thought. "Are you having fun?"

"Not as much fun as it sounds like you're having!" laughs Elliott as Gabby starts. What does he mean? How does he know she's talking to Matt? But it's only talking. How does he know?

"What do you mean?" she says slowly, attempting to sound as sober as possible, knowing Elliott will know.

"First of all, it was noisy as hell when you picked up, secondly, I know you're having a girls' night out tonight, and third, you're drunk, and don't try to deny it because I always know. I can hear it in your voice."

Gabby laughs. "You're right. I'm stopping now."

"What are you drinking?"

"Martinis."

"Aha! Just remember, martinis are like a woman's breasts: one is too few, three is too many."

"I'm on two and done."

"Who's driving?"

"Ella. How's the camping? How are the girls?"

"They're having the best time. They tried going swimming in the lake with Sasha and Jolie, but it was too cold. They're dying to get to the s'mores later. This was a great idea, even though we miss you."

"I miss you, too," Gabby says, out of habit, although she hasn't thought about Elliott for a second since he left early this morning.

"And you were right to suggest I do this with Tim. Not that we wouldn't have had a great time, but I know you feel a bit done with sleeping bags and tents."

"Damn right," laughs Gabby. "What time are you home tomorrow?"

"Not until midafternoon, I think. You go and have fun with the girls. I love you."

"I love you, too."

Gabby walks back inside, seeing Matt through the crowd, her stool next to him empty, and as she moves back toward the bar he turns and watches her, smiling, and she feels another jolt.

Don't be pathetic, she thinks. Don't think this is something other than a nice guy who's bored and lonely, eager to have a friendly face to talk to. Not that I wouldn't be enormously flattered if he were flirting, but look at you! Look at him, now look at you. Even if he were flirting, which he isn't, there would be no point. I'm happily married to the loveliest man in the world. But if he is flirting, even though he's not, it would be nice to feel attractive again. It would be nice to feel that I still have it, even if it's only for three more minutes.

"Gabby?" Her arm is grabbed as she spins to find herself face-to-face with Claire. "Who is that adorable guy at the bar? I can't believe you've been flirting with someone all evening! We haven't even seen you!"

"I'm not flirting," Gabby says, certain that she is not. "I don't flirt. I don't know how to flirt anymore. I'm just having a really interesting conversation with a sweet young guy."

"He's not sweet." Claire glances at him. "He's a stone-cold fox!"

"Right." She nods. "And he's twelve."

Claire squints as she looks across the room. "He's not twelve. He's at least twenty-seven. Old enough to know what he's doing. . . ."

"Claire!" Gabby reprimands. "First of all, he's ten years younger than me, and secondly, hello? I'm married. Remember?"

"We're all married." She winks. "Doesn't mean we can't have a little fun."

Gabby doesn't ask her what she means by "fun." She shakes her head with a laugh as if Claire's suggestion is ridiculous, then moves toward the bar, where Matt is waiting with a big smile.

On the way there, Gabby is aware she is standing straighter, smiling more widely, giving off an aura that is causing the other men to turn and look at her in admiration.

Because tonight, thanks to this younger man who is paying her attention, Gabby feels beautiful. Despite her incredulity that he may be flirting, deep down she is aware of a connection between them. She has no plans to do anything about it—Gabby would never be unfaithful—but it has been years since she felt desirable; years since she felt sexy, beautiful. It is a powerful, heady feeling, and once tonight is over, it will be gone. Once tonight is over, she will once again be a middle-aged suburban housewife, caught up in the pots and pans of life.

What's the harm in dragging it out just a little bit longer? She isn't going to do anything.

Absolutely not.

Everything okay?" Matt flicks his eyes to her phone.

"Just my husband. Checking in." Now she has said it. She has a husband. "He's with our girls, camping in Vermont." She breathes a sigh of relief, knowing she is safe now the information is out there. There is no pretense at being available anymore, and what man would not respect the presence of another?

"What's your husband like?"

This was unexpected. "You'd love him," she says. "Seriously. The two of you would get on like a house on fire."

"I'm sure we would. He's a man of excellent taste." Matt grins, as Gabby teasingly smacks him on the arm.

"Flatterer," she giggles.

"Truth teller." He grins back. "So what *is* he like?"

How does she describe Elliott? From the moment she met him, both of them sitting at the same table, at the same time, at a coffee shop in New York, she knew he was exactly the kind of man she had been waiting for. She was twenty-three, working at a bookstore in the city; he was five years older, a doctor, doing his internship at New York-Presbyterian.

He had asked if he could share her table, even though there were several empty ones; he spent the next two hours distracting Gabby from her work, and making her laugh with his impromptu stories about the people waiting in line, so that eventually she shoved her sketchbook and pencil into her bag and gave up any attempt at drawing.

The next day she met him at Central Park for a walk. He showed up with a basket that had belonged to his grandmother stuffed full of badly made sandwiches and packets of chips in every flavor because he didn't know which flavor she'd like, and didn't want her to be disappointed.

"I am married to the most wonderful man in the world."

Matt smiles. "What makes him wonderful?"

"He's brilliant," she starts. "And kind. He's curious about everyone and everything, and is the kind of man that everyone feels instantly relaxed with. He's warm, and caring. And a great father. We have two girls, and they're the apple of his eye. He's a great husband. I'm lucky. . . ." She trails off, aware she is doing a hard sell, unsure suddenly of who she is doing the hard sell for.

"He sounds wonderful."

"He is."

"What does he do?"

"He's a doctor. Gastroenterologist. So, obviously, the good bedside manner helps."

I am a doctor's wife, she thinks. Which is exactly what it sounds like. Stable. Safe. And just a tiny bit dull.

For a second she indulges in a fantasy. What if she were a dotcom billionaire's wife? What then? She sees herself padding around a glass house in Malibu, in one of Matt's shirts, her legs having suddenly become miraculously tanned and toned, her hair a good six inches longer than it could ever be, given that she has been trying to grow it for ten years and it still doesn't reach much farther than her shoulders.

Imagine the parties they would go to! She and Matt, laughing together as they lean on a deck overlooking the ocean, the wind blowing her very long hair around, no sign of cellulite, children, or ex-husband, no sign of anything from her former life.

She shakes her head. What are you doing? she thinks. Are you completely mad?

"Another martini?" Matt is about to gesture the bartender over.

"God, no!" she says. "A martini is like—"

"A woman's breasts." He smiles. "I know."

"I should probably think about leaving," she says regretfully, not wanting to leave, but feeling as if they have reached the end. What is the point in staying, after all. There is a ripple of danger just below the surface of her consciousness, and she knows she has to go home.

"How are you getting home?" Disappointment is in his eyes. "You can't drive."

Gabby laughs. "Trust me, I know that. One of the girls is

driving." She looks over to where her friends are, were, but there is no sign of them. "Oh shit," she mutters. "Where are they?"

Matt is amused. "They deserted you? What kind of friends are they?"

"Crap ones," Gabby says, annoyed, as she gets her phone out to text them. Matt laughs.

> WE DIDN'T WANT TO DISTURB YOU ;) TELL US EVERYTHING TOMORROW!

"They've gone?" Matt doesn't see the text, but he sees the look on Gabby's face.

"I can't believe they left without me. That's just awful."

"Tell you what," Matt says. "Why don't you come to the hotel. We can have some coffee and they'll call you a cab."

Gabby studies his face. There is no ulterior motive; it is just a coffee, and she could do with a coffee right now.

He pulls notes out of a wallet and lays them on the bar, refusing to let Gabby contribute, then stands up as Gabby does the same. He is tall, much taller than her, and her heart does a small flip as she sizes him up.

Despite being twelve, he is unutterably gorgeous. Oh if only this were several lifetimes ago. She looks up at him, at the thick brown hair, the strength and breadth of his shoulders.

Matt checks in to the hotel while Gabby curls up on a sofa in the lobby, feeling, suddenly, unsure. Why is she here? Why is she having coffee in a hotel with a stranger while her husband is away? Of course she's not going to do anything, but hasn't this gone far enough? Wouldn't it be so very much better if she went home now?

Matt turns round and smiles at her from across the room, and her heart does that thing again, that flip. Not because she's planning on doing anything, but because being with him makes her feel beautiful again. It's been so long since anyone has noticed her; so long since Gabby has been *seen*.

She will not be unfaithful, she would never be unfaithful to Elliott, who she loves with all her heart and soul. But her self-esteem, already so fragile, can treasure this evening, this gentle chemistry, this feeling of someone as gorgeous as Matt being interested in her, for years to come.

And what would be the harm?

I've really had fun tonight," Gabby sighs, a couple of hours later. Coffee became Irish coffee, and she is aware that her sobriety said goodbye a very long time ago.

"For the record," Matt says, "I don't make a habit of sitting at bars and flirting with lovely looking ladies. Especially when I'm traveling for work. You have made a boring business trip completely delightful."

Gabby says nothing, too busy twisting the words he just used over and over in his mind. "Flirting!" "Lovely looking!" I wasn't imagining it!

"I'll have them call you a cab." He doesn't move.

There is no one else in the hotel lounge. It is now the early hours of the morning. One receptionist is there, the lights dim.

Matt and Gabby stare at each other, as Gabby wills herself to move, to get up, to get out and go home before . . . before it's too late. But she can't move. Her heart is pounding, an unfamiliar heat is coursing through her body, and she knows she has to go, but she can't do anything other than stare into the eyes of this man as she lets out a deep sigh.

"Why are all the women I like unavailable?" he whispers, as

Gabby's heart threatens to jump out of her body. She doesn't know what to say. She wants to leave, knows she has to leave, but oh how she wants to stay.

"I should go." Her voice is a whisper, and mustering all the strength she can manage, she reluctantly climbs to her feet.

Two

Minutes stretch into hours as Gabby thinks about getting out of bed. When she was a student at Bristol University, hangovers were a way of life. Her group of friends would pound back shots on pub crawls, then somehow manage to crawl out of bed the next morning and make it to lectures.

Despite the hangovers, the nausea, she didn't stop drinking. It was part and parcel of university life in England, part and parcel of growing up. She hasn't been drunk in years, not since she and Elliott first started dating. Perhaps a handful of times—less—since the girls were born.

She now knows her limits. Being drunk may be fun, but it isn't worth it. This isn't worth it. She had no idea, last night, that she had drunk enough to make her feel as bad as she does now. Martinis. Irish coffees. Mixing drinks. That's what did it. That's why she feels like living death this morning.

The bathroom used to be so close, but overnight it seems to have moved three miles farther away. If I can get to the shower, she thinks, I'll feel so much better. She can almost feel the cold water pouring over her head, the relief the shower will bring, but the journey from the bed to the bathroom feels like an impossible feat. She actually doesn't think she can move, and although she wants to think about last night, thinking about it means thinking about the martinis she drank, and if she thinks about that she may very well throw up. Instead she imagines jumping in a swimming pool, feeling the cool water surround her, bringing her back to normality. It helps.

Her head is pounding, her throat dry. She squints at the curtains, then at the clock, knowing there is nothing to do but wait until she feels strong enough to make it to the bathroom, the shower, life.

Hours later, she stands under the water, making it as cold as she can bear, finally starting to feel human again. She scrubs her hair, wraps herself in a terry-cloth robe, and goes downstairs to make some strong black coffee. Years ago, watching *Cabaret*, she remembers Sally Bowles swigging a Prairie Oyster—a raw egg swirled with Worcestershire sauce—as a hangover cure. As a teenager, she would do this regularly, with no idea whether it worked or not, because she wanted to be like Sally Bowles.

As a forty-something mother, she's pretty certain a Prairie Oyster would make her throw up. Instead she brews strong black coffee, so thick it's almost Turkish, and intersperses coffee with sips of ginger ale.

Elliott and the girls will be back later. She has hours for herself, but wishes she didn't feel quite so awful, wishes she could actually do something with this afternoon off, rather than slump on the sofa with coffee and the remote control.

Her phone buzzes.

"I've been trying you all morning!" Claire says. "Where have you been?"

"I had the ringer switched off and the phone was in my bag. I didn't hear it. What's going on?"

Claire barks with laughter. "Never mind me, what's going on with you? Or should I say, what was going on with you last night? We left and you were engrossed with the totally hot guy at the bar. Tell me you were a good girl. . . ."

There is a smile in Claire's voice, only because she *knows* Gabby was a good girl. Were she to suspect anything else, she would never ask with this lilt in her voice, never dare tease over something so serious.

For a second Gabby is tempted to tell her how close she came, and how confusing she finds this today. She loves her husband, so how could she be attracted to someone else? And this morning she is quite clear: she was attracted to him.

A problem shared is a problem halved, and even though this isn't a problem, there is a part of her that wants to shout out that she is still desirable; that she isn't as middle-aged and dowdy as she might appear, that someone young and hot wanted her.

But she could never tell anyone what she's thinking. Not even Claire, who she trusts above everyone else. Except Elliott.

"Of course I was a good girl." Gabby forces a laugh. "But God, he was so cute! And so young! If ever I was going to be a bad girl, please let it be with someone who looks like that. . . ."

"Aw," grumbles Claire. "We were taking bets on whether you'd be a bad girl."

"That's terrible!" Gabby says. "This is me you're talking about, remember? I'm the last person in the world who'd misbehave."

"Exactly! That's what I said, but Ella said you were in the zone, and once you're in the zone, rational thought goes out the window.

She was convinced you would have made out with him, even though I told her you'd never do that."

"What does that mean, in the zone?"

"When lust takes over and you forget everything except the person sitting at the bar next to you," Claire explains. "I have to say, when we left, you were engrossed. We were all trying to get your attention from the other side of the room, but you never even looked up."

"Of course I didn't look up," blusters Gabby. "How could I have done when the view was so pretty. Have you heard from the boys?" She changes the subject, too much noise in her head, needing quiet to process what happened, or didn't happen, last night. "Any idea when they're getting back?"

"Tim just called. They're going to leave in a couple of hours or so after some off-roading. I'm glad the two boys did this. It's good for them to have some time together, and even better for us to have quiet time. Don't you love it when the house is completely quiet on a weekend? This just feels like luxury. I'm exhausted. I'm still in my pajamas, and I'm not sure I'm going to get dressed at all. I may just lie on the sofa and watch *Downton Abbey*, eating chocolates. Want to come and veg with me?"

"I think I may veg on my own sofa," Gabby says, unsure that she can face more interrogation. "I'm feeling a day of back-to-back *Mad Men* coming on."

"Okay. I'm going to call Ella. She had to practically push that guy off her last night."

"Which guy?"

"That guy Nick? Oh, you weren't with us. He's apparently one of the dads from school, but he was there with a bunch of guys, and he totally came on to Ella. Can you believe it? I mean, I know Ella was flirting, but we all were. It was just fun. This guy thought she was up for it, and Ella knows his wife!"

"Who's his wife?" Gabby is relieved someone else is the focus of the conversation.

"Jeannie? Quiet, kind of mousy. Her kid is Phoebe?"

"I know her. And I know the husband. I always thought he was a sleaze."

"Now we know for sure. He invited Ella outside for a cigarette, then he grabbed her and tried to stick his tongue in her mouth! Can you believe it? Isn't that the grossest thing you ever heard?"

"Oh my God!" Gabby says. "Ella *smokes*?"

The truth is, she can believe it. She can believe all of it. When they first moved to the suburbs, in their late twenties, with one baby, no one would have dreamed of being unfaithful. Too busy building their families, shuffling to mommy-and-me groups, bleary-eyed from lack of sleep, the women she knew were either wearing maternity clothes as they waited for babies to arrive, or because they weren't able to get their prepregnancy figures back.

No one had time to exercise, unless it constituted a leisurely walk around the beach with children strapped safely in a stroller. They certainly didn't have the time, energy, or inclination to have an affair.

Even the marriages that perhaps should never have been, the marriages kept together by the glue of their children, the routine of making new friends, building a home in an unfamiliar town, trucked along with no question of either husband or wife ever being unfaithful.

The years have passed, and Gabby and her friends are no longer the newcomers to town, young women with babies, convinced they are the only women in the world to have babies, demanding the world stop to accommodate them.

Gabby often finds herself standing in line at CVS as a young mother with a baby stresses out over the lack of the right formula. Everything in her body language, her speech, announces that she is a mother! She has a baby! She is more important than everyone else! Gabby looks around and catches the eye of other middle-aged mothers, their grey roots beginning to show, puffy shadows under their eyes, fleeces and clogs because they can no longer be bothered to dress to impress, and they exchange understanding smiles at these young, entitled women.

I remember when I too thought the world revolved around me, says the smile; I remember when I too thought I knew everything, deserved everything, was entitled to everything and more.

Oh how little we knew.

Few of the mothers worked, when Gabby moved to town. They were, they announced proudly, "stay-at-home moms." They volunteered to be room mothers, joined the PTA, accompanied the children on every field trip, showed up in the classroom having spontaneously baked twenty-four nut-free, lactose-free, gluten-free cupcakes.

These same women were left stranded by the time their children entered middle school. The women who didn't work suddenly longed to have something to do all day, longed to reinvent themselves, or perhaps find themselves again. They would invariably take up Zumba or yoga, meet friends for lunch daily at the Organic Market before slowly rejoining the workforce: some working part-time, others attempting to run businesses from the comfort of their kitchen table.

Gabby was lucky in that she was able to follow a different path. Using her long-forgotten creativity, she started restoring furniture, initially for herself. When the other mothers saw how she picked up cheap tables at the consignment store and stripped them, refinishing them to look like beautiful antiques, they wanted her to do the same for them, and soon she had a business.

A few of her friends have worked all along. Trish, one of the other mothers, was one of the first women Gabby knew to divorce. Soon after her fourth child was born, her husband announced he was leaving her for his secretary. She started designing accessories for the home—vases, trays, boxes, cachepots—and is now stocked throughout the country. Every time a new range comes out, she has a house sale, each time hosted by a different woman who lives in town, with various friends working for the day to help sell, each of them leaving with a renewed sense of purpose, ideas for businesses of their own.

The bodies of her friends have changed. Once soft and squishy, elastic from the stresses and strains of childbirth, those bodies have, in their forties, suddenly been honed into toned shape, from Pilates, yoga, spinning.

Dowdy during the days of her kids' early childhood, Gabby is surrounded by two extremes of women now that she is approaching the afternoon of life: the women like her, in their shapeless, comfortable clothes, secure in their husband's love, in their place in the world, who have not yet felt the need to reinvent themselves as time slips slowly away; and the glamourpusses like Trish, who have reinvented themselves in middle age, although Trish has doubtless been perfect since the day she was born.

The glamourpusses may be forty-something, but they are fitter, prettier, far better dressed than they were back then.

Partly because they have to be. In this affluent town, at this age, there is always someone around the next corner who could take their place. And it isn't just the women who need to be worried. In the last year, four women Gabby knows—not friends, but women from the neighborhood she has known for years—have suddenly left their husbands. They say they have been unhappy for years, tell stories of how terrible the husbands are, even when the husbands have always seemed delightful, before everyone discovers that in each of the cases, there were other men involved.

In one case, the husband of her best friend. In the others, random men, picked up at the gym or, at an AA meeting, the contractor.

Gabby found herself sitting in living rooms for coffee as these women told tales of how terrible their husband had been, before swooning with delight as they lit up describing the perfection of their new man.

"But nothing happened," they each swore. "He was just a friend until my husband and I split up."

Each time, they described these men as their soul mates. Why else would they have broken up their marriages, exploded their lives, alienated, or at the very least caused immeasurable pain to, their children? No one likes to think of themselves as the kind of person who would have an affair; who would ever betray their spouse so monumentally, so unforgiveably, so heartlessly unless they had no choice? Unless they found the one person the Gods had chosen for them, the one person they were supposed to have married, had circumstances not got in the way and slipped their boring old husband in instead.

Of the four wives that had left, three of them were no longer with their "soul mates." One of them had confessed to Ella she had made a terrible mistake. She would do anything to turn the clock back, but her husband had met someone else. He was not only happy, but happier than he had been with wife number one. It was too late, and now she spent her kidless weekends at bars much like the one last night, wondering how her life ended up such a mess.

Gabby, who had always thought of it as a midlife crisis, hadn't ever really understood why these women left their stable lives, their loving husbands, their comfortable homes. Until today, as she slouches back on the sofa, blankly staring at the television screen, knowing exactly how these things happen.

"You have a choice," she was fond of saying. "Just because you're married doesn't mean you're not attracted to anyone else. You're married, not dead. We're all going to be attracted to other people at some point, but ultimately it comes down to a choice." So easy to say when you have never been presented with a choice, and honestly? Gabby had never felt an attraction to anyone other than Elliott since the moment they met.

Last night, Gabby had a choice; she had many choices. She could have gone home with her friends. She could have called a cab from the bar, not gone back to the hotel with him, because however much she may try to deny it, even to herself, she knew the possibility was there.

That moment in the hotel lobby, late, quiet, when their eyes locked and held, neither of them speaking, chemistry surging in waves. She had a choice then. She could have so easily stayed, let him lean forward, kiss her gently on the lips. He didn't, but she knows he would have. She sits, playing this moment in her mind over and over again. He didn't, but he would have. He didn't, but he could have.

And if he had, how would it have felt?

And if he had, how would she be feeling now?

She shudders, lust and guilt replacing the small smile that unbeknownst to her has been playing on her lips since she started thinking about him.

She didn't do anything. She has nothing to feel guilty about. She is married, not dead. This isn't nearly the big deal it could have been, and if she can't stop thinking about it, so what? This is just . . . flattery. This is just . . . pleasurable: having the undivided attention of someone other than her husband, feeling the sparks of attraction fly between them, was . . . exhilarating.

Even now, she is torn between feeling sick with guilt at even considering the thought, and elated at still being desirable, still having a sexual power she's not sure she was ever aware of having. She and Elliott have always had a great sex life, but it is great partly because they are so comfortable with each other. Making love with Elliott is a tried and tested routine, with little variation. She has never wanted more variation, has been perfectly happy with the routine they have had, is almost always brought to orgasm, feels entirely sated afterward.

But it doesn't light fires anymore. She's not sure it ever did.

Last night was a blaze of glory. She pictures Elliott moving inside her, his eyes filled with longing and love, and feels . . . content. She pictures Matt, imagines him flipping her over, his fingers inside her, mouth on her nipple, and she gasps, her entire body flooded with desire.

Thank God nothing happened, she thinks. For if he were to phone, now, and say come with me, I need you at my side, she honestly isn't sure she'd be able to say no. There was no talk of them staying in touch. Even though Gabby could get hold of him—his email flashes up on the home page of his website—she knows already she will not.

He is too dangerous, she decides. She cannot be in touch with him. She may have mentioned her email in passing, but he'll never get in touch. Why would he? He must have thousands of women flocking, and she was just a passing fancy. Perhaps he has a penchant for older women; perhaps he is attracted to the unavailable. Either way, last night has to be written off as a fun flirtation that needs to filed away and never thought of again.

Three

Elliott tries to pull away, but Gabby is holding on tight, and he laughs, stepping forward again and lifting her up.

"Wow!" he murmurs into her hair. "You really missed me, huh? I should go away more often."

"No!" Gabby says into his shoulder, pulling back to gaze at her husband, the man she loves, welling up at what she could so easily have done, at the shame of even having the temerity to daydream about another man when Elliott is here, with all the familiarity, and comfort, and love that she needs.

How could she possibly have thought about anyone else? "I missed you."

"Liar," he teases. "I heard you last night. You were having a great time with the girls. I bet you didn't even think about me."

"I'm just glad you're home," she says, kissing him full on the mouth as he smiles in delight and raises an eyebrow, gesturing toward the house.

"Ewww." Olivia brushes past them, scowling the typical scowl of a sixteen-year-old. "Can you not do that in front of us? That's gross."

"Kissing is entirely natural," Elliott says. "And we are your parents. It's not like there's anything illicit going on here."

Gabby quickly looks away. Why did he say that? Why would he choose those words? She looks at him carefully, but there is no way he knows anything, not that there's anything to know, merely a harmless flirtation. Thank God.

"Hi sweetie." Gabby puts an arm around Alanna and pulls her in to kiss the side of her head. "Did you have fun?"

"Uh-huh," Alanna manages, her attention focused on her phone as Gabby suppresses a pang. Grief would be too strong a word for it, but oh how she misses the days when her girls were tiny, when they adored everything she did; when they wanted nothing other than to spend time with their mother.

Looking at them now, Alanna so petite, with her dark blond hair streaming down her back, the image of her father, and Olivia, tall and curvy, her dark curly hair just like Gabby's, just beginning to find comfort in her skin, it is hard to reconcile them with the small girls they once were.

Olivia, when young, wouldn't let her leave the bedroom at night. Gabby would go in to snuggle, adoring how her tiny body fit so perfectly into hers, adoring how Olivia would chatter away, using everything she could to make her mother stay longer. Gabby never wanted to leave, and only ever did when the clock ticked on, and she knew Olivia had to go to sleep.

Now, at eleven, Alanna barely lets Gabby in her room, and Gabby doesn't remember the last time she snuggled in behind Olivia and gave her a cuddle. Even Alanna, so calm, so wise, is now far more interested in her friends than in her mother. Gabby knows so little about what is going on with Alanna in school, she has started doing the unthinkable and going through her texts. Still, she learns nothing.

Oh how she misses the early years, the delicious all-consuming love, the hours and hours of doing nothing other than playing with the babies, watching them with wonder and love, unable to believe she had created these two miraculous little lives.

"Tell me she didn't spend the entire camping trip on the phone?" She turns to Elliott.

"Not the entire time," he says, as Alanna looks up.

"I'm not on the phone. I'm on Instagram," she says.

"Oh." Gabby nods. "Well that's okay then. So how many followers do you have now?"

"Three hundred and forty two." Alanna grins.

"Wow. You are popular!"

"Mom." She rolls her eyes. "It's not about popular."

"So what is it about?"

Alanna shakes her head dismissively as she disappears inside. "You wouldn't understand."

"You wouldn't," Elliott corroborates, pulling their bags from the car. "Neither would I, apparently. We're too old."

Usually Gabby would laugh and agree, except she didn't feel old this weekend. For the first time in years, she didn't feel like she was past it, and she's not ready to relinquish the feeling that life still holds possibilities, that there are still adventures to be had, even if she will never repeat the adventure of last night.

"How was Alanna? Was she sweet?"

Alanna, always known as the good one, has become more of a handful over the past few months. Middle school, not easy for anyone, has seen Alanna occasionally accepted by the girls she has always referred to as the Populars, and with that occasional acceptance comes an attitude that Gabby and Elliott have not welcomed in the slightest.

"She was pretty crabby when we got there, but she settled down. We really did have a lovely time. Tim and I think you and Claire should come next time."

"I thought you said you understood sleeping bags weren't my thing anymore."

"We could get a blow-up mattress. It was amazing, being out in nature."

"I'm totally happy being out in nature, as long as it's at a spa." Gabby grins.

"By the way, Tim said we should go to their house for dinner tonight. He's got a ton of burgers and dogs he needs to get rid of."

"Perfect." Gabby sets the bags down on the floor of the hallways and starts to unpack, pulling out clothes for the laundry. "I'll ring Claire and see what I can bring."

"First I think you should come upstairs." Elliott puts his arms around her from behind, nuzzling her neck, as Gabby, who so often pushes him away, telling him no, insisting she's too busy, or his timing is horrible, or she's not in the mood, allows herself to be led to their room.

With the door locked, Gabby sinks to her knees, unbuckling Elliott's pants, as he murmurs in surprise and delight.

It is, she realizes, the least she can do.

Years ago, when they were first married, they swore they would never become the kind of couple they so often saw around town. Couples who sat in restaurants together, looking around the room, with nothing to say to each other. They swore they would never become like the friends they knew who would laughingly relate how little sex they had: Who has the energy? they'd say. Who has the time?

Gabby and Elliott have never been a couple to sit in silence. Elliott wakes up in the morning and turns to Gabby, invariably starting a conversation about something he's been thinking about since he woke up. It could be politics, the solution to the town parking problem, his fears for the future of the world.

In turn, Gabby shares everything with Elliott. Unlike so many of her friends whose husbands are gone for most of the day, who turn to their girlfriends for everything in their lives, Gabby has never needed much more than Elliott. She has Claire, her closest friend, and is included in the group of girls, but would never phone any of them for a chat, wouldn't think to turn to them if ever there were a problem in her life. The only best friend she has ever really had, has ever wanted, could ever truly count on, is Elliott.

He says it's because they have been together twenty years, but there are plenty of couples Gabby sees who have been together as long—longer—and they are not friends in the way she and Elliott are.

When they met, Elliott was talking about marriage by the end of their third date. Everyone told Gabby she was crazy, and much too young, at twenty-three, to even think about settling down.

Which is why she waited to get married until she was twenty-five. And still, everyone was wrong.

Although, and it is only grudgingly she will admit this, their sex life is not what it was. Gabby loves the smell of Elliott, the warmth and closeness their lovemaking brings, but, and she would never say this to him, if they only had sex every once in a while, it really wouldn't bother her.

It isn't that she doesn't think about sex. It isn't that she doesn't get turned on reading certain books, or watching certain films; it isn't that she doesn't masturbate. It's more that Elliott is her best friend, her family, and although she always enjoys their lovemaking once they start, the thought of making love with him is just one she rarely entertains.

Frankly she'd rather read a good book and have an early night.

Claire and Tim watch porn together, which Claire says has transformed their sex life. Tim has no idea that both Gabby and Elliott know this, and although Elliott suggested they do the same, the few times they tried Gabby found herself critiquing the acting, the fake boobs, the thrusting that goes on for hours that she finds exhausting.

It didn't do anything for her, although Elliott was demonstrably more imaginative for a little while.

Oral sex, while an imperative part of their lovemaking during those early years, rarely happens anymore, and for Gabby to initiate it is unheard of.

Until now. Naturally Elliott doesn't think to question why. Doesn't wonder if this is the female equivalent of the guilt gift—women get jewelry when their men have strayed, or thought too seriously about straying.

And the men? They get blow jobs.

He just closes his eyes and succumbs to the waves of pleasure washing over him.

Four

Pushing open Claire's back door, a door they know almost as well as their own, Gabby, Elliott, and the girls walk through the mudroom, gingerly stepping over the sneakers and backpacks littering the floor, through to the kitchen, where Claire is making a salad.

"Hi girls!" She greets Olivia and Alanna first. "Sasha and Jolie are outside on the trampoline, and I think Sydney's upstairs. Go on out. Or up. Did you have fun camping . . . ?" she calls after them as an afterthought, but they're already out the back door.

Gabby puts her bowl on the table and slides out of her fleece, as Elliott walks outside to find Tim. She is grateful to be here tonight, to do something as familiar and normal as a barbeque at Claire and Tim's. Each normal step she makes is a step away from the events of last night, from thinking about what could have happened, in what is rapidly becoming obsessive.

"What did you make?" Claire peers over at the bowl Gabby is carrying.

"Asian slaw."

"Yum! I love that slaw. Trish is coming, too. She's made some kind of meringue dessert."

"Oh God. It's going to be some kind of perfect dessert. I wish I'd known she was coming. I would have made more of an effort," says Gabby.

Claire laughs. "Will you stop? Why do you always have this thing about her? You think she's judging everyone else by her standards, but she really isn't looking to see what other people bring, and before you say anything, she doesn't care what anyone looks like either. Despite what you're always saying. You know it's your insecurity and nothing to do with her."

"I know. She's so nice, but she's so perfect, and really, how is it possible for one person to be amazing at *everything*?"

"I don't know, but she's bringing some guy she's dating. Ella said he's gorgeous."

"Of course he is. As if she'd date anyone less?" Gabby peers at Claire. "Speaking of gorgeous, you look good. Did you spend the entire day in bed? You look totally well-rested."

Claire smiles. "I feel good. Hang on." She goes to the back door. "Tim? Will you come in? You too, Elliott."

Tim walks in, leaning down to give Claire a kiss before standing next to her with his arm around her shoulders.

"O-kay." Gabby looks at Elliott, then back to her friends. "Would someone mind telling me what's going on here?"

"We have some news." Claire grins. "We wanted to tell you together and we wanted you to be the first to know."

Gabby frowns. It can't be what she thinks, because Claire is older than her, and it wouldn't be fair, and she has never talked about it, and she knows Gabby wanted—

"We're pregnant!" Tim says, as Claire's eyes fill with tears.

"Can you believe it?" she says to Gabby, opening her arms to embrace Gabby in a hug.

"Oh boy!" Elliott embraces Tim, then Claire, Gabby doing the same, as a dagger of pain slices her heart in two. It's exactly what she was dreading, exactly what she had always wanted, but for her. "That's huge!"

"It's huge!" Gabby says. Her eyes are filled with tears, but she smiles through them, leading Tim and Claire to believe she is as overwhelmed with joy as they. "When did you find out?" she asks.

"About an hour ago!" Claire grins. "I'm not telling anyone else because God only knows what'll happen. I mean, I'm forty-four! But I told Tim I had to tell one person because I just can't keep this excitement in, and you're our closest friends. So. We shouldn't celebrate, not yet, but I couldn't get through the evening pretending everything was normal."

"I'm glad you told us," Gabby lies, hugging Claire before excusing herself to go to the bathroom.

She doesn't go to the bathroom off the kitchen. She walks through the house to the formal powder room, for it is quiet, and secluded.

She doesn't want anyone to hear her cry.

Six months ago, Gabby finally did the unthinkable, sorting through her closet and boxing up all her maternity clothes, tearful, numb, finally reluctantly acknowledging there wouldn't be another child; her baby days were done.

She pulled the baby seats, and strollers, and bouncy chairs out from the attic, the brightly colored toys her daughters had long outgrown, and piled them in the car, then she dropped them off at Goodwill, feeling nothing.

She had never been able to get rid of the baby things before, knowing she wasn't done with having children, no matter what Elliott thought. Her two girls were wonderful, but three was the magic number, the number she had always dreamed of. She didn't care whether the third was a boy or a girl, only that there would be a third.

After Alanna was born, she and Elliott decided to wait for a while when the girls were small. Elliott was getting settled, and a doctor's salary isn't what it used to be. He always said they should wait until they had some more money in the bank; until they could really afford it.

The years went by, and it never seemed like the right time. Gabby wondered whether she should accidentally-on-purpose get pregnant; say she was on the pill but forget to take it, deliberately puncture a condom, tell him the timing made pregnancy impossible, that she had finished her period that morning, when in fact she was at the height of ovulation.

But she couldn't lie, couldn't deliberately deceive the man she loved. Not then. So she waited for the right time, for Elliott to decide that they could do it. At thirty-nine she started to panic, and Elliott started to voice his second thoughts. They were already settled, they had two beautiful girls; he didn't want any more children.

Other people fight about money, disciplining kids, in-laws. The only thing Gabby and Elliott fight about, have ever fought about, was this. Once Elliott voiced his not wanting more children, his stance grew ever firmer. Gabby thought she could change his mind, persuade him otherwise, but he was clear: there were going to be no more children.

And even though Gabby knew she could never deliberately trick him into having a baby, she knew she could be a little less . . . careful. She learned to be forgetful about taking the pill; she welcomed going on antibiotics, knowing it reduced the efficacy of the pill, praying each time she would become pregnant.

In the back of her bathroom cabinet is a paper bag filled with pregnancy tests, and each time she had been "forgetful," she would unwrap a test, on the first day her period was due—as the years went by her periods were more and more erratic, sometimes disappearing altogether for a month or two—holding her breath with excited anticipation as she peed, her whole body flooded with disappointment when the tests had a negative result.

Six months ago, Elliott announced he was having a vasectomy. He had been thinking about it for a long time, and there was no question in his mind it was the most efficient form of birth control. He couldn't ask her to have her tubes tied, and frankly, it was bad enough that she had to take the pill. She had gone through childbirth twice; now it was his turn.

It was the fair thing to do.

The operation, minor, was booked, he said. They sat down to discuss it, and Gabby expressed her upset, her reasons for not agreeing, her wanting to have another child. However many times they talked, and fought, there was nothing Gabby could do to change his mind. He was only able to see his point of view: once she got over her disappointment, how did she not see how much easier it would be—they could make love spontaneously! No more pills! No more condoms! It would free them to truly enjoy the rest of their lives.

"How dare you make a decision so momentous unilaterally!" Gabby had burst into tears. "You can't do this without my agreement."

"But you know I don't want more children." He was confused, had no idea how serious Gabby was about her need for another child; had no idea she had a stash of pregnancy tests, was still hoping against hope for another baby, despite her advancing age making it unlikely. "You knew this. You knew I wasn't going to change my mind."

Gabby ran out of reasons for him not to do it, the subject eventually becoming a no-go area. Every time they tried to talk about it, it ended up as a fight. It was easier to stop talking about it and sweep it under the table.

Elliott went ahead with the appointment, figuring he would ask forgiveness, not permission. This was the right thing for their family.

Gabby, silent with resentment for a week, finally boxed up her maternity clothes, gave away her baby toys, weeping the entire time.

And still she hasn't forgiven him. It is done. The deed cannot be undone, nor can any amount of apology heal her pain in knowing she will never again hold a newborn baby in her arms, smell its new-baby smell as it suckles at her breast, blow raspberries on a chubby little belly as a tiny person waves its arms and legs in the air, giggling with delight.

Gabby loves Elliott. She will never not love him, but nor is she certain she can forgive him for going ahead and having the vasectomy. It is akin to how he would feel had her machinations worked, had she suddenly found herself pregnant, but that is irrelevant.

It is the fly in the ointment that has made the past year such a hard one. Gabby knows that time will heal, that as each day goes by she will feel less anger, less resentment, but standing in the kitchen, looking at Tim and Claire aglow with joy, she felt, just now, nothing other than overwhelming fury.

It should have been them.

In the bathroom, Gabby sobs. She puts the lid down on the toilet and sits, her head in her hands, her entire body wracked with sobs. She is quiet, but not so quiet that she can't be heard by anyone who should happen to be standing directly outside the door.

"Gabby?" Elliott leans his head against the wall, his face a mask of sadness.

"I'm okay." Gabby tries to compose herself. "I'll be out in a second."

"Let me in, Gabs," he says, and she unlocks the door, unable to look at him.

"I'm sorry," he whispers, taking her in his arms. "I am so sorry. I never realized how much you wanted this. I thought you'd be okay, you'd get over it. I was wrong." Gabby bursts into a fresh round of sobs, her head against his chest, her tears soaking his T-shirt.

That he finally admitted it should make it better, should make the pain go away.

But it doesn't.

Five

Gabby emerges from the bathroom to see Trish, a sweep of streaky blond hair, a perfect white smile beaming as she deposits on the table a white china cake plate holding a meringue piled with whipped cream and strawberries, a plate of raspberry bars, and a platter of chocolate chip cookies.

"Gabby! It's so nice to see you!"

Gabby smiles as Claire reaches for a cookie, swooning in delight as she takes a bite. "Tell me you didn't bake all these yourself."

"I did. It was nothing. Gavin helped." They all turn to look approvingly at Trish's date, standing outside with the men.

"He's that handsome and he cooks, too? Are you kidding me?" Claire murmurs. "In my next life can I come back and be you?"

"Oh silly," trills Trish, looking over at the chopping board. "Can I help? I can finish off the salad if you want."

Gabby steps forward. "Don't worry, I'm doing it." She moves

over to the board and picks up the knife, slicing the onion as Trish watches her with a frown on her face.

"Ooh. Careful of your fingers," she warns, just as Gabby cuts herself.

"Shit!" She immediately sticks her finger in her mouth, as Claire spins to open a drawer, pulling out the Neosporin and a Band-Aid.

Trish picks up the knife and carries on, tucking her fingers into a claw and slicing the onion into perfect, paper-thin rings at the speed of light.

"Where did you learn to do that?" Gabby asks.

"I went to cooking school." Trish shrugs. "It was ages ago, but I picked up some good knife skills."

"Is there anything you can't do?" Claire says. "There must be something you're really, really bad at."

Trish stands still, thinking, as Gabby and Claire exchange secret smiles. That she even has to think about it is extraordinary, thinks Gabby. Eventually Trish's face lights up.

"I'm really bad at math," she says. "Like, I don't get numbers at all. I can never work out tips in restaurants."

"Thank the Lord!" whoops Claire. "The woman isn't perfect! So." She glances out the window at the men standing round the barbeque. "Where did you meet the gorgeous Gavin?"

"Match dot com," Trish says confidently.

"Really? Do you do a lot of dating on Match dot com?" Gabby's surprised she is so open about it.

"It's really become one of the only places. People do occasionally set me up, but out here in the suburbs the singles scene is very small, and you have to cast your net wider. I used to struggle with people knowing, but the stigma really doesn't exist anymore. Everyone who's single does it. It's either that or the bar scene, which is pretty horrendous. The last thing I'd want is to meet the kind of man who's doing that kind of scene."

Claire gives Gabby a knowing look. "They're not all awful. . . ." She grins as Gabby flushes.

"No?" Trish turns to Gabby, who shrugs and looks away, as if she has no idea what Claire is implying.

"Oh, come on, Gabs." She turns to Trish to explain. "Ella organized a girls' night out last night at the Grey Goose. We were all there, surrounded by middle-aged cheesy men, except for Gabby, who got totally hit on by this rather adorable young guy. I'm telling you, if I wasn't married, I'd have snapped him up. He was delicious!"

"What?" Elliott appears in the kitchen. "Did I hear you just say my wife got hit on by a hot young guy?" He's smiling. "Gabs! You didn't tell me that!"

"I didn't want you to feel threatened," she says, lightly, mortified that anyone is talking about the evening, instantly guilty, wishing they would just keep quiet and move on, yet thrilled, too, that they are talking about her! That she should be the one who was noticed that night, that perhaps Elliott, perhaps all of them, would see her in a new, flattering light.

"Apparently your wife is a MILF," laughs Claire. "The rest of us were stuck with the lecherous old sleazeballs. You should count yourself lucky you have a wife who's still got it."

Elliott puts his arms around Gabby as he kisses her neck. "Oh I do," he says. "I absolutely do."

Alanna appears, sidling quietly up to the counter as she attempts to slide a large handful of chocolate chip cookies into her pocket.

"Alanna!" Gabby is shocked. "Put those back right now! Those are for after we've eaten."

"They're not just for me," she protests. "I was sent inside to get them for everyone."

Gabby shakes her head. "And I suppose if they asked you to jump you'd say, 'How high'?"

Alanna just stares at her. "What?"

Gabby sighs. "Never mind. Put them back. Everyone can wait."

Alanna grumbles in a way that seems far too teenage for an eleven-year-old, but puts the cookies back as Trish walks over.

"How is Alanna finding middle school?" she says. "My girls had such a rough time, and I hear it's gotten worse. Such a difficult transitional phase."

Gabby would love to be able to say that everything is fine, but everything is not fine and she has never been good at lying. Alanna seems to be the same girl she has always been, only quieter, but Gabby knows she has given up trying to be in with the group she calls the Populars—girls Gabby has known forever, who are sweet as pie with the adults, and vicious minxes as soon as they are on their own—and in middle school has found a new group of friends.

A new group of friends who were clearly the Populars in their own elementary school, who are exactly the same as the old girls Gabby never liked, only couched in different clothes, with different names.

Alanna refuses to talk about it, and when Gabby encourages Alanna to find different friends, ones who are not obsessed with boys in sixth grade, ones who aren't given the iPhone 5 as soon as it comes out, Alanna doesn't want to hear it. She isn't interested in the girls on the softball team, or the girls from art class. She wants only to be accepted by the cool girls in school, and nothing her mother says or does will make her want anything else.

Gabby takes a deep breath. "Alanna's a tough cookie," she lies to Trish. "I think she'll be fine."

Six

The sheets are refreshingly cool as Gabby slips between them, pulling the covers up and reveling in the comfort of her bed, the comfort of her life, which is effectively rendering the fact that last night she met a man to whom she was attracted more and more dreamlike.

In the bathroom Elliott brushes his teeth, walking into the bedroom still brushing, leaning against the doorjamb.

"I like that Trish," he says. "And Gavin seems like a great guy. Young, though. How old do you think he is?"

"Thirty-five?" Gabby ventures, before making a face.

"What? You didn't like him?"

She sighs. "It's not him. It's Trish. She's always pleasant enough, so why do I feel so damned inadequate around her?" Gabby laughs, knowing how ridiculous she sounds.

"Why would you feel inadequate? I'll admit, she's great at a lot of things, but so are you."

Gabby gives a bark of laughter. "You are kidding, right?"

"You don't have a business, but other than that, you cook pretty well, you're fantastic at restoring furniture, which I bet she can't do, and you're a great mother. You . . ." He pauses.

"See! You're struggling. Me, too. That's the point. Look!" She grabs a handful of her belly. "She's perfect! She doesn't have this! Or these!" She vainly tries to show Elliott the two prickly hairs she's recently found on her chin, but he doesn't have his glasses on and can't see them. "I bet Trish doesn't have any chin hairs!" They both laugh. "Seriously! She's there with her taut yoga-honed body, and I get hives just driving past the damn place. Everything about her is perfect. There isn't a wrinkle on her face or a grey hair on her head, and look." Gabby bends her head down. "Look!" She sounds like she is joking, but there is a touch of hysteria in her voice as she points out her grey hairs.

"I can't see anything," Elliott says gently.

Gabby puts her head up. "Oh. I just dyed them. Still. They're there. And I'm never going to get into my size sixes again. I'm not even going to manage the eights. I can just about squeeze into the tens, but only when they're stretchy. Oh God. When did I turn into such a fat, frumpy mess."

"First of all, you're not a fat, frumpy mess, and second of all, even if you were, you're my fat, frumpy mess, and I love you exactly as you are."

"No you don't," grumbles Gabby, as Elliott moves toward the bed and sits down on her side. "You always used to say how sexy I was when I was thin."

"You're even sexier now." He smiles, pulling the covers down and reaching a hand to cup her full breasts. "You never had these when you were thin, and I don't want to have to say goodbye to these." He smiles, as Gabby rolls her eyes. "And apparently I'm not the only one who thinks you're pretty damn hot," Elliott reminds her, astonished to see her blush.

"What do you mean?" she says, embarrassment rising for she knows exactly what he means.

"Whoa! Relax. I just meant that you were a hit last night, right? Some young guy? Whatever insecurities you may have, and however much you refuse to believe me, you're still beautiful. Even Claire said it. How did she describe you?" He laughs. "A MILF! See? You've still got it."

"Maybe," Gabby grumbles. "But only for about three more minutes."

"That's okay. I'm not going anywhere, not when my wife is so gorgeous," and he unbuttons her nightgown as he tips his head to kiss her right breast.

DAD!" The door handle is rattled. "Open the door! Why is the door locked? Mom?"

"Jesus," Elliott hisses through his teeth, rolling off Gabby, who pulls the covers back up. "Go back to your room. I'll be there in a minute."

"Why is the door locked?" Alanna persists, rattling the door back and forth. "Mom? Will you come say goodnight? Let me in!"

"She'll be in in a minute," Elliott says. "Go, Alanna."

"But just op—"

"NOW!" Elliott barks, and they both listen to Alanna's footsteps stomping down the corridor. "Whose idea was it to have children?" He turns to Gabby, reaching for his shorts as Gabby smiles and reaches for her robe.

Elliott pauses by the bedroom door. "We've lost the moment, haven't we?"

"What do you mean?"

"I mean you're not going to want to finish what we started. I know you. You'll get back into bed and grab your Kindle, and there'll be no more passion tonight."

Gabby grins. "You're the one who always refers to the children as passion killers."

"With good reason."

"Actually, I think tonight you may get lucky."

"Really?"

Gabby moves toward him and pulls him down to kiss him deeply. "Meet you back here in ten minutes."

She couldn't say no to Alanna's request to have her mother tuck her in, not when Alanna wants so little to do with her these days.

"Is everything okay?" she asks, sitting on the bed as Alanna climbs in. "Want me to snuggle?" This was never their thing, always hers and Olivia's, but to her surprise, Alanna nods.

Gabby lies down and draws her daughter close, burying her nose in her hair, feeling her solid small body as she wraps her arm around her and holds her.

"Is there anything you want to talk about?" she whispers, sensing there is something going on for Alanna to be so affectionate, but wordlessly Alanna simply shakes her head, shuffling back to fit perfectly into the safety of her mother's body.

Gabby knows there is something wrong, suspects Alanna is struggling with middle school, but also knows there is nothing she can do until and unless Alanna chooses to share it with her.

As hard as everyone warned her it would be, Olivia had sailed through middle school, despite being her more challenging child. There was no question in her mind that Alanna, easy since the day she was born, would bypass the social pressures and bitchy cliques Gabby was grateful to have avoided with Olivia.

But Alanna, at eleven, is not the sunny, happy child she used to be. She is suddenly determined to be in with the right crowd, seeing middle school as the opportunity to reinvent herself. Abandoning her old friends, she has excitedly been making new ones since she started middle school in September. Gabby misses Alanna's old friends, who have been deemed "uncool" by Alanna and her new friends, and these new friends make Gabby nervous. They seem too sure of themselves, too advanced, all of them flicking straightened hair around their shoulders, posting provocative poses online, chewing gum as they check their iPhones for texts.

Gabby wants to talk to Elliott about her fears, but Olivia has now talked him out of bed and back downstairs to watch an episode of *The Voice*, and Elliott, who can resist anything except his daughters, is now sitting on the sofa discussing the pros and cons of a one-hit wonder who came on the show desperate to prove he was more than that singing his one-hit wonder.

Gabby tucks Alanna in and heads back to her bedroom, alone. She reaches for the iPad rather than the Kindle, idly flicking through her Facebook newsfeed, before going onto Trish's page. She has a personal page, and a business one, with 84,000 likes. Which upsets Gabby.

She and Trish were always friendly without being friends, but there is a chasm between them now that won't disappear. Gabby knows exactly when the tide turned.

It happened a couple of years ago, when Alanna was nine. Trish had phoned Gabby to organize a playdate, asking what her schedule looked like in three weeks' time. Gabby had resisted the urge to laugh. She barely knew what day of the week it was, let alone what the girls were doing in three weeks. The playdates she organized tended to be last-minute, with neighborhood kids, and more often than not the girls arranged it all themselves with little or no input from the mothers, other than picking up or dropping off at the end of the playdate.

She dutifully looked in the book and came up with a day. Trish explained she would be dropping Alanna back at five p.m. as she had to take her son to basketball at five-thirty on the other side of town.

"Are you sure I can't pick her up?" Gabby offered, knowing it would have been impossible, for Olivia had a dance class in Fairfield, twenty minutes away, which ended at five.

"It's no problem," Trish said.

"Fine. My sitter will be home," Gabby said confidently. Gabby didn't actually have a sitter, but made a mental note to make sure to find one for the day.

A week before the playdate, Trish phoned again to check if Alanna had any food allergies. "Don't worry about snacks," Trish had reassured Gabby. "We're a gluten-free, sugar-free household so it's only healthy snacks!" Gabby eyed her own snack drawer, stuffed with Pirate Booty, Fruit Roll-Ups, chips, and individual packets of chocolate chip cookies.

She forced a smile. "Great!"

It was too late to cancel the playdate—Alanna was so excited, but Gabby already suspected these preliminary checkup calls didn't bode well.

Trish's daughter, Skylar, had always seemed lovely, but Gabby had learned not to have playdates with kids whose parents didn't share the same sensibilities. Gabby was not a helicopter parent. She was not the kind of parent who desperately sought opportunities, any opportunity, to muscle her way in to her kid's classroom.

She was busy restoring furniture, painting old pieces she picked up at the consignment store, sometimes the dump, repurposing them, and friends had started buying the occasional piece. She went to a knitting class at the local yarn store. She volunteered at the town farm. She cooked from scratch every day, proper family suppers so they could all eat together as a family. Her days were busy; she figured the kids were perfectly fine without her showing up at school all the time.

Her friends tended to be other mothers who were equally laid-back. They let their kids ride around the neighborhood on bikes; they pushed the children out the back door, telling them to play, not worrying about them, or giving them a second thought, until they came home because they were hungry.

Sure enough, on the day of the playdate Alanna went home on the bus with Skylar, and Gabby took Olivia to dance, only remembering she had meant to find a sitter when her cell phone rang at 5:02 p.m., her own home number flashing on the screen. Her heart plummeted to her stomach.

She'd forgotten to book a sitter.

"Mom? Where are you? Skylar's mom just dropped me home and there's no one here."

"Oh honey. I'm sorry. The sitter must have forgotten. I'll be home in five minutes. I know Skylar's mom has to be somewhere so tell her to leave you. It's only five minutes."

Gabby listened while Alanna relayed this to Trish, who then came on the phone.

"Gabby? Hi. There's no sitter here."

Was it Gabby's imagination or was there judgment in her voice? A wave of defensive panic washed over her.

"I don't know what happened. But I'm literally five minutes away," she lied, knowing she was twenty-five minutes away. "Just leave her. She'll be fine for five minutes. I know you have to go."

"I'm not leaving her by herself," Trish said. "I'll just wait for you."

"No, really. I'm so close and I know you have basketball to get to. Alanna's fine."

"I'm not leaving a child on her own," Trish said. "We'll wait." She didn't sound happy.

"I'm so sorry," Gabby said again, now feeling sick, knowing she'd been caught. There was no way in hell she'd be home in five minutes, or anything close.

In the end, she phoned her neighbor and begged her to run over so Trish could leave. She did, but Gabby knew Trish knew she'd lied, and there was no more talk of another playdate, nor did Gabby reciprocate.

It was, as she said to Claire at the time, too much pressure.

She is happy to be friendly at social events, but they will never be friends; of that she is certain.

Scrolling through Facebook keeps her busy until Elliott comes back up to bed. On a normal night, she might well curl up in bed, read a couple of pages on the Kindle before going to sleep, leaving Elliott's bedside lamp on for when he gets up. But tonight she needs to make love with him, needs to erase, finally, the evidence of her mental infidelity—and thank God it was merely in her head—and the only way to do that is to feel him inside her.

"You're still awake?" He crawls onto the bed, pleasantly surprised.

"I told you we had unfinished business." She smiles, pulling him to her and kissing him deeply. Her concerns for Alanna can wait.

Their lovemaking has become a well-worn routine. Tonight Gabby pulls out all the stops, pushes him back on the bed, climbs on top of him, feeling a passion for her husband she hasn't felt in years.

She closes her eyes and moves on top of Elliott, moaning, as she gives in to the temptation of fantasizing it isn't her well-worn husband underneath her, but the smooth, strong body of a thirty-something; it isn't her husband moaning as she kisses his neck, but Matt.

Seven

This house was not a house they were ever supposed to have looked at when they were looking to upgrade to something bigger. They had a long list of houses to visit—mostly '50s and '60s ranches and splits, which was all that was affordable given Elliott's new residency at Norwalk Hospital.

Their Realtor, flapping and stressed, announced they would have to make a quick pit stop at a house—she needed to change the lockbox.

Elliott was in the front of the car, Gabby in the rear as their Realtor pulled onto a pretty street close to town, with picture-book cottages lining each side.

The house was grey shingle, with a natural wood barn in the backyard, a large copper star hanging on the side. Once upon a time it had been a horse barn, but was now used for storage. The house was a small Cape, too small, the Realtor pointed out, seeing how excited they were, for Gabby and Elliott and their two young girls.

The downstairs had been added on to extensively—light-filled rooms, a sunroom, a playroom, but the upstairs had just two bedrooms and one bathroom, all of them tiny.

"Couldn't we add on above the sunroom?" Elliott had peered out the window, pointing out the flat roof.

"You could," she said doubtfully. "But I just don't know how much you want to put into this house."

"Surely adding a bedroom and bath would be an investment?"

"Yes, but only if you got it at the right price. They're asking about thirty thousand too much, and so far they've refused to move."

Elliott had turned to Gabby, whose face had lit up. "I love it," she said.

"Me, too."

They made their offer, raised it twice more, only to have it rejected. Losing heart, they settled on a '60s ranch on the other side of town, with a huge backyard and no charm whatsoever.

The day they were going to contract, their Realtor phoned. The owners of the cottage had rethought. They would now accept the third and final offer if Elliott and Gabby still wanted the house.

"We do," Elliott said, "but I have to offer lower because of the money we've spent since then." He named his price, shockingly low, even to the Realtor, while deciding not to tell Gabby until and unless the offer was accepted.

Three months later, they moved in.

Empty, the house needed more work than they had imagined. Paintings that had been removed left huge rectangular stains on the walls; the wooden floors were stained and thirsty after emerging from where they had been hiding underneath rugs for twenty years.

They worked evenings and weekends to restore the house, while the builders worked during the day to build Olivia's bedroom and reconfigure and enlarge the rooms that were there. The job became larger, the contractor pointing out how easy it would be to cut off a chunk of the now-oversized master bedroom, to create an en suite bathroom and a walk-in closet. How could they not?

The walls were covered with fresh paint, the floors sanded and stripped before being stained a dark brown, oiled with tung oil for a glossy, rich finish. Gabby ran up simple curtain panels in a pale mushroom linen, the same panels in a fuchsia pink for the girls' rooms.

They had little money back then. Their furniture was a mix of consignment store and castoffs. If ever anyone said they were getting rid of anything, Gabby and Elliott took it, regardless of what it was, what it looked like, or whether they had room.

What they couldn't use was stored at one end of the barn. The other was turned into a workroom where Gabby would restore furniture for their home. A huge old pine dresser they found at the dump one day, covered in an ugly green paint, was transformed into a beautiful bleached pine, lined with linen to hold their Crate and Barrel plates and bowls.

Gabby became an expert at stripping furniture and repurposing it. Where others would see an ugly dark, heavy chest of drawers, she would see an object of beauty: once stripped, painted a soft ivory, the intricate and ugly brass pulls replaced with pretty crystal antique knobs, these pieces of furniture were invariably more beautiful than even she expected.

Elliott made the outdoor table, and the pergola under which it sits; Gabby collected old Mason jars, all shapes and sizes, filled them with votive candles and hung them at varying lengths underneath the pergola.

It has become a house others describe as magical. Tiny lights twinkle from the pear tree in the front garden, and the two apple trees in the back. It is a house that feels happy, feels like it is home to a happy family, and everyone who comes over immediately feels comfortable.

This has always felt like Gabby's haven, a place where she is safe from the world. It is the quietest, most peaceful house she can imagine, a world away from the house in which she grew up.

Gabby grew up in England. She moved to the States just after university, at twenty-one, initially just for the summer, as a camp counselor at a girls' camp in Maine, but life seemed so filled with possibility here, she never went home. First, she applied for a student visa, working as a nanny and studying in the evenings, before meeting, and marrying, Elliott.

The London house in which she grew up was always filled with people. Her mother, once well known as a stage actress, had, in the afternoon of her life, retrained as a therapist. Never a woman who fully understood boundaries, Natasha de Roth (no one is ever sure where the "de" came from) offered up their home as a safe harbor to waifs and strays, anyone who had nowhere else to go, including an assortment of rather scruffy dogs and unhappy cats.

Once a rather large and grand house at the top of Belsize Park Gardens, the Roth/de Roth (her father only went by Roth) house always felt a bit like a game of Russian roulette to Gabby—opening the front door after school, you never knew what you were going to get.

There might be a woman standing in the kitchen shouting, being coached through a bipolar rage fit by her mother, who would smile cheerily and wave Gabby along, as if this were perfectly normal and she should come back later.

Impromptu group therapy sessions around the kitchen table were normal. Gabby would walk home longing for a quiet hot chocolate and some digestive biscuits, only to find the larder empty, the biscuits having been eagerly consumed by the seven people currently weeping, chairs pulled in to the old, scrubbed pine table next to the Aga.

Gabby learned to stop at the newsagents in Belsize Village on her way home from school and buy some chips, or cookies, going straight up to her bedroom to avoid the mayhem.

She'd sit cross-legged on the floor, leaning back on her beanbag, plugged in to her Sony Walkman surrounded by posters of the Police, Madness, the Specials, eating two or three Jaffa Cakes, putting the rest away for another time.

It was peaceful, in her large, sun-filled bedroom at the back of the house with views over the treetops. Occasionally she'd hear a door slam downstairs, or the bark of laughter, but mostly, when plugged in, she was able to lose herself in daydreams.

She dreamed, even then, of a peaceful life. She dreamed of a life when she wouldn't be surrounded by drama and chaos, by a mother who needed so desperately to be needed herself, she couldn't possibly be there for the one person who truly did need her: her daughter.

Her father, a quiet, scholarly man who made his living as an editor on one of the broadsheets, had little to do with either of them. His way of dealing with the chaos was to remove himself, if not entirely physically, then certainly emotionally. He worked late hours at the newspaper, and would, when home, drift through the house, spending hours sitting in a cracked leather wing chair by the bay window in the living room, methodically working his way through a large pile of newspapers on the floor next to him, cigarette always in hand, bottle of Scotch resting on the table.

Gabby adored him, even though she had little to do with him. He would always light up in delight when he saw her, and might, if in the mood, briefly engage her in a discussion about politics, or Ethiopia, or what her thoughts might be about the situation in Northern Ireland.

But soon he would be back to his papers, and Gabby would disappear off to her room, grateful to have had any kind of attention at all.

America. The very word seemed to be lit up, heralded by angels singing. Everything about America seemed larger than life, exotic, magical. Her favorite films were American, as were her favorite film stars. She watched *Happy Days,* and longed for the nostalgia of a life she had never known, a life she was certain existed across the pond, where everyone was always happy; they had perfect big white teeth, they had mothers and housekeepers who were always smiling, who paid them attention, thought everything they did was perfect, baked them fresh cakes every day for when they got off the bus—the yellow school bus! Oh how she wanted to travel on a yellow school bus!—after school.

They had one family vacation when Gabby was twelve. To New York, which was the most vibrant, exciting city she had ever been to, and Shelter Island, to stay with friends of her mother's.

That was when Gabby fell in love, plotting then and there to make her way back. After university, she knew she couldn't live under her mother's roof, and a camp counselor job was a perfect stepping-stone until she figured out what to do next, and how to stay in the States.

When she moved to New York, there were a few dates with dull men. On a semiconscious level Gabby knew she had only agreed to go out with them to prove her mother wrong: you re-create what you know, her mother had once said, gesturing around what even her mother had begun to call the Madhouse. Or, she'd shrugged skeptically, you go the other way entirely, but often that only happens after an intervention, years of therapy usually. I wonder, she'd fixed her gaze on Gabby, which way will you go?

"Duh!" Gabby had rolled her eyes. "I'm up in my bedroom desperately trying to find peace and quiet. I hardly think there's any question about which way I'm going."

"You say that now"—her mother smiled knowingly—"but you're a teenager. Wait until you're out in the world. You're going to be attracted to men who are reminiscent of your parents, whether you like it or not."

God, no! Gabby had thought. I love my father, but I'd hate to be married to a man so distant. And as for marrying a man anything like my mother . . . she'd shuddered in horror.

The dull men were to prove her mother wrong. They were more present than her father, more interested in her, just not . . . very interesting. Gabby would be interested in them for all of about five minutes, before realizing she could never spend her time with people so disinterested in any of the things she was interested in.

"What are you looking for?" other people would ask, curious about this bright-eyed English girl with the curly hair and large smile.

"I'm looking for peace," she'd always say.

"No!" They'd shake their heads. "That's not what I meant. I mean, do you want someone tall? Short? How old? Funny? What? What are you looking for?"

"Peace," she'd say again. "Someone who makes me feel peaceful."

Few knew what to say after that.

Elliott was what she was looking for. From the minute he started talking to her, he made her feel peaceful. It was as if she recognized him. There were no violins or halos, no crashing stars and bolts of lightning. It was simply a quiet recognition.

You, she thought. I *know* you.

And it is peace that has been the defining factor of their relationship. Unlike during her childhood, when she never felt particularly wanted, or noticed, or happy, or safe, she feels all of these things with Elliott.

They have built a beautiful life together, with beautiful children, a beautiful home.

Why on earth, Gabby thinks, as she closes the front door after the girls have gone to school, would I do anything to screw this up?

What the hell am I thinking, even fantasizing about another man? Even in my head, this isn't okay. Even in my head, this has to stop.

Eight

But she can't stop thinking about it. In the car, driving to Claire's, she has an imaginary conversation, out loud, as if she were explaining herself to Claire, having confessed to what has, up until now, remained a fantasy: sleeping with another man.

"I wasn't thinking." Gabby's voice is quiet but clear. "I didn't think about my husband. I didn't think about anything other than how good it felt to be wanted, how alive I felt, knowing that someone, and someone like him, even noticed someone like me."

"Why didn't you stop before you went too far?"

"I tried. There was a part of me that kept going, just ten more minutes, just a few more, I'll go home soon, but it was, I don't know. Heady. It was like taking drugs. I was high, and I just wanted the high to keep going."

"And if Elliott ever found out?"

"He can't ever find out. It would kill him. It would kill us. This is a secret I'm taking to my grave."

Gabby exhales loudly and sighs as she climbs out of the car and pushes open the gate to Claire's house. Thank God, she thinks, I didn't do anything. Now I just have to get the whole bloody thing out of my head.

"Are you ready?" she calls in the front door, not bothering to knock. "I'm waiting in the car."

Claire bounds out seconds later, giving Gabby a quick hug. "Was it my imagination or were you just sitting in the car outside my house talking to yourself?"

Gabby flushes. "Oh God. I can't believe you saw that."

"You were! Gabs! That's hilarious. So, what were you talking about? Anything good? You looked pretty intense."

Gabby sinks her head in her hands in shame. "I can't believe I got caught," she mumbles, before looking at Claire. "It's just something I do sometimes to clear my thoughts. I treat myself as my own therapist."

"O-kay," laughs Claire. "So how's that working out for you?"

"Surprisingly well." Gabby turns the car on, and laughs.

"I do have an amazing therapist if you need one. I've told you this a million times, but if you ever do need someone to talk to I could totally get you in, and you'd love her."

"And I've told you a million times"—Gabby shudders—"no therapists. Only the one in my head. I've still got all this mother stuff to get over. The poor woman put me off for life."

"Yes, well, not all of them are crazy."

"I know that. But my mother is. And I just can't go there. I love that you keep offering, though. I just hope that things are never desperate enough for me to want to take you up on it. What are you having done at the doctor today? You're not having a scan, are you? Isn't it too early?"

"Just a checkup. They'll do a blood test to confirm everything.

Thank you so much for driving, Gabs. I just feel kind of jittery, what with my age. I know it's too early to get excited, and the risks are huge, but it's all I'm thinking about. I couldn't sleep last night so I went online and started reading up about pregnancies in women our age. It's pretty scary, but I just have this really strong belief that everything's going to be okay. Is that weird? Or wrong? I'm just so sure that this is supposed to be, and that I won't have anything to worry about. Do you think everyone feels this way, even when it doesn't turn out to be the case?"

"I don't know," Gabby says. "But I absolutely believe positive thinking can change the world. And the IVF wouldn't have worked if you weren't supposed to have this child, that much I'm sure of."

"I know," Claire says. "I'm one of the lucky ones. It was such hell when we were going through it, and we so nearly gave up. This was our last shot and it worked. Can you believe it?"

No, thinks Gabby sadly. I can't.

Claire turns her head slightly to watch the streets flash by out of the car window, before speaking, as if reading Gabby's mind. "You always said you wanted another child. You're younger than me, you could still do it. Imagine if you and I were pregnant together! It would be so much easier if I had someone my age going through it."

"I can't," Gabby says quietly. "I wish I could. I wanted it so badly, but it just isn't meant to be."

"Who knows?" Claire turns back to her with a smile. "Accidents can happen. And there's always IVF."

"Not when your husband's had a vasectomy."

Claire's eyes open wide. "Elliott had a vasectomy? Oh God. I had no idea. And you were okay with that?"

Gabby pauses before answering. She wasn't okay with it then, and she isn't okay with it now. But there is nothing she can do about it, and the best she can hope for is to learn to accept it.

"It is what it is," she says lightly, ignoring the pain that wraps itself around her heart.

In the waiting room, Gabby flicks through *Parenting* magazine, not taking any of it in—she has moved so far away from babies, and toddlers, and micromanaging her children's lives in a bid to be the best mother, produce the best children.

How different she would be now, she thinks sadly. How much better, in so many respects.

Her phone buzzes. A text from Elliott: "Just telling my wife how much I love her . . ."

She smiles. "Love you more," she texts, starting a game of Words with Friends just as a black strip appears at the top of her screen announcing she has received an email.

From Matt@Fourforsight.com.

Her heart jumps into her mouth as she scans the email, unaware of the delighted smile now stretching from ear to ear.

To: Gabby
From: Matt
Subject: To be continued . . .

Gabby—
What an unexpected and truly great surprise it was to meet you the other day. You turned a boring business trip into what felt like a much-needed fun-filled break. Every time I think of your green eyes sparkling I start to smile—we could all do with more friends that make us feel like that. I hope your husband made it home safely and had fun with your girls.

Life here in Malibu is as dull as ever—sand, sun, surf.

It's good to be home, although I always find myself yearning for the changing seasons when I've been to New England. I should have brought back a bag of gold and russet leaves to put in a bowl on the table—it might have done the trick.

As it stands, I have to come back in a couple of weeks, and was hoping we could grab another drink

Take care. M x

Gabby's face lights up as she reads, rereads, rereads again. Is he flirting? What does this mean? No. Impossible. He says quite specifically he could do with more friends . . . but . . . "sparkling green eyes"? Who says that if they're not interested? *Gabby!* She sits up, shaking her head. *What are you doing? You're married.* There's nothing inappropriate in this email, yet it feels . . . inviting. Exciting.

She reads it again, not noticing Claire until she is standing right in front of her.

"What on earth are you reading?" says Claire. "You look like you're about to explode with joy."

"Oh. Nothing," Gabby says. "Just an email from a friend."

"Really? Because you look like you've won the lottery."

"I'm fine." Gabby puts her phone away. "So tell me, how was it? What did the doctor say?"

It is hard to concentrate on the way home. Gabby finds her thoughts drifting back to the email as Claire talks, desperately wanting to reach into her bag and read it again.

She drops Claire off, declining to come in for coffee, before driving straight home, where she can read the email in solitude.

Dear Matt, she writes, before deleting it. Not dear. He isn't dear. *She* wasn't dear.

Matt—

What a lovely surprise to receive your email—I'm glad you got home safely and I know what you mean about the seasons here. California is a place I sometimes dream about, but I couldn't live without the spring and the fall. Fall is, in fact, my favorite season. I'm looking out the window now at a huge old maple tree whose canopy spreads over the entire front yard, and there is a blanket of red and orange leaves beneath, which is really quite beautiful. If I knew your address, I'd send you some leaves. . . .

I'm waiting for a chill in the air, because nothing's better than lighting fires. I'm always up early, and usually downstairs with a fire lit by seven. Sometimes six. We go through wood . . .

No. She deletes it.

I go through wood like crazy from this time of year onward. I also turn into something of a sloth—I could curl up on the sofa with books for the rest of my life.

How exciting that you're coming back, and the leaves will be glorious in two weeks.

She pauses. She should invite him over for dinner, have him meet Elliott. Isn't that the way to have a proper friendship?

Does she want, in fact, a friendship? Wasn't she the one who always said that once you are married, you do not get to make new friends of the opposite sex—ever? You are allowed to befriend other couples, and if you get on particularly well with the husband, that is allowed, but single members of the opposite sex?

No. It's just not done.

But why not? Why should she not have a new friend? He's by far the most interesting and glamorous person she's met in ages. Elliott would be fascinated by him, even though she doesn't yet want them to meet. Matt met her on her own, and this friendship has to develop on that basis before she is ready to reveal her true self.

She doesn't want him to see her as a wife, a mother, a middle-aged housewife. She wants to keep the illusion going, for just a little while longer, that she is, as he thinks, clever and strong, with sparkling green eyes.

My schedule's so crazy, I don't know if I'll be able to get away, but if I can, I definitely will. It would be fun.

She takes a deep breath.

Just as long as you promise not to get me drunk and take advantage of me . . . :) Gabby x

One kiss. That's enough. That wasn't flirtatious, was it? Maybe just the tiniest bit, but really, Gabby's just having fun. It isn't as if she's going to actually *do* anything—she isn't the slightest bit interested in actually doing anything, but what fun to play at being the sort of woman other men want. What would be the harm?

Two emails arrive, back-to-back, two minutes later:

The first:

33624 Malibu Cove Colony Drive, Malibu, CA 90265. xxx

The second:

I can't promise anything of the sort . . . ;)

With a spring in her step, Gabby grabs a Ziploc bag and runs out to the front lawn, grinning as she stuffs the bag full with the most perfect golden, russet, and red leaves. Sealing it up, she jumps in the car to run over to the post office, feeling younger than she has in years.

Gabby slips the Ziploc into an envelope, then seals it tight, scribbling Matt's address on the front.

Handing it in at the counter, she walks out checking her email, hoping there might be an additional response. She holds the phone in her hand for the rest of the day, glancing at it every few minutes, wanting to feel the exhilaration of earlier, of seeing his lovely, and unexpected, email.

By eight-fifteen, sitting on the sofa with her family watching television, present in body but a million miles away in her head, she starts to feel depressed, berating herself for being so ridiculous, for acting like a lovelorn teenager when she is a forty-three-year-old married mother of two.

"Mom? Mom? Mom!" She breaks out of her reverie to see three sets of eyes staring at her.

"Hmmm?" She is still worlds away.

"What's the matter with you?" Olivia's voice is filled with teenage disdain as she tilts her head, her dark hair tumbling over her shoulder, her full lips in a pout. Gabby sees, suddenly, the beauty she is becoming.

"Nothing." She smiles. "Sorry. Just thinking about everything I have to do."

"Can you take me to Benefit tomorrow? I need some makeup," Olivia says.

"Benefit?" Gabby blurts out. "What's wrong with CVS?"

Olivia gives her a withering look. "At seventeen? I need the good stuff for my skin now."

"I'll go to CVS!" pipes up Alanna.

"For makeup?" Gabby looks at her eleven-year-old in horror.

Alanna shrugs. "Just mascara. And maybe lip gloss."

"First of all, no," she says to Alanna. "You shouldn't be wearing any makeup at this age, and Olivia, I don't know about Benefit. That stuff's expensive. Can't we please just go to CVS?"

"No!" Olivia says. "Everyone goes to Benefit, and I can't wear the stuff from CVS anymore. It gives me allergies."

Gabby looks at her skeptically. "Since when?"

Olivia doesn't break eye contact. "Since it started giving me allergies."

"Well, what do you need? Maybe we can go to Benefit, but it depends how much you need. I don't mind buying one or two things."

"Thank you, Mom!" Olivia leans over and plants a kiss on Gabby's cheek. They both know they will be walking out of the store with a bag filled with makeup, Olivia delighted she will get her way, and Gabby happy to not have a fight on her hands, to go back to thinking about Matt.

The more she thinks, the more humiliated she becomes. She wishes she hadn't sent the leaves, wishes she wasn't sitting here feeling stupid for having done so, wishes she hadn't responded to anything, and certainly not with the overt flirtation she now deeply regrets.

"I'm going to bed." Gabby leans over to kiss Elliott, then the girls, all transfixed by *The Voice*.

"Stay!" Elliott says. "You always watch this with us."

"Not tonight." She stands up. "I'm tired. I'm going up to read."

. . .

Her book manages to take her mind off the lack of response, although she allows herself another read of Matt's emails before she switches off the light. Perhaps it is her turn to write back, she thinks suddenly, making sense of his silence throughout the afternoon. Perhaps that's what he's waiting for?

But no. She can't. Stop this, she tells herself. You are a grown-up getting yourself worked into a state over a man you don't care about. If you're getting attached to some outcome here, it's you that's doing it, not him. This is ridiculous, and I'm not going to respond anymore.

Feeling much better, she switches off the light, curls up, and goes to sleep.

At 2:34 a.m., Gabby wakes up. Next to her, Elliott lies on his back, snoring loudly.

"Ssssh," she says loudly, close to his ear. He doesn't move. "Roll over," she says, pushing him over as he gently rolls, still fast asleep.

Gabby slides her iPhone off the nightstand and scrolls through her emails. Junk, mostly. And one from Matt.

Her heart pounds as she creeps out of bed and into the bathroom, refusing to read the email until she is alone and safe, a treat she is saving.

Ms. Sloth,

I love your description of curling up on sofas in the fall, but thanks a lot for making me long to be there—I'm going to have to start marking the days off like an advent calendar.

I went surfing today, which is the greatest advantage

of living here. I'm enclosing a picture taken with a group of my surf friends. Surfing, to me, is the greatest feeling in the world. You can probably tell by my smile that the waves were awesome today. So however much I miss the changing seasons, take me away from the water for any length of time and I suspect I'd die.

I had an ex-girlfriend who was just like you. She loved winter, and warmth, and just didn't understand surfing. No surprise why that relationship didn't work out, although had she had sparkling green eyes, things might have ended differently . . . who knows. :)

I must stop flirting with you! I'm sorry, I know it's inappropriate. You just make me smile.

M x

Matt, or as I now think of you, Surf Dude,

Um. Your friends look great, but . . . wow. It was hard to focus on them when . . . I mean . . . good LORD! Well, thank you for sending me a half-naked picture of you with a surfboard and a tan—I'll say this for you: you definitely know how to brighten up the day of a middle-aged housewife. I'm tempted to print it out and put it on the fridge—you'd be next to the local firefighters calendar, and you definitely give them a run for their money, but then I might have some explaining to do. . . .

I have no idea why I'm awake in the middle of the night. It seems to be the curse of middle age (I know, I know, I'll shut up about it in a minute), but no one I know sleeps anymore. Oh, all the men do—they're sleeping like babies, but all us women are up at 2:46 writing emails and reading the *Huffington Post*.

I should really get up—there'd be so much I could get done, but bed is so warm and cozy, I'm quite happy lying here letting my mind play havoc and losing myself in fantasies. . . .

Oh no. I think I'm giving away all my innermost secrets. I'm supposed to let you think I'm super fit and healthy, and interested in all sports, especially surfing, and instead I'm revealing that I'm happiest either curled up on the sofa or in my bed. It's pathetic. I don't know what's happened to me. I did used to be filled with energy. When I was your age (I know how patronizing that sounds and I'm sorry, bear with me), I wasn't surfing, but I was skiing, and ice skating, and in summer I'd go hiking all the time. I got completely addicted to spinning, for about five minutes, but it was a pretty intense and happy five minutes.

The last couple of years have been . . . harder. It used to be that my husband was paid a decent salary and was able to be home tons, and now his salary has been cut, and in order to make anything like he used to, he has to work every hour that God sends.

Gabby presses Delete, and erases that last paragraph in its entirety.

I keep thinking that one day I'll wake up and feel alive again, instead of sleepwalking through my life, but I'm still waiting. . . . Maybe I should take up surfing?

Sorry to be a downer. Clearly I need more sleep . . . am off to try and trick my brain into thinking it's tired.

Big hug,
Ms. Sloth xo

P.S. I didn't even realize you were flirting! Keep calm and carry on. . . .

Ms. Sloth
I wish I were there to give you a big hug and make you feel better. The only thing I know for certain is that everything passes. The good times, the bad times . . . not that these are bad times, but if you're feeling down, it will pass.

Did I ever tell you, by the way, how much I love your accent? I've always wanted to go to London, but the timing's never been right. I think you said that's where you're from. Do you miss it?

If I plan a trip, you'll have to tell me all the places to see and things to do. One of the things I hate is seeing anywhere as a tourist—I always try and go with contacts ready so I can see the real city, rather than the tourist version.

I want to know what the locals do, where they eat, what pubs they go to. Even writing this now is getting me excited—I'm thinking London needs to be next on my list.

And now I have to be serious with you. Listen very carefully. YOU ARE NOT A MIDDLE-AGED HOUSEWIFE. God, woman. Will you listen to yourself? You're gorgeous! I don't want to hear those words from you ever again. Seriously. You're doing yourself a massive disservice every time you think those words, and I can tell you think them all the time, which is nuts.

So, I am sending you a sandy hug from Malibu—I hope the blues go flying out the window tonight. . . .

SD x

SD,

The blues did indeed fly out the window last night. You obviously have the magic touch. I slept incredibly well after my small interruption, and I have to say, I feel better today than I have done in years. I'm also mortified at revealing quite so much to a relative stranger on email. I'm truly sorry, and I promise to keep things light from here on in.

You asked if I miss London. I never miss it when I'm here. My life is here, my friends, my family, although my parents are still in London, but I have always felt as at home here as I felt over there. Often more so. But I have to be honest, whenever we visit, as soon as I touch down at Heathrow, I start to get desperately homesick. I miss the cabbies that start chatting to you about politics as soon as you get in the cab; I miss the cafe culture—sitting around for hours drinking cappuccinos and putting the world to right. I miss Europe—hopping over to France or Italy for the weekend, mixing with other cosmopolitan people who have traveled, seen the world, are interested in everything around them.

But there are pros and cons to everything. It's shockingly expensive, and I suspect I couldn't raise my kids there even if I wanted to. The British love children as long as they're basically seen and not heard, and I can't imagine my very American children going down too well—they're much too loud and opinionated.

Actually, that's not strictly true. Olivia, the eldest, has always been loud and opinionated, and as stubborn as an elephant. Alanna was always my baby, and so easy, but she's at that awkward age where the social pressures of school are starting to get to her, and she's becoming more and more moody by the day.

Despite all, and particularly despite missing how easy it was and how lovely they were when they were tiny, I wouldn't change a thing.

One of the things I have always adored about this country is how easy it is to live here, particularly with children. You can park everywhere, and we live an hour outside of New York City in a town that has fantastic beaches and a municipal country club! What's not to love?

I guess, if I had to pick one thing, it's the lack of sophistication of Europe. I miss the culture. It's very easy to get lazy living in a small suburban town, and I worry I've become very lazy. Why go anywhere else when you have everything you need on your doorstep, and that doorstep is so pretty?

So . . . changing tacks entirely. You mentioned an ex-girlfriend. I imagine you're extremely busy playing the field—a different girl in every port, and probably more than one, you charmer, you!

My dearest Ms. Sloth,
How very wrong you are about a different girl in every port. I will admit, I'm not exactly a hermit, and yes, I certainly do manage to go out and party quite a bit, and yes, I'll also admit that I like women. A lot. But as much as I like

having fun, there's a part of me that would love to settle down.

In many ways, dating was much easier before the company. When I was just "Matt," I never had to question people's motives in wanting to befriend me, or flirt with me. The hardest thing about having any kind of public profile is that suddenly everyone knows who you are. You find yourself surrounded by people, and yes, by people I mean women, and they're fun, and gorgeous, and all over you, but there's this part of your brain that's always asking, are they with me for "me," or because of who I am, because they think I have power, or money, or whatever. . . .

Sometime during the last year I started to think very seriously about settling down. I come from a big family—I have four brothers and sisters, and I'm the last one to not be married. My mom keeps hinting that she'd love grandchildren from me, and I have to say, when I'm around friends with kids, I start wondering if I might be getting closer. . . .

What are your girls like? How old are they? I bet you're an amazing mother. I see you as being really fun, but probably quite strict. I have a great friend here, Eleanor, who's English, and she's really stern with her kids, but they all adore her. They also all have the greatest manners of any kids I know. They actually shake hands and look you in the eye, and always say please and thank you. I've asked Eleanor if she might consider having my kids, because when I have them I want them to be exactly like hers, but she said her husband wouldn't be too happy.

You apologized for revealing so much to a relative

stranger. The weird thing is, you don't feel like a stranger. I know we hardly know each other, but you feel like a really close friend. In fact, I don't think I've revealed this much of myself to anyone before. I have no idea why that is—you're just really easy to "talk" to. When I read your emails I can picture you talking, and it makes me happy. I like having a new best friend on email. I like even more that I get to see you in a couple of days. . . .
SD x

SD,
First off, rest assured I have no ulterior motive. Well, I may insist the martinis are on you, but that's as far as it goes. Luckily for all of us, I'm married, so you're safe from my evil advances and plans to kill you off and steal all your money.

I do understand how hard it must be. A boy I knew from school days has become a hugely famous actor. I haven't seen him for years, but we have a really good mutual friend, and apparently he only fraternizes with people he's known forever, or with other famous people who understand what it's like. And he also says he resents how distrustful he's become, but he's been burned too many times. Years ago some young tart he had a thing with sold her story to the Sunday papers, and he just retreated after that.

I like what you said about children. It seems I misjudged you, my Surf Dude friend, and thank you for saying such nice things about what you think I must be like as a mother. My children would disagree entirely! In truth,

I do adore being a mother, but it isn't, as it seems to be for so many of the women around here, the be-all and end-all. I love my children, but I don't need, or want, to be involved in every aspect of their lives. There's a woman in town, Trish, who has a hugely successful business and manages to be at the school pretty much every day. I have no idea what she's doing there, but she volunteers for everything, and if there's nothing on offer, she'll just show up with a tray of cupcakes and a large smile.

It makes me furious! Bitch that I am, I am firmly of the belief that what your children do at school is in the hands of the school. There are so many women here that are defined solely by their children—they're not women who exist anymore in their own right, they only see themselves as X's mom. I've always done stuff outside of motherhood, even though I haven't had a "job" for years. I restore furniture, and paint, and can make pretty much anything if you give me a wood bench and a jigsaw.

Oh, the things you're learning about me! Nothing quite so sexy as a woman with a hammer. Kidding! But I am reaching the point where I've started to want to actually do something. I've talked about being defined by something other than my kids for years, but now I'm feeling that I need a job. And it's more than want . . . it is NEED. The truth is, I always thought I was going to have another child. I just never felt done, and even though the window of opportunity was narrowing, I kept thinking it would happen. But what's become very clear over the last six months is that there will be no more babies in my future, and that dream has left me with an emptiness inside that needs to be filled by something.

I need something to fill my mind, something to keep me busy. I've thought about turning my hobby into something bigger—I have sold restored pieces to friends over the years, and Claire, who's my closest friend, has always said I should open some kind of a store. We have a barn on our property where I work—I turned half of it into a workshop, and she thinks I should open it as a store. I love the idea, but get a little overwhelmed when I think of all I'd have to do.

But I do know I need something to fill the void.

G x

Ms. Sloth,
It isn't lucky you're married. I'd say it's hugely unlucky. For me. ;)

Also, I beg to differ about a woman with a hammer. . . .

And finally, I know you have no ulterior motive. That's why I like you. I'm leaving now for the airport. I'll email when I land!

M x

Nine

Gabby is not a woman who particularly enjoys shopping. Most of her clothes are bought online; when forced to buy in person, she is most likely to run to Main Street for stretch pants and some long-sleeved T-shirts at the Gap, rarely anything more sophisticated. Dressing up has never been very interesting to her.

When she was young, growing up in London, she would watch movies about American teenagers, and long to wear the clothes they wore. She wanted faded jeans and Converse, baseball shirts and Top-Siders.

She was something of a tomboy back then, and even now, she is rarely out of her Converse sneakers, although she will team them with yoga pants and a cute hoodie.

She pulls her curls back into a ponytail and jumps in the car, actually looking forward to shopping, hoping she will find the outfit she's looking for, because she has it in mind, she knows exactly what she wants to project: rumpled, sexy, confident; a woman who is fully aware of the power she holds.

Leggings and boots made of the softest leather, that reach up to her knees, maybe over. The long, sky-blue sheer alpaca sweater she noticed in the window of Great Stuff, with the sweet charm necklace they paired with it, and the fine cashmere scarf in the same color, twisted loosely around the neck.

That's what she wants to wear when she meets Matt for a drink this week. Nothing too overt. It isn't as if anything's going to happen—it certainly isn't as if she's going to be unfaithful—but how lovely it is to be noticed, to be flirted with. This is an outfit that Gabby has carefully put together in her mind, hopeful it will be beautiful and sexy without shouting anything out, without sending any messages to Matt that she is interested in anything other than a friendship.

Not that she hasn't imagined something happening, but she has only done this a handful of times, and is trying very hard to stop. She knows this is an indulgence, a fantasy. This isn't what their correspondence is about, and even if there may be a chemistry, that doesn't mean anything.

Gabby thinks of all the times she and her friends have discussed people who have been caught having affairs. She, and they, have never understood it. Just because you're married doesn't mean you'll never be attracted to anyone else, Gabby had always said. The point is, you have a choice, and you do the right thing; you don't act on it.

She still believes those words to be true, but at that time, she hadn't ever been attracted to anyone else. It is very easy to say things like that when temptation has never crossed your path.

Temptation is crossing her path now. She absolutely wants to believe she won't do anything, is telling herself over and over that she and Matt are just friends, but if he were to lean over and kiss her, she honestly doesn't know if she would have the strength to resist.

In her mind, she pushes him away. Not before she feels his lips, his tongue, holds his top lip between her own. She will push him gently back while shaking her head. "No," she will say, regret and desire etched on her face. "We can't. I'm married. I love my husband."

He will understand, and let her go, knowing that he may have lost the one woman who could make him happy. They will resolve not to stay in touch, and Gabby will be weighed down with sadness for a few days, but will then be buoyed by the rightness of her decision, will fall in love with Elliott all over again.

Where is Elliott in all this? He doesn't feature much. Her thoughts have been wholly and all-consumingly filled with Matt. She wakes up in the night with his name dancing on her lips, carries her cell phone with her all day, glancing at the screen every few minutes to see if there is a new message.

Elliott is accusing her of daydreaming all the time, and it is true; she may be going through the motions, but she is not present in her life. Half the time she has a dreamy smile on her lips, which, when asked, she will put down to thinking about a funny TV show, or something that the girls said (and she is getting used to having stories ready), or she is trying not to feel blue that six hours have gone by and still Matt hasn't responded. She will feel embarrassed, and angry, will vow not to respond to his next email, but then it will arrive, and it will be so lovely, she will stop whatever she is doing to find a quiet corner to send him back her innermost thoughts.

Gabby pulls into a spot behind Main Street, then cuts through the Gap, this time not glancing around, going straight to the shoe store. The boots are inside—no heel, but beautifully cut, narrow,

Italian leather. She pulls them on, then tucks her yoga pants in as she studies herself in the mirror, a smile on her face.

This morning she had told Elliott she was thinking of going shopping today. Because she is so bad at it, because she dislikes it so much, on those rare occasions she announces she is going to spend some money, Elliott always encourages her.

"What are you looking for?" Elliott had asked, watching her as she pulled off her robe to get dressed.

Gabby had shrugged. "I just feel like all I wear is jeans or leggings and sneakers. I have no idea why I grew up to be a teenage boy, but I feel like I need some more feminine clothes. I saw a sweater on Main Street that I'm slightly obsessing about, and I thought I might get some knee-high boots."

Elliott's face lit up. "Mmm, sexy." He pulled Gabby over, holding her naked body close as he murmured in pleasure.

"Oh stop." Gabby stepped back, laughing.

"Why stop?" Elliott said, moving back in as Gabby's smile disappeared.

"I'm serious, Ell. I have a ton to do. I need to get dressed."

Elliott put his hands up. "Okay, okay. Sorry. Forgive me."

Gabby got dressed quickly and silently, not looking at Elliott again. There were times, of late, when he had been getting on her nerves, and she found herself snapping at him far more than she would like.

She knows her hormones are raging, and does plan on seeing a doctor, an endocrinologist, someone to help, but life is always so busy, and tomorrow never comes. And so she is left to take it out on her husband, filled with remorse afterward, as she tries to make it up to him, only to find she is still irritated.

Gabby is not stupid. She knows this is her resentment at him deciding to have the vasectomy, a resentment that is choosing to come out now because she is projecting perfection onto an alternate man. Which doesn't mean the resentment isn't real. This is the resentment she has been trying to push down so hard, for so many months; a resentment that is refusing to disappear, is instead growing stronger.

In the store she tries on the sweater. It is even better than she had imagined. The girls in the store crowd around complimenting her, layering jewelry, scarves, a shearling vest, running to the other side of the store and coming back with the perfect pants, another wonderful sweater that would look perfect on her.

She leaves with three large bags, and walks straight into Claire on the street outside.

"What are you doing here?" Claire looks at her bags, aghast. "Am I sleepwalking? I'm looking at three bags of clothes from my favorite store, and you hate shopping. Actually, you hate clothes."

Gabby laughs. "I know! Can you believe it? Elliott gave me permission to feminize my wardrobe, so what's a girl to do? I had to take him up on it."

"Great. You finally decide you want to be a girl, and I can't even enjoy it with you." She proffers her own bag, "A Pea in the Pod. That's all I've got to look forward to."

"Want to grab a coffee?" Gabby grins.

"Only if it's decaf. So what's up with you recently? You look all glowing. If I didn't know better I'd say you were pregnant."

"Sadly not. Must be menopause," Gabby says. "Haven't you ever heard of the menopausal glow? No? Me neither. I think it's just that life is going well. I feel . . . happy. You know how you always said you loved being in your forties because you felt truly comfortable in your skin, that you didn't need to prove yourself to anyone anymore, and I never quite felt that way? Well, I get it. I do. I've just suddenly found myself feeling really good."

"That's great. I remember a couple of months ago you were

saying you felt really middle-aged. It's great you're feeling better. Is this what the whole makeover's about?"

"Makeover?"

"Your grey hair has disappeared, and you're spending fortunes. If I didn't know better"—Claire peers at her as they stand in line in Starbucks—"I'd think you were having an affair."

"Oh ha-ha." Gabby rolls her eyes. "Yes. I am having an affair, for I am exactly the type. In fact, I'm having three affairs, all at the same time. Why do you think I had to cover the grey hair? It was the only way I could attract all three gorgeous lovers."

Gabby may not be having an affair, but she is about to have a drink, with a man who isn't her husband. She has no idea what to say, how to explain it to Elliott. It occurred to her that she could orchestrate another girls' night out, and, coincidence!—the same man would be at the bar and the two of them could, as they had before, spend the evening talking together.

This time her friends would grow suspicious. Who even knows if Gabby and Matt would be left alone. She doesn't want to lie to Elliott. A lie, however small, feels like the beginning of a slippery slope, but how can she possibly explain it? Can she tell the truth, couched in a white lie, so she will still be able to live with herself?

Are you sure you don't mind?" Gabby now feels guilty at buying so much, even though Elliott is delighted with her new wardrobe.

"Are you kidding? Gabby, you look incredible! I feel like I have a new wife! I had no idea you were this sexy, honey!"

"Great," she grumbles. "Thanks a lot."

"Gabs, you know what I mean. Everything you bought looks incredible. You know, usually you wear such shapeless clothes, no one can even see your figure, but everything you bought just shows it off. You are seriously hot."

"I've lost a couple of pounds." Gabby turns to look at her side view in the closet mirror. "I kind of needed these pants because the ones I have are swimming on me."

"I can see," Elliott says approvingly. "Not that you needed to lose anything, but it suits you. How much have you lost?"

"About six pounds," Gabby says. "I wasn't even trying. I just haven't been hungry."

Elliott looks down at his own stomach, more cuddly than ever before. "I wish I knew what that felt like," he says. "Oh well. At least there's more of me to love."

Gabby, looking at him, feels a surge of love. "The more of you to love, the better." She leans down and kisses him before sitting on his lap and sliding her arms up around his neck. "Anyway, you're still as gorgeous as the day we met."

"Liar," he laughs.

"Oh! Guess what!" She stands up and starts to undress, carefully folding the scarf. "You know that Fourforsight website I joined?"

"No."

"It's another social media thing."

"I know that. I just didn't know you joined it." Elliott shakes his head with a laugh. "Isn't that like a Facebook for hipsters? You and the girls with all this stuff. I don't know how you find the time. What was your last obsession, Pinterest?"

"Yes. Over it. This one's the new one, and they contacted me and asked me if I wanted to take part in a focus group study! Isn't that exciting? The guy who started it is flying around meeting people and talking to them about the website and what changes they'd like to see!"

"Okay." Elliott shrugs. "If you say it's exciting, then I'm excited for you."

"Well, I am excited. I feel like I could be part of a huge change. So it's Wednesday night. I have to go to some hotel in Greenwich."

"Sounds great. Just make sure you wear some of these new clothes—you want them to think you're a hot mommy, right?"

"You better believe it." Gabby's smile is large as she turns to slide the scarf onto a shelf.

Ten

Gabby walks through the lobby of the hotel, aware that each of the three men sitting and standing around by the front door is following her with their eyes. She isn't so much walking as sailing, a confident smile on her face as she takes long strides, her new boots click-clacking on the marble floor, her hips swaying, her hair, styled into soft sexy waves instead of the more usual unruly curls, bouncing gently on her shoulders.

She has a quality tonight that is more than mere beauty. It is clear to anyone watching that this is a woman well aware of how powerful, sexy, and gorgeous she is, who exudes confidence from every pore, and it is this that makes her so compelling.

Gabby walks through to the bar, and stands for a few seconds in the doorway, squinting slightly as she looks around for Matt. She has made sure to be fifteen minutes late, so she wouldn't be the first one here.

And there he is. At one end of the bar. Her heart jumps into her mouth, and at that exact moment he turns and sees her, his face lighting up. Gabby falters suddenly.

Oh *God,* she thinks. Look how . . . *gorgeous* he is. What am I *doing* here? What the *hell* am I doing here? I need to leave.

But she doesn't. She walks toward him, the smile on her face matching the smile on his, and they stand for a second or two, grinning at each other, before he extends his arms and wraps them around Gabby, who closes her eyes as he holds her tight.

This is fine, she thinks. I can do this. We are friends. I'm just going to be chatty and friendly while still retaining my distance. I'm the one in control here, and I will not let this stray into territory that might get me into trouble.

They sit down, at the bar, Matt swiveling his stool so he is facing her, and they look at each other and both start to laugh, Gabby shaking her head and looking away.

"I don't know why I'm laughing," laughs Matt.

"I don't know either," laughs Gabby. "But I'd love a drink."

"Coming right up." He orders before sitting back to gaze at her.

"What?" Gabby is self-conscious. "Do I have something in my teeth?"

"No. You look great." She notices his eyes darken as he says this, knows this means he's aroused, and feels waves of embarrassment, pleasure, before remembering her manners. "Thank you. How was the flight?"

"Good. How's the piece you're working on. Didn't you say it was a desk?"

Gabby smiles. He remembered. She had found a dark wooden desk at the consignment store and had stripped it with the intention of painting it a soft dove grey, replacing the handles with small black iron knobs, reinventing it as a Gustavian-style desk, perfect for the study. "It's going well," she says, getting out her cell phone and scrolling through for pictures.

As she scrolls, she realizes Matt is looking at the screen, at all the evidence of her life, her real life, which she doesn't want him to see. She doesn't want him to see her husband, her children, the signs of a middle-aged housewife, however much he may want to think otherwise. She tilts her screen slightly to prevent him seeing, but it isn't enough.

"Wait! Is that your husband?"

They haven't talked about Elliott. Gabby isn't even sure Matt knows his name. It wouldn't feel right to discuss him, nor does she want Matt to see him. "No," she lies. "Just some friends back home."

"Oh come on, let me see," he insists.

"No." She is firm, dropping the phone back in her bag. "Can't find the desk, sorry. Take my word for it, though, I'm doing an amazing job."

"I don't doubt it." Matt raises his glass, dropping the subject. "Cheers!" he says, as Gabby raises hers. "To us."

Gabby says nothing as she drinks. Us? To *us*? What us? There is no "us." And yet she can't deny a thrill at hearing him say the word, and she can't deny a thrill as her eyes unconsciously move across his body, remembering the picture of him surfing. She can't deny a thrill as he watches her looking at him, gives her a slow, sexy smile that makes her tingle down to her toes.

What am I *doing*? she thinks. I need to leave.

She doesn't. Of course she doesn't. She has another drink.

Their smiles do not fade, each of them high on the other's company, and it is only as Gabby sips her third drink that she realizes Matt is talking, has been talking for quite some time, and she has no idea what he is saying.

"I'm drunk," she says suddenly, staring at the glass as she tries to focus, pushing it away and shaking her head as if to clear her thoughts.

Matt laughs. "You haven't had that much."

"I know. I'm a total lightweight," she says. "Drinking on an empty stomach has never been good for me."

"Or, perhaps, it's very good for you. Depends which way you look at it."

Gabby snorts with laughter, then shakes her head, looking up at him from under her eyelashes.

"What? Why are you looking at me like that?"

"Because you," she says, shaking a finger at him, knowing she is only saying this because she has had too much to drink, knowing she would never dare say this when sober, "are dangerous."

Matt sits back, feigning dismay. "Me? *Me? Dangerous?* I'm not the dangerous one." A slow smile spreads on his face. "*You're* the dangerous one."

Gabby shakes her head. "I'm an old married woman," she says, only able to say these words because for the first time in years she doesn't feel like an old married woman, knows she doesn't look like an old married woman. "You're the sexy younger man flirting with a woman he can't have."

"Oh?" Matt sits forward and leans very close, his lips brushing her ear as a shiver runs through her entire body. "Are you absolutely sure I'm flirting with a woman I can't have?" His voice is a whisper of desire as Gabby closes her eyes, her whole body on fire, knowing this is too much, this is more than she can handle. His hand is on her knee, and it is as if it is burning through her skin; she can feel him in every bone, every fiber, every tendon of her body, and it is so delicious, so intoxicating, she wants to just sit like this forever, his breath brushing her ear, his hand on her leg.

She is married. To a wonderful man. The thought of Elliott, his face were he to see them, his devastation were she to be unfaithful and were he to find out, is sobering.

She opens her eyes to see Matt, his face inches from hers. A few seconds go by as they stare at each other, before Gabby shakes her head.

"Matt. I . . . I can't do this. I'm not the sort of woman . . ." She stops. She doesn't know how to say this. "I'm married. This feels like too much. I'm sorry."

"It's fine." He jumps back, his face filled with apology. "I didn't want to make you uncomfortable. I'm sorry. It's my fault."

"Oh Matt. If I were ten years younger, and single . . ." Her voice trails off.

"You're perfect exactly as you are," he says. "You are. Truly." He gives a wry smile. "It's my bad luck to have found the perfect woman, who's unavailable."

"We can still be friends," Gabby says.

"Absolutely," Matt says. "Friends."

He calls Gabby a cab, as she mentally kicks herself. She did the right thing, of course she did the right thing, but he is slightly distant now. The playful flirtatiousness, the dangerous edge of earlier, has gone, and Gabby would do anything, *anything*, to get it back.

When the cab arrives, Matt puts his arms around her in a perfunctory hug, but Gabby steps back, then moves forward again, taking his face gently in her hands, opening her lips as she kisses him slowly, softly, moving back when she feels his tongue. No tongues. Just . . . teasing. She just needs him to keep wanting her. She needs to continue feeling as beautiful as he has made her feel, and if that requires a tiny bit of teasing, so be it.

This time she pulls back to see a smile of delight on his face.

"Friends?" he whispers.

"Friends." She nods, climbing into the cab, her heart threatening to pound right out of her chest.

The girls are fast asleep when she walks in. Olivia sleeps in the dark, her face as soft and peaceful as when she was a baby. Gabby brushes her hair out of her face and kisses her on the forehead, then the cheek, then the cheek again. When the girls are asleep, at their most vulnerable, not fighting, not looking at her with disdain, not being the vocal, confident children they are, she is reminded of their innocence, falling in love with them all over again, every night.

Alanna's light is on, her iPod touch still clutched in her hand. Gabby prises it out, then hesitates, clicking the screen on. In the last six weeks Alanna has set up an Instagram account, and Gabby, not allowed to look under normal circumstances, could perhaps find out more about what's going on.

But the iTouch is suddenly password protected, and nothing Gabby can think of works. With a sigh and several kisses on the forehead and cheeks of her younger child, she turns off the light and moves quietly down the hallway to her own bedroom.

The television is on when she walks in, Elliott illuminated by the bluish light of *Homeland*, his mouth open as he snores gently, the covers mussed up around him, his T-shirt ridden up to expose the rounded belly she has always loved so much.

And suddenly Gabby feels like crying. The familiarity and comfort in seeing Elliott, the thought of having come so close to doing something so terrible—she did come close, as close as she has ever come—pricks her eyes with tears.

Kicking her boots off, she snuggles into Elliott's side, wanting to smell him, feel him, wanting the safety of her husband to somehow negate the danger of the evening. She nuzzles into his neck just as he stirs.

"Oh, hey! What time is it?"

"Elevenish. I just got back."

"It must have been fun." Elliott stirs, pushes himself up on the pillows and smiles at his wife. "Did they think you were a total hot mommy?"

"You know what?" She is coquettish. "I think he did. This kid, Matt, who started it, definitely seemed to think I was a MILF."

"He's clearly a man of excellent taste." Elliott grins, tracing a hand lazily along the collar of her shirt, moving down to unbutton the top button, then the next as he pulls her toward him.

Gabby kisses him, helps him shrug off her shirt, pulls his own T-shirt off.

"Did you lock the door?" he whispers.

"No. Hang on." She jumps off, comes back seconds later, and pulls him on top of her. His fingers are between her legs, her own stroking him to hardness as she closes her eyes, and once again—please let this be the last time—imagines that it is not her familiar, loved, teddy bear of a husband on top of her, but a hard-bodied, virile, unbelievably sexy thirty-something.

It is Matt's fingers she feels inside her, Matt's body she moves her lips down until she takes him in her mouth, and she is more active, more energetic, more turned on than she has been in years.

Afterward, Elliott cradles her in his arms and laughs. "What got into you tonight? You were amazing."

"Isn't that how MILFs are supposed to show their husbands the love?"

"I don't know, but I sure as hell hope so," he laughs, turning the television back on. Within five minutes, he is gently snoring, leaving Gabby to replay every single thing that happened tonight, before she came home.

Eleven

Gabby hadn't realized quite how obsessed she had become until the emails stopped coming.

She waited, the next morning, for Matt to send one of his customary emails, determining he should be the one to make the first move, not her, but by lunchtime she was worried. She had changed everything when she said no. Why did she say no? Why could she not have just kept it going for a while longer?

At two o'clock she can't take it anymore. She can't focus on anything, and with shaking hands she sends him a text, attempting to keep it light, fun; attempting to stay in the spirit of their correspondence before last night.

But nor does she want to assume the intimacy that has existed between them, not until she is reassured that he feels the same way. No "Surf Dude" today, no easy jokes. She needs to wait to see where she stands.

MATT, JUST WANTED TO THANK YOU FOR A WONDERFUL EVENING. HOPE YOUR MEETINGS GO WELL. SPEAK SOON . . .

Delete. Much too formal.

DEAR MATT, GREAT EVENING! THANK YOU! LET'S DO IT AGAIN.

Delete.

M—DELICIOUS, DANGEROUS NIGHT. THANK YOU. XX

Send.

Hi Liv." Gabby comes into the kitchen just after Olivia has got off the bus. "How was school?"

She doesn't know why she asks this question. Every day, when the girls get home, Gabby has a need to ask them how school was. Perhaps, she reasons, this is because she was never asked. Somehow this has become cemented in her head as being symbolic of what kind of a mother you are; a good mother, an interested mother, always asks how your day was.

Alanna always says fine, even when Gabby can see the day hasn't been fine. She is quieter than she used to be, frequently going straight upstairs to do her homework, rather than sitting at the kitchen table, as she has always done.

Even when her teen and tween both grunt in response, Gabby has to ask the question. There are other things she tries to do in order to be a good mother: freshly baked cakes sit on the cake stand for when her children get home, although of late Olivia has announced she is on a diet and will not eat anything with sugar or flour in it. Still, there is something about a kitchen that smells of cinnamon, and sugar, and caramelizing butter, that Gabby thinks is what a home should be.

Olivia grunts in return before dumping her backpack in the middle of the floor and opening the fridge, peering in at the shelves.

"There's nothing for me to eat," she says, belligerent, as Gabby slides her out of the way to point out the cheese, the yogurts, the fruit.

"I don't want fruit."

"So have a yogurt."

"I don't eat yogurt. I'm vegan."

"What?" Gabby stares at her. "Since when?"

Olivia shrugs. "I've been avoiding meat for a while. I just decided today to go completely vegan."

"Great," Gabby says, not unsarcastically. "What am I supposed to feed you?"

"Vegetables. Salads. Gluten-free pasta. Quinoa."

"Eggs?"

"No. Nothing from an animal."

"Cheese?"

"No. Dairy products are the worst."

Gabby sighs dramatically. "What am I supposed to do with the macaroni and cheese I made for dinner tonight?" She suppresses a smile as Olivia pauses, her mother's homemade macaroni and cheese being her favorite food in the world.

"Are you just saying that?"

"No!" Gabby opens the fridge and pulls the foil off an oval dish to show her.

"I guess I could eat it tonight. I'll start again tomorrow."

"Absolutely." Gabby turns away, knowing this will, as with all of Olivia's fads, last approximately two weeks, at most.

"The garden guy wants to see you. He's outside," Olivia offers nonchalantly as an afterthought.

Gabby grabs her checkbook from the kitchen drawer and runs outside, writing "$50 made payable to cash" to the mow, blow, and go guy in the driveway, going straight back inside to check her phone, except it isn't where she left it, on the desk above the check drawer. Damn. Where the hell is it? She turns, running her eyes over the counter, until Olivia's voice pipes up from the family room, filled with suspicion.

"Mom? Who's Matt?"

Her heart thumps in her chest. "What do you mean?"

Olivia stands up from where she had been hidden, slumped down in an armchair facing the fireplace, and turns to face her mother, her expression one of distrust and confusion, of wanting to be reassured, of pushing down a distrustful anger.

"Ur wicked sexy when drunk . . . wink, Matt kiss kiss hug kiss." Olivia cocks her hand on her hip as she reads, before staring at her mother accusingly.

Gabby is aware the color has drained from her face. How should she play it, what should she say, what the fuck was she thinking, leaving her phone around unlocked. But, wait . . . she didn't leave it unlocked.

"How did you unlock my phone?"

"Alanna and I have both known your code for ages. Which doesn't explain why you're getting these texts from someone other than Dad."

"It's not what you think," Gabby says quickly. "Dad knows

about it. It's the guy who interviewed me and we were joking he fancied me. Let me see." She holds out her hand for the phone, reading the text. "Wow, it sounds like he really did fancy me." She feigns surprise. Badly.

"What about your text before? I'm not stupid, Mom. 'A delicious and dangerous night'? What the fuck does that mean?"

"Excuse me?" Gabby's voice rises in guilt and shame. "Don't you dare speak to your mother like that."

"Don't you dare send texts like that to someone who isn't Dad!" Olivia's voice rises.

"I'm not doing anything," Gabby says weakly, deflated, overwhelmed with shame.

"Tell that to Dad," Olivia spits.

"You know what, Olivia? I plan to. This isn't what you think." Gabby snatches the phone away and deletes the text, going upstairs to her bedroom and shutting the door.

First she emails Elliott.

Our daughter seems to think I am having an affair with the child I met with last night, and is now being a teenage bitch from hell. Incidentally, though, he did send me a text saying I'm sexy!! You were right—the hot mommy clothes worked! Meanwhile, I'm flying high that I've still got it (you lucky man, you). Will you talk to Olivia? She seems to think I encouraged him, which is laughable. What time are you home tonight?

Love you,

G xxx

And next, Matt.

My dangerous friend, it might be wiser not to text. My fault entirely, as I texted first, but seems my daughters are adept at breaking codes to unlock my phone. I truly did love seeing you last night. I don't remember the last time I had so much fun. You are utterly delicious, which you know, and you have brought sunshine into my life all day today. Thank you.

G xoxox

Gabby keeps her phone tucked into the rear pocket of her jeans for the rest of the night, going to the bathroom to pull it out and check for a response, but none comes. The high from the night before starts to wane. By the time Elliott comes home, she is feeling a mixture of depression and anger.

Why hasn't he responded? What's wrong with her? Why did she have to send that email to him? Why does she now feel so humiliated? Elliott walking in just before seven raises in her both relief and guilt.

"Where are the girls?"

"Alanna's in the basement watching TV, and Olivia's in her room, still not speaking to me. She thinks I wrote something provocative to that guy, Matt."

Elliott cocks his head. "Did you?"

"No!" Gabby looks away, shaking her head with a dismissive laugh. "I wrote it was delightful and dangerous because I had to reveal stuff about myself with the questionnaire. I think she thought it meant something else."

"Oh." His voice is drawn out as he laughs. "Okay. She phoned me, upset, and did tell me you had written a text saying something about dangerous."

"See? I think she thinks I'm having an affair."

"Yup," Elliott laughs. "That's exactly what she thinks. And she thinks I'm an idiot for not seeing it."

"Well she's right, because I am exactly the kind of woman to have an affair. After all, I'm married to a terrible man, and really, my life is so awful, why not blow it up? Just for fun?"

Elliott shakes his head with a sigh. "Teenagers. Their frontal lobe isn't fully connected. As we well know, it leads to all kinds of disasters. I'll go and talk to her, because she was really upset. You should talk to her afterward. Don't be hard on her, just reassure her."

"Okay," Gabby says, although at this moment in time, she'd be just as happy not having to look her daughter in the eye.

Twenty minutes later Elliott comes downstairs with Olivia, who's looking both grumpy and sheepish.

"Anything you'd like to say to your mother?"

"Sorry," she mumbles.

"And Gabby? Anything you'd like to say to Olivia?"

Gabby frowns at Elliott, no idea what he means. "Sorry?" she attempts.

"Right," he coaxes, "and we both want Olivia to know that you are not having an affair, nor would you have an affair."

"Exactly," Gabby says, wishing she could be as certain, although there is still no response from Matt, and anger is starting to set in.

"Come on." Elliott gives his elder daughter a kiss. "Go get Alanna and let's have dinner."

Their evening is uneventful, Gabby aware she has had something of a lucky escape. She has to stop. She wants to stop. But all she can think about, all she has been thinking about for weeks, is Matt.

She is finishing off stacking the dishwasher when Elliott walks up behind her.

"Gabs, by the way, I have to be at a GI conference in April. Harvey was going but it turns out it's his anniversary and one of us needs to be there. I know it's a while away, but you don't mind if I go, do you?"

"Of course not. Isn't that the weekend the girls are going to see Jill?"

"We're going to Aunt Jill's?" Alanna's face lights up. "You didn't tell me."

"I forgot," Elliott says. "Sorry. Your cousins are desperate to see you so we were going to drop you off and have a romantic weekend." He turns back to Gabby. "I'm really sorry, sweetie. The conference is in New Mexico, at a big hotel. Maybe you could come. We could turn it into a romantic weekend there."

"Right." Gabby shakes her head. "A romantic weekend during which time I wouldn't actually see you."

"Probably not, but you could have massages and spa treatments, and I think the weather's great."

"It sounds glorious, but not nearly as glorious as being in my own house, all by myself!" She shudders with pleasure. "Now that's a treat that almost never happens. I get to sleep in our great big bed with no one stealing the covers, I can eat sandwiches from Trader Joe's for two whole days if I feel like it, I can work in the barn without worrying about having to come in and cook for anyone, or clean, or do laundry. Bliss!"

"Great, Mom," Alanna says. "Why don't you just say you hate being a mother."

"Okay." Gabby shrugs cheerfully. "I hate being a mother."

"Mom!" Both girls look at her, horrified.

"I am so kidding." She smiles. "I love being a mother. Especially when you were little. How did the two of you get so big? When did you stop needing me so much?"

"Uh-oh," Alanna flashes a look at Olivia. "Mom's getting sentimental."

"I'm sorry." Gabby blinks, aware her eyes are glistening. "I just miss those days so much. Meanwhile, I love the two of you more than anything, but I so rarely have time that's just for me. And count yourselves lucky, girls. I had a mother who really did hate being a mother."

"No!" says Olivia, who adores her grandmother. "Grasha says she was just busy."

"That's the point," Gabby says. "Grasha was far more interested in everyone else than she was in me. But," she concedes, "she is a much better grandmother than she ever was a mother, it's true."

"When are we going to see her?" Alanna says. "Can we go to London again by ourselves?"

"I think maybe Grasha should come here next time." She and Elliott exchange a look. They had sent the girls over to London last year, as unaccompanied minors. All had gone extremely well until the girls actually reached the Roth/de Roth house, at which point it became clear that Grasha was a far better grandmother than mother only when not on her own turf.

Once on her own turf, she hadn't changed at all. The girls came home excitedly reporting the streams of freaks sitting around Grasha's kitchen table. Because their grandmother was "so busy," they were left to explore London by themselves, which they adored, although Gabby had blanched at a ten-year-old and a fifteen-year-old making their way around London alone.

"Darling, *you* did it," her mother said innocently, when pressed. But, as Gabby pointed out, she had been *raised* in London; she wasn't a naive child from the suburbs of Connecticut who had never been to London before.

To their credit, and much to Gabby's pride, the girls had not spent all their time in Topshop and Primark, but had been to Tate Modern, ridden the London Eye, been to various markets, and even—and of this Gabby was most proud—watched *A Midsummer Night's Dream* in Regent's Park. All by themselves!

Going to stay with Jill, Elliott's sister in Manhattan, is a far safer proposition.

Being on her own, given Gabby's recent obsession, may, on the other hand, turn out to be the most dangerous proposition of all.

There is no response from Matt by bedtime, leaving Gabby in a haze of anger and insecurity. She is tempted to email, asking if she did something wrong, but manages to resist, telling herself not to act like a crazy woman; telling herself she is married, she has to let this obsession go; telling herself to grow up and move on.

"Are you okay?" Elliott has been standing in the doorway, watching her.

"Fine. Why?"

"You keep putting the Kindle down and frowning. It looks like you're either very worried or very angry about something."

Gabby puts the Kindle down and holds her arms out for Elliott. "I'm sorry, sweetie. I guess I was just thinking about Olivia, and the teenage stuff. I've always felt that we've managed pretty well, but I really didn't like the way she spoke to me tonight. I've noticed this a few times recently. I was thinking about whether we're in for a rocky ride."

Gabby hugs Elliott, knowing how he is loving being in her arms. She is aware she hasn't been as affectionate of late, has been distracted, and she can feel him relax, happy to have her back.

"She just misinterpreted and she was angry," he says. "I understand. Perhaps she was rude, but she was scared. All in all Olivia's a great kid, and I think we've gotten off pretty unscathed. If she has a few moments of rudeness, I think we're doing pretty damn well. Compare her to Jolie, Gabs. Look at what we could be dealing with."

Claire's daughter, Jolie, once one of Olivia's best friends, has gravitated toward the fast crowd in school. Once one of the brightest, she is now far more interested in drinking and partying. Her clothes have gone from classic cute prepster—J. Crew, Sperry's, cashmere cardigans—to juvenile hooker: micro skirts, five-inch platform heels, tight shirts to show off the cleavage pushed up by her Victoria's Secret leopard-print bra.

In the last two years Jolie has become surly and truculent, screaming at her parents for no apparent reason. Claire, often despairing, has confessed she hopes to God this baby she's carrying is a boy, for she never wants another one like Jolie.

Gabby sighs. "You're right, you're right. I know you're right. It just . . . worries me when she acts like that."

"Don't worry." Elliott smiles at his wife and traces the frown line on her forehead. "It ages you and I can't have my hot wife looking old."

"There's always Botox," Gabby says, half-joking. She had long denigrated the many women she knew who suddenly appeared looking not younger, exactly, but . . . smoother. There was something almost indefinably different about them, and it took her and Claire a while before they figured it out. Botox had smoothed their foreheads, in many cases unnaturally arching their eyebrows, giving them a look of permanent surprise; cheekbones had miraculously grown into Marlene Dietrich–style high apples, their skin strangely taut and shiny, thanks to chemical peels.

Claire was desperate for Botox but had a fear of needles and would never do it, and Gabby had never wanted any of it, until very recently, when she started to think it might be rather wonderful if she were able to look younger. Why not erase the frown lines, eradicate the crow's feet? Would her lips not look better if slightly plumped? Her face more radiant if some filler were added to raise her cheekbones to where they would have been had the good Lord been generous enough to actually grace her with any in the first place?

But Elliott would not allow it. The very idea of injecting anything unnatural for vanity was anathema to him. The side effects were unknown, he said. Wait ten years, he said, and we would find out terrible things.

The lure was getting stronger. Gabby stands in the bathroom, staring at her face in the mirror, fingers pulling her skin ever so slightly taut, pouting to see what her lips would look like bigger.

"You're not having Botox," Elliott says, moving to his side of the bed and reaching for the remote control to turn the television on.

At 4:23 a.m. Gabby is wide awake, and has been for two hours. She had woken up, as she so often does these days, and grabbed her iPhone, now kept charging next to the bed, to see if Matt had responded, her heart leaping with exhilaration when she sees he has.

> Gabrielle who is perfectly dangerous . . . do you know that song? Shades Apart? You ought to listen to it. . . . I'm sorry I've been out of touch—things have been a little crazy over here. I had a wonderful time with you last night. You are just as beautiful, bright, clever, and special as I remember. Actually, more so. And that "friendly" kiss goodbye? What can I say. WOW. Your husband is a lucky

guy and I'm jealous as hell. I'm flying off to Cincinnati this week and have a ton of meetings so I may be a little out of touch. What do you have going on this week? I'm hoping to be back in about a month—cannot wait to see you again. xxxx

Gabby takes her iPhone into the bathroom, shuts the door, and reads the email yet again. What does it mean? He can't wait to see her again, yet the earlier part, the mention of her husband, seems so light, as if he doesn't really care, as if he's already written her off, already realized she is truly out of bounds.

But she is, as she keeps reminding herself, out of bounds. She is happily married, with no idea why she has this desperate need to keep this young man interested, other than to inflate her ego, which is both sad and shameful.

Aware of all this, Gabby still can't help the soaring of her heart when his emails come in, the ensuing obsessive picking apart of every paragraph, every word; looking for meaning between the lines.

Going straight to iTunes, she downloads the Shades Apart song, playing it over and over in her bathroom, looking for meaning in the lyrics, hoping Matt has deliberately picked this song because it will tell her how he truly feels about her. She listens, and she smiles.

Finally she knows she'll sleep well.

My friend, Cincinnati sounds . . . Midwestern. I've never been. That's where you can tell how very English I am—I've lived in Connecticut for years, but other than California, New York, Massachusetts, New Hampshire, and Vermont, I'm a disaster with the rest of the country—

couldn't tell you anything about it. Oh. Missed Arizona. We once had a wedding in Tucson. My husband's off to New Mexico for a conference the weekend of March 23rd. I was thinking of going too, but the girls are away that weekend, and the prospect of a weekend alone, in my own house, is just too tempting. Wouldn't it be fun if your schedule coincided with that weekend (even though it's ages away)? Think of the martinis we could drink! The fun we would have! Hope you travel safely, and don't worry about being out of touch—I have a busy week too. xxx

It is a test. Of course it is a test. She hits Send with a smile on her face, a clutch of anticipation around her heart. Will he rise to meet the challenge, and if so, what does that mean?

Gabby glides back to bed, plugging her iPhone back in to the charger, lying down, eyes closed, thinking about the weekend she'll be alone, fantasizing about Matt coming here.

Would she have him over to the house? No. That would be far too inappropriate. Would she sleep with him? No! Absolutely not. She just wants the flirtation to continue a little longer, wants to continue the high she gets from feeling appreciated, desired, by someone other than her husband.

Maybe she'll even get Botox. She'd never tell Elliott, but would go to the dermatologist, tell Elliott it's because she's having moles removed. On the night she sees Matt she'll wear something devastatingly fabulous, and will undoubtedly have lost ten pounds by the twenty-third.

If Matt visits on the weekend she's on her own, Botox it is.

Twelve

I can't believe you're actually doing this." Claire turns to study Gabby's face as she drives. "And behind Elliott's back! How are you going to explain it?"

"Moles and skin tags removed."

"No! I mean how are you going to explain your sudden lack of lines?" Claire bursts out laughing.

Gabby looks at Claire in disbelief. "Do you know my husband? Hello? He's a man. They never notice things like that."

"True," Claire says. "Trish said the first time she got Botox, her husband—she was still married at the time—just kept saying how beautiful she was. He had no idea, just thought she'd woken up one day looking years younger."

"She *would* have Botox," mutters Gabby. "I knew she wasn't that beautiful naturally."

"Stop being jealous. She is that beautiful naturally. Botox just erases the lines—it doesn't change your features. God I'm jealous.

I can't even dye my hair while I'm pregnant. Will you look at this?" She dips her head down to show the grey.

"I can't see," Gabby says. "I'm driving."

"You know I won't be able to actually come in and watch while they put the needles in, right? Even the thought of it makes me feel woozy and nauseous. But I cannot wait to see. You know it doesn't have an immediate effect, it takes a few days."

"I know. But you have to swear not to tell anyone, ever, I did this."

"I swear. I only told Trish. . . ."

"What!"

"Kidding. This stays between you and me. It's only Botox. It's not like you're getting a face-lift, although I suppose these days Botox is the equivalent of a facial. Really, it's no big deal. If I didn't have my needle phobia I'd be on that Botox wagon quicker than you can say 'frown.' "

The dermatologist, her long blond hair pulled back in a ponytail to frame her exquisite face, steps back to gaze at Gabby's face. "Have you ever thought about a little filler?"

"Filler?" Gabby asks dumbly.

"Restylane or Perlane. Just here in the cheekbones. Look." She hands her a small mirror, gesturing for Gabby to look at her face. "See these lines from your nose to your lips? As we age our faces drop, but if we added just a tiny bit of filler here"—she touches her cheekbones—"it would not only add back the volume you've lost, but would pull your face up and erase those lines. See?" She pulls Gabby's face up, Gabby's eyes widening with pleasure as the lines disappear. "I wouldn't do too much."

"You couldn't do too much," Gabby says. "I can't stand seeing those women with applelike cheekbones."

"Absolutely," says the dermatologist. "You just need a touch to restore volume. I do it on myself and do my cheekbones look bad?" She turns her head slowly from side to side, knowing how beautiful she is, how perfect her cheekbones. "I'm forty-seven but these treatments have helped me stay young."

"Forty-seven! No! What else do you do?" Gabby breathes in awe, wanting to look exactly like her.

"Sculptra," she says matter-of-factly. "You'd be a wonderful candidate for Sculptra, and you'd love it. Everyone I do it for loves it. You do it twice, all over the face, and it stimulates your body to start producing collagen again, so you immediately start looking younger. Even better, the effects are cumulative and last a couple of years. The more time goes on, the better you look. You'd look fantastic with Sculptra. It's the best thing I've ever done."

"I want it," Gabby bursts out, feeling entirely unlike herself. "When could you do it?"

The dermatologist laughs. "We'll do it all right now. And the Perlane, too?"

"Yes!" Gabby finds herself saying. "All of it!"

What took you so long?" Claire throws down a three-month-old copy of *Better Homes and Gardens*, grumbling as Gabby finally appears in the waiting room, a series of small, raised red bumps on her forehead.

"Ouch!" Claire winces. "Did it hurt? Was it awful?" She squints. "You did something to your cheekbones! Oh my God! What's the matter with your mouth?"

"It's numb. I had some other stuff and they gave me a local anesthetic. Do I look freaky?"

"What other stuff? Yes, you look freaky. What did you do?"

"Let's get out of here. I've just forked over a shocking amount of money. I need to recover and figure out a new story. There's no way in hell Elliott's going to believe I had a few moles removed for that price. It's at least a leg. Maybe both. Jesus, Claire. What the hell was I thinking?"

"I don't know. What *were* you thinking?"

"I wasn't. I just got completely carried away when I saw the dermatologist. Have you seen her? She's forty-seven! The woman looks thirty. I asked her for everything she has."

They are in the parking lot as Claire starts laughing uncontrollably, crossing her legs as she holds on to the trunk of the car for support. "Oh no," she weeps, "Don't make me laugh. I'll have an accident."

"I wasn't making you laugh. I'm telling you what happened."

"I know." Claire calms down enough to stand up straight, wiping her eyes. "I think you're having a midlife crisis."

Gabby doesn't say anything until they are in the car and driving. Claire's words keep reverberating through her head. Is that really what is happening? There is no question she feels as if her days as an attractive woman are numbered, but does that explain all that she has been going through? Is it really something as predictable as that?

"Do you think women *have* midlife crises?" she asks, as they approach traffic lights. "And does this mean I'm going to be going out and buying a red sports car and chatting up twenty-year-old hunks?" She tries to sound flippant, but images of Matt fill her head, his impending trip back to Connecticut, the way he smiles at her, the way his eyes darken when he looks at her, which makes her heart, even now, skip a beat.

Claire raises an eyebrow. "You were chatting up a rather gorgeous young man at the bar that time we went out," she says.

"I wasn't chatting him up." Gabby is indignant. "*He* was chatting *me* up."

"Are you still emailing him?"

Gabby, unable to keep it to herself, desperate to talk about him to someone, if only to tell her he was a new friend, had confided in Claire when he sent the first email.

"Sporadically," she lies. "I actually saw him last week. He was in town and we had a drink."

"No!" Claire's eyes are wide. "Gabby! You're so bad!" She peers at her. "Just a drink, right? Tell me nothing happened." Her face becomes stern.

"God, no!" Gabby says. "Just a drink. He was flirting, though."

"And how about you? Were you flirting back?"

"Maybe just a tiny bit. But I wouldn't do anything. I'm married, and I love Elliott. There's absolutely no way in hell I would ever have an affair, nor do anything to jeopardize my marriage."

"Did you tell Elliott you were having a drink with a guy you met in a bar?"

Gabby shifts uncomfortably in her seat. "Sort of. I told him I was meeting a guy. I didn't tell him how we met initially."

Claire shakes her head. "Oh Gabby. You know this is how these things always start, right?"

"What do you mean?"

"No one thinks they're going to have an affair. Everyone starts thinking it's just a fun flirtation, or a new friendship, that they'll never let anything happen. So they pretend to be friends, even though the only thing these two people have in common is a mutual lust, which eventually has to ignite. It's one of the laws of the universe. They have an affair, and mitigate it by deciding that it isn't just an affair, this is their *soul mate*. They aren't supposed to be married to the lovely, stable lawyer in boring old Connecticut, but are instead meant to be living with the dangerous, unstable, inappropriately young surfer in San Diego, or wherever it is the interloper happens to be from. They blow up their marriages, leaving devastation in their wake, to run off with said surfer, only for them both to discover, several weeks, months, but no more than a year down the line, that in fact they have nothing in common other than that lust, which has now, shock and horror, completely disappeared.

"They realize what a terrible mistake they've made, which is when they go back to their husband, tail between their legs, begging to come back, telling them how sorry they are, what a terrible mistake they made. The husbands have invariably moved on, and these women spend the rest of their lives beating off sad middle-aged professional singles at the handful of bars around town. It happened to Alison, and Denise. Oh, and Cathy. Same story. There. That's my cautionary tale for you. I shall say no more about it."

"You're so convinced. You don't really know what happens behind closed doors."

Claire shrugs. "It happened to my sister. Who's now in a crappy walk-up apartment in Pelham Manor, taking any job she can find and bitterly regretting leaving her rather wonderful husband for her metal teacher. The thing with Rodrigo lasted six months. Her husband has now remarried and had a baby, and the new wife, ten years younger, is living the life my sister should be living, in the Upper East Side apartment with doorman, nanny, and housekeeper. I've seen it happen time and time again."

Gabby laughs nervously. "That is so not going to happen to me."

"So stop the email," Claire says. "How would you feel if Elliott were emailing a younger, gorgeous woman? Him insisting they're just good friends wouldn't make you feel any better, would it?"

Gabby shakes her head. This has occurred to her. Particularly the last email referencing their "friendly kiss." It wouldn't do for

Elliott to read that. Not at all. And there's no way Matt is her soul mate. This would never follow the trajectory of Claire's sister. How ridiculous.

Although . . . she has indulged in the odd fantasy of what it would be like to live in Malibu, to be Matt's . . . partner. Not at the expense of leaving Elliott, more along the lines of if her life were something else entirely.

Sober, reasonable Gabby knows these are only fun fantasies, that she is not seriously thinking she and Matt may be an item. Sober, reasonable Gabby recognizes she is obsessed in an unnatural and unhealthy way, and that it can't go on much longer.

Sober, reasonable Gabby is hoping that perhaps, after the twenty-third, she'll be able to let go of it entirely.

Thirteen

Darling? Your car's here," Gabby calls up the stairs before opening the front door and gesturing to the driver, holding her fingers up to let him know Elliott will be down in five minutes.

"I wish you were coming," Elliott says, as he comes down the stairs, carry-on bag in hand. "I know we wouldn't have seen each other much, but we could have had dinner together at night. Now I'll have to go out with a bunch of boring old doctors."

"Yeah, right." Gabby snorts. "The last conference you went to you ended up drinking and dancing all night. If I recall, you came home saying something like you hadn't had so much fun in years."

Elliott laughs, dropping his bag on the floor to encircle his wife's waist. "Have I told you lately how beautiful you are?"

"Yes. You told me yesterday." Gabby smiles, still delighted.

"It's true. The older you get, the more beautiful you become."

Gabby declines to point out that this is, in fact, largely due to the

Botox, Perlane, and Sculptra, grateful only that it worked, and that he hasn't realized.

"Have a safe flight," she says, kissing him deeply. "I love you. And behave yourself."

"I will." He grins, picking up his bag and taking it to the car, blowing her a kiss as he is driven out the driveway, leaving Gabby, finally, entirely alone.

I want to see where you live," came the email. Gabby had already planned dinner, coming up with a small, hole-in-the-wall place in Bridgeport, a place where they were unlikely to run in to anyone she knew. But Matt was saying he wanted to see her home. Where she lived with her husband and daughters. That didn't feel right. That felt . . . inappropriately intimate.

"Why would you want to see where I live?" Gabby wrote. "I've already described it to you."

"Why wouldn't you want me to see where you live?" he responded. "I want to see the books you read, the paintings on your wall, the food in your fridge."

Gabby had smiled when she read that. She'd love to see his home, for exactly those reasons. She wants to see who he is when he isn't out in the world, composing himself, carefully contorting himself into the man he wants others to think he is.

And who is *she,* she wonders, walking around her house, trying to see it through his eyes, looking at what a newcomer might infer from what he sees.

The paintings in the house are, indeed, reflective of her. Elliott, never interested in art, has indulged her love of line drawings. Sketches of people, delicate renditions of cities she has been to, life studies in pen and ink fill every available space.

Books line the bookshelves, with various *objets* they have collected over the years. Ammonite fossils, small pots, porcelain sculptures of chickens that make her laugh. A bronze hand, fingers outstretched, filled with yearning. A bottom shelf crammed with the paperbacks she reads in between the heavier, hardback, literary tomes that are required reading for local dinner parties. She takes the paperbacks and stuffs them under the sofa. No one needs to see those—they make her look flighty and insubstantial.

Why do you even care what he thinks? she wonders. You are, after all, ten years older than he, which automatically makes you substantial. Less substantial, she smiles to herself, than she was three weeks ago. She hasn't weighed herself, but her jeans are loose, and her cheekbones more pronounced than ever; surely they would not be that pronounced from Perlane alone. Getting down on her knees, Gabby pulls the paperbacks from beneath the chair and puts them back.

I'm not doing anything, she thinks. We'll have a quick drink here, then go out. No romantic fires, no candles. This is not a seduction. I'm not even that comfortable having him here, she realizes, as the day progresses and her butterflies start to increase. I can't wait to see him, but in my own home? Not so much.

Gabby is ready by 6:45. Tonight she is dressing down. Tonight she can dress down, for her weight loss has given her a confidence she was missing before. In jeans and a T-shirt, she adds great boots with a heel, and a long thin strand of tiny labradorite and seed pearls looped around her neck.

She looks at herself in the mirror, and even she is impressed. But the boots have to go. Barefoot is better, at least when he gets here. That way she will look as if she's made no effort at all.

Her heart jumps into her mouth as she hears a taxi pull up and a door slam, then her doorbell is ringing; she is suddenly so nervous, she feels as if she might throw up.

She doesn't. She walks downstairs, forcing herself to take deep breaths as she opens the door to find Matt grinning at her. And then she is grinning back, and she isn't scared, or nervous, just truly, madly, deeply happy to see him, and they step toward each other and hug, and it doesn't feel inappropriate, or wrong. It feels lovely, and very, very right.

"You look amazing!" Matt steps back and looks at her. "Did you change your hair? Something's different. You look so beautiful."

"I lost some weight," Gabby says. "And I'm having a good hair day. That's it."

"I love that I'm here! Your home! I can't wait to get the full tour."

"Do you want some wine first?"

"Sure," he says, following her into the kitchen, admiring the Aga stove she insisted on having to remind her of her childhood home, even though it was the most expensive thing in the kitchen.

"I'm sure I have a bottle in here," Gabby says, rooting around in the fridge, knowing there is a bottle in there, for she placed it in there that morning. She turns and reaches for the corkscrew, stepping back as Matt steps in, taking both corkscrew and bottle from her and smiling down at her as he uncorks and she goes to get glasses.

On the other side of the kitchen, Gabby is aware Matt is watching her walk. It makes her feel sexy, and young, and more alive than ever before. There is a charge in the room, touching everything; a charge that has given both Gabby and Matt permanent smiles, smiles that occasionally dissolve into embarrassed laughter as they catch each other's eyes: both relieved, excited, drunk on the chemistry. Gabby is busy pretending to be someone she may not be, and Matt is too caught up in the thrill of the chase, the lure of the unobtainable not being quite so unobtainable as he once thought.

"Do you want nuts?" Gabby pulls out a packet, but Matt shakes his head.

"I'm good. Here." He hands her a glass of wine. "Cheers."

"Cheers." She holds eye contact with him as they both sip, the first to look away. "Do you want to see the house?"

"You know what I really want to see?"

Please don't say the bedroom, she thinks. That would be so predictable, and so sleazy. And I would have no idea what to say.

"What?"

"The barn. I want to see your work."

Gabby's shoulders instantly relax as they step outside, Gabby wrapping her arms around herself to stay warm as they cross the garden to the barn.

"Are you sure you're ready for this?" she teases, pausing by the door.

"This is your space, right? This is the place where I'm really going to be able to tell who you are."

"Oh God," she groans, as she pushes the door open. "You're going to think I'm a disorganized, crazy mess."

She stands there, Matt next to her, as he slowly looks around in delight. He takes in the old beams, the workbenches, the furniture. He asks her questions about the furniture, exclaiming with delight over her work, the painting techniques, the notice board on which she has pinned her before and afters.

"What's up there?" He points to the staircase.

"Bedroom and bathroom," she says. "Supposed to be for guests, but they always end up staying in the house. It's too far away for most people. I love it, though—I sneak in a nap from time to time."

"Let me see!" he says, heading for the stairs.

"Matt, there's nothing to see. It's very dull."

"Come on. I want to see." He's upstairs, and in the doorway of the bedroom before she can say anything else.

Gabby walks up, stands next to Matt in the doorway, surveying the room with pleasure. The rest of the barn is natural wood, but in here she color-washed the walls a pale grey, the same color as the pretty antique iron bed. An old pine dresser sits at one end, with an antique wing chair covered in a natural soft linen, by an antique Swedish Mora clock. The bed is piled with plush white pillows and a soft matelassé bedspread, with a sumptuous blue-and-white quilt folded at the bottom of the bed. It is picture perfect, and its simple charm gives Gabby pleasure every time she walks in here.

"See," she says. "Nothing to write home about."

"Not true." He walks in to the tiny room. "I bet that bed has a story."

Gabby laughs. "Only that I found it at a tag sale when we were first married. I fell completely in love with it and forced my husband to sleep in it, even though it was way too small. I painted the iron, and now . . . it's here."

"And the clock?"

"That was my mother's. They downsized a few years ago and my mother did something uncharacteristically generous, in sending me a few pieces that had been my favorites when I was a child. That clock had been in my bedroom, and I always loved it."

"Now it's in your bedroom here."

"Indeed."

The air is very still. Gabby knows she cannot step farther into the room, knows, in fact, she should leave now, and walk downstairs, back to safety, but everything is frozen, and she isn't able to move. She can hear everything. Even, it seems, the particles of dust flying in the sunlight; Matt's breathing; her own heart pounding in her ears.

It happens very slowly. Matt's head coming toward hers, bending, dropping the gentlest of kisses on her frozen lips. She stands, not moving, feeling his lips, on the edge of a terrible precipice, unable to go forward, definitely unable to go back.

And then she is kissing him back, and it is her tongue in his mouth, her groan of anticipation, of desire, of longing that comes out first.

They are tangled in each other's arms, and she is feeling his body, so young, so hard, such an unbelievable turn-on. When he pulls his T-shirt off, she actually gasps, unable to believe how smooth his skin is, how taut, how firm.

Gabby is no longer a forty-three-year-old housewife, no longer a mother, no longer dull, slipping into middle age. She is thirty, twenty, eighteen. She is wild and ferocious. She doesn't care about stretch marks, or sag, or pouches, cares only about pleasure, giving and receiving more pleasure than she had thought possible.

She tears off her bra, not thinking, not planning; nothing exists outside of this room, this beautiful man who is exploring her with his fingers, his mouth, who is writhing when she flips over and does the same to him.

This isn't lovemaking. This isn't the safe, same routine she has with Elliott. This is raw, animalistic. Gabby slides her fingers in places she would never dream to with her husband, laughing as Matt moans in surprise. And pleasure. She licks, and swallows, and engulfs, her appetite insatiable, her energy unstoppable.

Finally he is above her, his eyes locked with hers as he slips inside, seamlessly moving slowly inside her as she closes her eyes, groaning in pleasure before she opens them to lose herself in his gaze.

There is nothing in the future, nothing in the past. Just the two of them, just this moment, and let this moment, these moments, go on forever and ever, for she can suspend her life during this, can suspend everything as long as they are here in this room together, releasing all the pent-up attraction, longing, the weeks of flirtation; but after this?

After this?

Afterward, Gabby gets up from the bed and goes to the bathroom. She may have lost ten pounds, but naked she knows she cannot pull it off quite so well. She has no butt anymore, just a flat slab where there used to be a peach; her varicose veins are clearly visible. Undressed, she looks like the middle-aged woman she is.

She doesn't care.

Numb, she walks to the bathroom, staring deeply into her eyes in the mirror as she washes her hands, unsurprised that all she sees is shame.

Fourteen

Something is different about his wife, but Elliott is too frightened to ask what it is. It started a few months ago, around the time she went to be interviewed by the man who started that website. *Man*. Hardly. Elliott Googled him extensively and is pretty confident that "boy" is the right term for him.

It was clear to him that Gabby had developed a crush. In some ways he understood it; almost in her midforties, she was delighted this young fellow had clearly flirted with her, and she had reacted to it inappropriately. Not that he knew this for certain, but she had a lilt in her step she had never had before, started taking care of herself in a way she hadn't before.

Gabby had worn makeup and fluffed her hair and done those things when they were first married, but after years of him telling her he preferred her natural, with no adornments, nothing artificial, she finally believed him. Up until a few months ago, he couldn't remember the last time she'd worn makeup.

What that man, *boy*—Matt—had obviously done was woken Gabby up, made her nostalgic for her youth. Why else would she suddenly start wearing tight jeans, high-heeled boots, and makeup, blowing out her hair? Why else would she stop eating carbohydrates and turn down chocolate, even her beloved Butterfingers?

Why else would she spend as much money as she did at the dermatologist, then lie about the procedure? Elliott had phoned the office to question the bill, which seemed outrageous for a minor procedure, even in this day and age, even in this town.

Botox, Perlane, Sculptra. He hadn't even heard of the last two and he's a doctor. No wonder she had looked so fresh, so young. For weeks she seemed to glow, and suddenly, she plummeted.

She stopped wearing the makeup, put all the weight back on, and more. She can barely rouse herself out of bed in the mornings, and it is not unusual, when he calls in the afternoons, for Gabby to be fast asleep.

He has found her, on occasion, in tears. Other times, she snaps at him or the girls in anger, swiftly apologizing, which doesn't explain these outbursts. She can be loving, affectionate, overaffectionate even, before quickly flaring up into a rage over nothing.

"Have you been to see a doctor recently?" he asked, gently, just the other night.

"You're a doctor," she snapped. "What do *you* think is wrong with me?"

"Have you had a period recently?"

"Why? What's that got to do with anything?"

"I think you're menopausal. I think you might actually be going through menopause. When was your last period? I don't remember, which means you need to get your hormones checked."

The tears came. "Thank you. Thank you. I thought I was going mad. You're right. I'll make an appointment tomorrow. What would I do without you?"

"Find someone else to pick on?" Elliott joked, only he wasn't joking.

"I'm sorry," she laughed through her tears. "You know I love you and only you?"

"You'd better," he said, surprised.

Of course she loves him and only him. He could see she had had an infatuation, but it had passed. He was grateful it hadn't become anything he would have to worry about.

Fifteen

Gabby is trying very hard to pretend her night with Matt never happened. Immediately afterward, when they had consummated their lust, when the full impact of what she had done was already hitting, Gabby found it hard to even look at Matt.

They moved around each other awkwardly, until Gabby dropped the pretense that they would even spend the rest of the evening together, inventing a headache so she could drive him back to the hotel.

Matt was puzzled. Hurt. He tried to comfort her, could see how uncomfortable she was, but she couldn't be comforted, and in the end, he gave up trying. He understood she was doing what she had to do.

She went home and stood under scalding water in the shower for twenty-five minutes, attempting to wash away the stain of her betrayal. She put on her fluffiest, most comforting nightgown, and curled up in bed, phoning Elliott, wanting to be enveloped in the safety of his voice.

Every morning since that night, after she awakes, the shame and guilt of her betrayal come flooding back. Some days she feels so disgusted with herself, so filled with remorse, she can't look Elliott in the eye, screams at him over nothing, not because she is angry at him, but because she is so angry at herself.

Other days, overwhelmed with love, with fear that he will leave, she is sexually voracious, pushing him onto the bed, taking him in her mouth, desperate to prove to him how much she loves him, how much she still wants him, terrified that this is the only way she can keep him.

Never has she wanted Elliott as much as she has since she betrayed him. Never has she been more aware of the fragility of marriage, of a relationship that once seemed so unbreakable, so strong.

And now that it is over, she cannot believe she has spent months of her life obsessing over another man. The minute it was over, everything was over. She never wanted to see him again.

A week later Matt emailed her. He thanked her for a lovely time, said he hoped she was okay, that they would still be friends. There was nothing flirtatious in the email, nothing leading, but Gabby, sick with shame when she saw his name in her in-box, wrote back to say it was better if they didn't speak for a while.

She had tremendous affection for him, she said, but it should never have happened and she needed to refocus on her family. Matt didn't write again after that, and Gabby hadn't expected him to.

She had a sense that the email exchange—brief but warm—was closure for both of them. There was nothing further that needed to be said, and she was able to walk away without hating him, or blaming him, or wanting anything more from him than he had already given.

He had already given too much.

Or perhaps she had taken too much. Either way, Gabby knew,

even before it was over, that it would never happen again. Not just with Matt, but she would never jeopardize everything she cares about again, would never be unfaithful again, no matter how great the temptation.

She would have done anything to go back in time and change what happened, is hopeful that every passing day that brings normalcy with it helps her transgression feel more and more like a dream.

It still burns, the nugget of guilt each time she and Elliott make love. At times it feels as if she is playacting at being herself, at being the kind of woman who is loyal, faithful, who would never betray her husband.

She cannot change it, but she can hope to learn from it and protect those around her from being hurt by it.

She wasn't caught. No one knows. She does not have to live in fear of Elliott waking up and asking who she is typing to at three o'clock in the morning. It is something of a relief to look at her inbox now and not see an email from Matt. It is something of a relief to sleep through the night, not waking up several times throughout, reaching over for her iPhone to see if he has been in touch. It is something of a relief to not have to lie, or deceive, or withhold anymore.

Gabby did a terrible thing, but it was one time only. She did a terrible thing, but she has to try and forgive herself and move on. The terrible thing only served to prove how much she loves her husband; how lucky she is. She will never make that mistake again.

Three months later, and she is still feeling sick with shame, although she is convinced her hormones have something to do with her sickness, her crazy mood swings.

Finally, thank heavens, she has a doctor's appointment.

Please God, she thinks, let the doctor put me on something that will make this all better. Please let him have a pill that will make me feel normal again.

Please let me have my life back, and I'll never do anything wrong again.

The gynecologist comes back in the room with a large smile on his face before sitting behind his desk. "Do you want the good news or the good news?"

Gabby stares at her OB/GYN, mystified. "What's the good news?"

"The good news is you're not going through menopause."

She breathes a sigh of relief. As mentally prepared as Gabby thought she was, menopause meant she had crossed to the other side, and she wasn't old enough for that. Not yet. "Great. So what's the good news?"

"Congratulations, Gabby! You're pregnant!"

Part Two

Sixteen

It has been three days since Gabby's visit to the doctor. Three days since everything in her life was destroyed. Three days of acting as if everything is normal, trying to put off the pain she knows is unavoidable.

Each morning she wakes up with a glimmer of something not being right, the full force of what it is shocking her into consciousness.

"Mom? What's going on?" Even Olivia, usually so wrapped up in herself, had noticed. "You don't seem like yourself."

Gabby had forced a tight smile. "I'm fine," she said.

But she wasn't fine. How could she be fine? The doctor's words reverberate in her head, the horror of those words mixed in with the secret joy at carrying a new life, having the one thing she had always wanted. Just not in this way.

You're pregnant . . . you're pregnant . . . you're pregnant . . .

Gabby had stared at her doctor as the static built in her head.

"What?" Her voice was barely a whisper.

"I know," he had laughed. "A lot of my older mothers are surprised, particularly when they're convinced their lack of menstruation is due to menopause, but I'd say"—she remembers he looked down at his notes as she fought a wave of nausea—"judging from the date of your last period, you're about fourteen weeks. Obviously we can be more specific when we do the scan, which we'd like to do today, plus the blood work. You can talk to Jacqui outside about making an appointment with the genetics counselor before you go. Given how late you are, we need to get you in as soon as possible. This afternoon would be best." He looked at Gabby kindly. "I can see this is a shock. Do you have any questions you'd like to ask me?"

Gabby's voice was low and quiet. "What are the chances of getting pregnant after a vasectomy?"

The doctor stared at her, the smile sliding off his face as comprehension dawned. "Oh dear," he said, with no idea what to say next.

She had gone straight in for the nuchal scan, lying on the table, still numb, still unable to believe this was happening. The baby couldn't be Elliott's, and no further lies would change that or give her an opportunity to spin it in any way other than the awful, shattering truth. She had stared at the ceiling, blinking back the tears as the sonographer put the warm gel on her belly. She didn't want to look at the screen, didn't want any of this to be real, but it was. Burying her head in the sand wasn't an option anymore, but still. She couldn't look at the screen, wasn't willing to see the tangible evidence of what she had done.

Naïve enough to think she had gotten away with it, as she lay there Gabby knew, with sudden clarity, this was her penance. You do not get to betray a man such as Elliott and walk away scot-free. You do not get to play around with your marriage, your future, and expect to get away with it.

"There you are." She was aware that the sonographer gave her a worried glance. She would think most new mothers, particularly the older ones, do not lie staring at the ceiling, tears streaming down their cheeks, during their first scan. "What a perfect picture!" she said, as Gabby slowly, reluctantly, turned her head, not wanting to look, but unable not to.

There it was. On the screen, in a hazy blur of greys, an unmistakable life: a perfect curled-up baby, thumb brought up to his mouth, tiny legs furled inward. No amount of guilt and shame could prevent the magic of that moment stealing up and catching Gabby in its grasp.

"A good strong healthy heartbeat." The sonographer stopped moving for a few seconds as Gabby's eyes widened with wonder. A baby! *Her* baby. The life she had wanted for so long, a life she never thought she would be privileged enough to create. Not again, not after Olivia and Alanna.

She caught her breath, taking in every curve, wanting to stop time, wanting to lie there, on that table, and drink in the marvel of the moment forever.

"That's my baby," she whispered, everything else forgotten, as her heart exploded with maternal protection, devotion, joy.

The delight comes in waves. It is interspersed with utter terror for the moment she knows she cannot put off for very much longer. Gabby never was a very good liar, and she can't keep pretending this is menopause. She has done enough damage. The very least she can do now is step up and take responsibility for her actions.

Every time she tries to think of the words, tries to think of how to frame it to cause the least impact, to somehow make it palatable, ease the pain her actions will bring, her mind goes blank.

How do you tell the man you love that you have done the worst thing possible; that he will never be able to trust you again; that you will have to live with the evidence for the rest of your life.

Seventeen

I am not stupid, Gabby!" Elliott is back to shouting again, as Gabby sits on the small sofa by the window, her head hung, exhausted.

"I didn't say you were stupid. It's possible. It happens. There's a point oh-five percent chance—"

"Gabby, don't lie to me. All I'm asking for is the truth. If you're honest with me, I can deal with anything, but what I can't deal with are lies. The chances of you getting pregnant by me are, as you pointed out, infinitesimal. We are a family, and you know I don't believe families are necessarily blood, but if you lie to me and tell me that somehow, despite this vasectomy, this baby could only be mine, and I do genetics testing and discover that you are lying to me, I will never recover. Do you understand that, Gabby? I will never get over you lying to me."

"I'm sorry. I'm so sorry. I love you so much," Gabby blurts out, as she starts to sob. "I know you won't forgive me. I don't know how to . . ."

As he sits down on the bed, Elliott's voice is calm. "Just tell me. It's fine."

"It was nothing. It was just . . . once. One time. It didn't mean anything."

Gabby watches as Elliott's jaw starts to tick. "What? What are you saying?"

"I slept with him once. It was a mistake."

"You slept with who once?"

"The guy from the website."

"Jesus Christ!" Elliott's voice is a roar of pain as he leaps up. "Are you serious? You're pregnant with another man's baby?"

Gabby has never seen her husband like this. She cowers back against the sofa as Elliott looms above her, his face, always so loving and kind, now contorted with rage. He looks as if he is about to hit her, before he turns and whirls out of the room, storming down the stairs.

Gabby is right behind him. "Where are you going?" she sobs.

"I don't know," he says, slamming the door and gunning the engine before screeching off down the street.

There is a gentle tap on the door that Gabby doesn't hear for a while, her face buried in the pillow as she sobs.

She hears the tap, lifts her head, and attempts to calm down. "Elliott?"

The door cracks open. "No, Mom. It's me. Alanna. What's the matter?"

Gabby attempts to crack a smile. "I'm just having a bad day. I'll be okay."

"Mom, were you and Dad fighting?"

Oh God. Please let them not have heard what happened. "What did you hear?"

"Nothing. I was in the basement, but I heard raised voices. Did you have a fight?"

"Yes, but it's all going to be fine."

"Mom, I've never heard you and Dad shout at each other before." Her face falls. "You're not going to get a divorce, are you?"

"Absolutely not!" she says firmly. "Not a chance in hell." She holds her arms out to give Alanna a reassuring hug, preventing her daughter from seeing the fresh tears roll down her cheeks.

It is nighttime before Elliott returns. Gabby is freshly showered, has made pork chops and mashed potatoes, his favorite. The table is set for two, even though she has no appetite, and there are yellow flowers, freshly cut from the pot on the front doorstep, bravely pretending everything is sunny and bright.

Alanna is up in her room, getting ready for bed, Olivia out at the movies with friends. Gabby is exhausted, and terrified, feeling trapped in a bad dream, desperate to make it better, knowing that pork chops and mashed potatoes probably won't make all that much of a difference, not knowing what else to do.

She has sat at the kitchen table for the last two hours, waiting for Elliott to come home. He has switched his cell phone off, and there is nothing to do but wait. She cannot read, or watch television, or focus on anything other than the wait for her husband and what he might say.

Relief floods her body when she finally hears the car. He opens the front door and glances through to her, in the kitchen, before sighing and taking off his coat.

"I made you dinner," she says. "Pork chops and mashed potatoes."

"I'm not hungry," he says slowly, walking in.

"Can I get you a drink? Would you like a beer?"

"No."

He pulls a chair out and sits at the kitchen table, staring straight ahead, his jaw clenched. He keeps starting, as if he is about to say something, but then he stops. Finally, he takes a deep breath, and bursts into loud, wracking sobs.

"Oh Elliott." Gabby gets up and flies to him, cradling him in her arms, resting her forehead against his. "Baby. I'm sorry. I'm so sorry." She is weeping, too. "I never meant this to happen. Whatever I can do for you to forgive me, I'll do. Anything."

There is a long silence as they both weep, in each other's arms. Elliott makes no move to touch Gabby, but allows himself to be held by her until he is calm. Gabby goes back to her chair, but reaches out for his hand, certain this is a step in the right direction, that the very fact he allowed himself to be held means there is hope.

"The thing is," Elliott whispers, not looking at Gabby, "I'm not sure I *can* forgive you."

Gabby's voice catches in her throat. "What do you mean?"

"I want to. I want to be able to put this behind us and move on, but I don't know how to do that. It would be one thing if you had just been unfaithful, but you're pregnant. With another man's child. How am I supposed to get over something like that? How am I supposed to forgive a betrayal like that?" He looks up at her then.

"I don't know," Gabby says, careful to keep the desperation out of her voice. "Maybe the only thing we can do is try. You know how Harvey's always using that expression of his he learned in Al-Anon, the one about *acting as if*? Maybe that's what we have to do. Act as if everything's fine, and then one day we'll wake up and it will be fine."

"But it isn't fine. And it will never be fine." Elliott starts to tear up again. "How could you do this to me, Gabby? How could you do this to us? How could you take a marriage that was so damn good and drop a bomb? Was I not a good husband to you? Was I deficient? How could you sleep with another man?" His voice is rising in anger again as he speaks. "How could you?"

"I don't know," Gabby says. "It wasn't about you. I think it was about me feeling middle-aged. I know how awful that sounds, but it meant nothing. I swear."

"When did it happen?" Elliott, tortured by not knowing, will be doubly tortured by knowing, but cannot resist.

"It was the weekend you were away."

He shakes his head. "Jesus. You planned the whole thing. You waited for me to go."

"No. It wasn't like that. He was going to be in town," she says. "And it was coincidence. I was just meeting him for a drink."

"Where did it happen?"

"Elliott. Please. Don't do this. Don't do this. You don't want to know."

"Just tell me it wasn't in our bed. Tell me you didn't fuck another man in our bed."

"No, I didn't fuck another man in our bed. I . . . I wouldn't do that. It happened in the barn."

"In our barn? So he was here? He was in my home?"

"Elliott, I told you not to do this. He was barely here."

"You mean he came in, went out to the barn, fucked my wife, and left?"

"Elliott. Please. It was nothing."

"No, Gabriella. It wasn't 'nothing.' It was a betrayal. And now it's a new life."

Gabby turns pale, almost feels her blood freeze as he says these words. She has always been able to get through to Elliott, always been able to persuade him around to her point of view, but for the first time ever, she knows she has lost him. Permanently.

"I'm sorry," Gabby weeps. "I'm so sorry. I love you."

"You should have thought of that before." Elliott gets up, and wearily goes upstairs.

What are you doing?" Elliott is walking down the hallway with some clothes and toiletries under his arm.

"I'm going to sleep in the spare room."

Gabby's face starts to crumple. "Elliott, please. Don't leave our room. I won't touch you, I swear, but please stay in our room. I need you. Please."

He hesitates, and Gabby thinks she has got through to him, before he shakes his head. "I can't. I'm sorry. It's just too painful. I need to be on my own."

Gabby crawls into bed and sobs until her bedroom door opens and Elliott is standing there. Flooded with relief, Gabby looks up at him, her eyes puffy and red raw.

"I just had to ask," Elliott says. "Was he better than me?"

"What?" Gabby says in disbelief. "What are you talking about?"

"In bed. Was he better? More creative? Was he bigger than me?"

"Oh Jesus, Elliott. I'm not doing this. Please."

"Please? You owe me, Gabby. You fucked another man, so now you have to tell me. Was he?"

"No he was not better than you, and no he was not bigger. I don't even know. I barely even looked. It was over so quickly."

Elliott says nothing. Just stares at Gabby before backing out of the room and closing the door.

. . .

Elliott is gone by the time Gabby wakes up the next morning.

"Mom? You look terrible." Olivia glances up at her. "What's the matter with your eyes?"

"I had a migraine last night," Gabby lies. "It's still there. It's made me puff up like a balloon."

Alanna looks up. "Is that why Dad slept in the spare room?"

Gabby nods.

"So it wasn't because of that fight you had?"

"What fight?" Olivia says.

"Never mind what fight," Gabby says. "Don't worry about it. I've been very headachy and I get up a lot, which disturbs your dad. Can you please not ask any more about it?"

"Okay, okay," Alanna says. "Sorry I asked."

"I'm sorry, sweetie. I just get grouchy when I'm tired. Did you see your dad this morning?"

"Yes."

"How did he seem?"

Alanna looks at her mother weirdly. "Fine. Why?"

"Oh. Good. Just glad he slept well." Gabby turns to go upstairs, disguising a fresh round of tears. How can her husband, the love of her life, have turned into a stranger overnight, into someone she has to ask her daughter about in order to find out his state of mind?

This is the man she is supposed to know best in the world, the man she turns to when the rest of her life is falling apart; if she can't turn to him, if he can't ease her pain, what is she supposed to do?

Gabby thinks perhaps she should just end it. Terminate the pregnancy. She should have done it before she even told Elliott. Why didn't she? It's a question Gabby doesn't have an answer to.

Eighteen

Gabby and Elliott circle each other all week, as polite as strangers. Each time Gabby makes an overture, suggesting dinner, a walk, some time to talk, Elliott politely declines. He has made no move to leave the guest room, and Gabby is clouded with sadness and the knowledge that there will be no good ending to this, and that it is entirely her fault.

She makes dinner and they sit at the table with the girls, Elliott pretending to be his normal self, making jokes and asking them about their day, as Gabby sits quietly opposite him, attempting to join in, feeling him drifting further and further away from her.

Alanna came home from school yesterday and didn't run straight to her room. Instead she came to the kitchen and sat down across from her mother at the kitchen table.

"I'm worried about you, Mom," she said, her small brow furrowed with anxiety. "And I'm worried about Dad. Something's going on and I'm scared you're going to get divorced."

Gabby had gasped. "What?" she said, immediately tearing up.

"Oh baby. I'm so sorry. We're not getting divorced, we're just . . ." She had no idea what to say. "Sometimes grown-ups go through some hard times. It's nothing for you to worry about, and Dad and I will figure it out."

"So you're not going to get divorced? Promise me you won't get divorced."

Gabby winced at the prospect, but knew she couldn't lie. She didn't know herself what would happen. How could she make a promise to her daughter she knew wasn't hers to fulfill.

"I promise you this," she said. "I love your father more than any other man in the world and I do not want a divorce. I know it seems like the end of the world when your parents are having a rough time, but I do not want a divorce. We will figure this out."

It was as close to the truth as she was able to give, and seemed to placate Alanna. For now.

Gabby now makes mental lists of what to talk about at the dinner table, stories she can tell about her day, newspaper articles she can share to ensure they are not sitting in an awkward silence.

She studies Elliott, across the table, astonished at how fragile her marriage is, at how quickly and easily it can unravel. Of course this is her fault; she knows this is her fault, but it was one mistake, and now she will do anything, will fight with all that she has to save her marriage.

Why doesn't Elliott feel the same way?

He has to; he must; it will just take him a little longer. In the meantime Gabby will be the perfect wife, will cook him all the foods he loves, will tend to his every need, will show him that he cannot find better, that he must not leave.

On Thursday morning, she gets a text from Claire. "So excited for tonight—the four of us haven't been out for ages! I booked at Finalmente at 7:30. Okay?"

She had forgotten. It is Tim's birthday, therefore dinner with Claire and Tim. Oh God. The prospect of even leaving her house right now is terrifying, let alone seeing other people. But Claire and Tim don't really count as other people. They are almost family. Perhaps seeing them will be a good thing, will remind Elliott of the life they have built, the friends they have; perhaps it will give him a dose of reality.

"Sounds great," Gabby replies. "See you later. xx"

I don't think we should be seeing them," Elliott says, as they pull out the driveway. "We should have canceled."

"We can't cancel. It's Tim's birthday. We have to go."

"I'm not ready for this. How do we tell other people what's happened?"

"Elliott! We don't tell other people what's happened. No one needs to know anything. We're just going to have a nice evening with our closest friends."

"You don't think you need to let our closest friends know you're pregnant? With another man's baby?" He mutters the last part of the sentence, disgust in his eyes.

"I don't think we need to tell them anything. Maybe they'll just think I've put on weights."

Elliott rolls his eyes.

"Elliott, please. Can you at least pretend? Can you at least be civil to me tonight? I'm not asking you to profess undying love, but can you at least try to look at me with something other than disdain?"

Elliott says nothing.

"Elliott?"

"I'll try."

. . .

Look at me!" Claire proudly steps back from their hug, showing off her growing bump. "I'm in my first maternity pants! Can you believe the size of me? I swear this is because I'm so old."

"You look amazing," Gabby says, wishing she could tell Claire that she too is pregnant, feeling odd, and awkward, that she has to withhold such huge news. This pregnancy is so different from her previous pregnancies, when she was filled with excitement, and joy.

All she feels with this one, from the moment she wakes up until the moment she manages to gain some respite with a few hours' sleep, is dread. This isn't even a child she wants; in some sick way she harbors a small hope something will happen to end this pregnancy, to enable her to put this all behind her, carry on with her life, with Elliott, finally removing all evidence of her transgression.

But her scan, carried out this morning, was fine. She went to the doctor's office alone, wiping a tear from her eye as she remembered going to another doctor for a scan that produced the first picture of Olivia. Elliott was with her, perched on a stool at her head as the sonographer moved the slick gel around her belly, and they had both gasped at the sight of what was so clearly, already, a baby, her thumb at her mouth. He had been there for Alanna's sonogram too, but there was no question of him being there for this one.

She lay there silently, alone, as the sonographer moved that familiar wand, and thought about how much she had wanted one more baby, as she heard the words of her mother echo through her head: *Be careful what you wish for.*

She could never have imagined this is what would happen. The sonographer moved the gel around, Gabby looked at the screen, and saw the baby growing in her stomach. She watched as they measured the nuchal cord, the limbs, checked to see everything was growing normally.

It wasn't overwhelming in the way it had been when Olivia and Alanna had been scanned. She felt . . . detached. In much the same way she feels with Elliott. *Detached.* As if this is all happening to someone else. That is someone else's baby on that screen. The marriage breaking up is happening to someone else. Not me. It couldn't possibly be happening to me.

Her need to share news of her pregnancy with Claire is not to share her joy, but to cement the bonds of their friendship. What will Claire do when she finds out? And can Gabby, a terrible liar at the best of times, withhold the full story? Assuming she and Elliott can work through this and stay intact, will Gabby be able to keep the fact of the father secret?

She will have to. There is nothing else to be done.

"How do you feel?" She focuses her attention back on Claire, aware that Elliott and Tim are busy talking, knowing there may be a semblance of normality tonight if only because Elliott and Tim are always perfectly happy to talk, just the two of them, for hours.

"I feel exhausted. Terrible. I could sleep all day and all night. Honestly? I have no idea what I'm doing having a baby at my age. Tim was saying just the other night, we should be planning a retirement home, never mind saving for yet another one's college. I swear to God, we just canceled our vacation for spring break."

"We didn't cancel," Tim says, tuning in. "We just . . . rearranged."

"Yup. We were all going to Cancún, and now we're driving up to Vermont to stay at a friend's house. Big difference."

"At least you're going away," says Gabby. "We haven't had a vacation for years. Remember when we went away by ourselves?" She looks at Elliott, reminding him of the good times, the happier times. "To Antigua?" She turns back to Claire and Tim. "We went to Galley Bay in Antigua and it was amazing. A second honeymoon. Apart from when we got stuck on the yacht. Remember that?" She's smiling as she looks at Elliott, who shrugs.

"Vaguely," he says, before turning to Tim. "Are you going to coach softball again this year? I was thinking about doing it, but I figured I'd check with you first."

Gabby looks up to find Claire frowning at her. "I have to go to the bathroom," Claire says. "Gabby, come with me."

In the bathroom, Claire turns to Gabby as soon as the door is closed. "What the hell's going on with you two? Have you had a fight?"

And Gabby bursts into tears.

She cannot stop for a long time. Her body is heaving with sobs as a shocked Claire tries to comfort her. Eventually, Gabby manages to calm down, the odd shudder running through her body every few seconds.

"Gabby." Claire is awkwardly crouching next to her. "What is it? What's happened?"

"I think Elliott is leaving me," Gabby says, staring at the floor.

"Don't be ridiculous," Claire says. "Elliott would never leave you. You two are the strongest couple we know. Why would you say such a thing?"

Gabby looks up then, into Claire's eyes, and there is such pleading despair, that Claire feels a cold clutch of fear.

"It was the guy, wasn't it."

Gabby nods.

"You had an affair and Elliott found out."

"It wasn't an affair. It was one night. Not even. One incident. And Elliott can't forgive me. He won't ever be able to forgive me."

Claire sighs. "Look, it's terrible. We all know it's terrible, but you're human, Gabby. I don't condone it, but I understand that we all make mistakes, and no one understands that better than Elliott. He's the most compassionate man I know. I'm not saying it's going to be easy, but I truly believe that you'll be able to work through this together. Have you talked about seeing a couples counselor? Couples therapy can completely transform a relationship, and you already know I have someone amazing. Gabby, this doesn't have to be the end of the marriage." Claire takes her hand. "It's going to be okay."

"It's not," Gabby says, looking up at Claire again as she takes a deep breath. "I'm pregnant. And the baby isn't Elliott's."

Claire's mouth drops open. Confusion floods her face, then horror as the words sink in. She actually reaches out for the sink to steady herself, her face a whiter shade of pale.

"Gabby." Her voice is a whisper, her face now a mask of shock as her eyes flick to Gabby's stomach, registering the weight gain, the small bump. "You can't have it. You need to end this pregnancy."

Gabby, feeling an unexpected surge of anger at her friend, shakes her head. Who does Claire, pregnant herself, think she is telling Gabby to have an abortion?

"I know," says Gabby coldly. "But I don't think I can."

Claire blanches. "I . . . oh God. I don't know what to say."

"I'm not sure there *is* anything to say," Gabby's hands reflexively go to her stomach, protecting the baby she wanted so badly, but not like this. "It's the one thing I wanted so desperately. And it's the worst thing that's ever happened to me."

Claire regains enough self-composure to reach out to Gabby

and put her arms around her, but neither of them is comforted; neither of them is able to pretend.

They leave the room a couple of minutes later, Gabby imploring Claire to act normal, to pretend she doesn't know, but Claire, always a terrible liar, is still in shock, and truly doesn't know how to pretend everything's normal.

"You know," she says after the waiter has brought them their drinks. "I know this is terrible, and I was so looking forward to this evening, but I'm feeling really nauseous. I think I may have to go home."

"It's fine," Elliott is quick to say. "Of course."

Claire hugs Gabby, whispering in her ear, "I'm sorry. I love you. Let's speak tomorrow," and then they are gone, leaving Elliott to pick up the check for drinks.

They walk out to the car, Gabby part embarrassed, part grateful, for she knew Claire would not be able to act as if everything was fine once she had told her.

"You told her," Elliott says as they get in the car. Gabby is silent. "Gabby." Her name sounds strange on his lips. He is reluctant to even say it, to even taste the shape of her name since her betrayal. "I can't do this anymore."

Gabby's heart leaps into her mouth. "What do you mean?"

"I mean I can't be with you. I wanted to try, but I can't. Every time I look at you, every time I hear your name, I just think of you with another man, and his child growing inside you, and I can't stand it."

"Elliott." Gabby forces her voice to be calm. "I know how hard this is right now, but I think we should go and see a couples therapist. I know of someone who's meant to be fan—"

"No." He stops her. "I'm not going to see a couples therapist. It won't help. It won't change what you did or how I feel about it. Gabby, I love you. I don't want to feel this way, but I do, and no amount of talking about it will make a difference. I'm sorry. I'm moving out."

"Elliott?" Gabby's voice is shaking. "If I ended this pregnancy would you still leave me?"

Elliott stares at her. "Yes," he says. "Yes I would. I would still leave."

Nineteen

Elliott stands in Claire's kitchen, a kitchen that is starting to feel like home, as Olivia rails at him. The baby Gabby is carrying has nothing to do with Elliott, so he had decided not to mention it to the girls, but Gabby has evidently now decided to share at least part of her news, and Olivia has not taken it well.

"How can you leave?" she hisses, having just got dropped off here by her mother. "What kind of a father are you that you can leave Mom when she's having a baby? I'm just . . . disgusted. I can't believe you're doing this. I can't believe you're leaving her now."

"Olivia," he says wearily. "There are things you know nothing about. You may think you know the whole story, but you don't. I'm sorry that this has happened, I truly am, and if there were any other way, if there were any way for me to make this work, don't you think I would? Do you think I want to leave my family? Do you really think I want to be staying in Tim and Claire's house? Much as I love them, this isn't my home, and I would never, ever leave you and Alanna. I wouldn't."

"So why did you?" Olivia spits, her eyes welling up with tears. "You have a choice. This is all bullshit. You didn't have to leave. You don't have to leave. I will never be able to forgive you for this, Dad."

"You don't understand," Elliott, in pain, says wearily.

"No. You're right. I don't understand. So explain it to me. Help me."

"I can't," he says, after a pause. "It's not something that's for me to tell."

"Great." The sarcasm drips from her voice. "You're trying to blame Mom for this, but she didn't leave. Whatever fight you've had, the fact that you left, when she's pregnant with your child, is unforgivable."

"It's not," he says quietly, unable to help himself.

"It's not what?"

"Nothing."

"No. It's not nothing." Olivia's voice starts to rise. "It's not what? What do you mean? Tell me, Dad! Tell me!" She is shouting now.

"It's not my child."

Olivia stares at him in shock, before running out the front door. Elliott goes after her, calling her name, but she is faster than he, and she doesn't stop, and soon she is out of view entirely.

He shouldn't have said it. He knows he shouldn't have said it. But he cannot stand being blamed by his daughters when he is not the one at fault. He has tried to be the good guy, tried to protect his wife, tried not to talk about it, but he will not allow his daughters to portray him as the bad guy.

He will not allow Gabby to take away what little he has left.

. . .

Olivia bursts through the door of the barn, frantically looking for her mother. She finds her on a chair in the corner, sitting, staring into the distance.

"Is it true?" Olivia bursts out, standing in front of her mother with crossed arms.

"Is what true?"

"The baby isn't Dad's."

Gabby just stares at her daughter, stunned. She wasn't going to tell her daughters. Certainly not yet, not while they were still struggling with the fact that their father had moved out. She hadn't discussed this with Elliott, but she assumed she had a few months, time for them to get adjusted, time for them to get used to this new life before she dropped another clanger onto them.

"Well?" Olivia pushes. "Is it true?"

"What did your father tell you? Oh God. I can't believe he told you. What did he say?"

Olivia stares at her mother, disbelief and sadness in her eyes, as Gabby is filled with regret for doing this to her; doing this to all of them.

"You're pregnant with somebody else's baby? No wonder he left. How could you? How could you sleep with another man when you're married to Dad and he's so . . . he's so great. What are you thinking? What were you thinking?" Olivia is shaking her head in disbelief, trying to comprehend. "How could you do this to him? To us? I have no idea who you are because my mother wouldn't do that. My mother would never do something so hurtful and wrong."

Gabby is not sure she has ever been in so much pain. She wants to explain to Olivia how it happened, that it didn't mean anything, but Olivia is seventeen, not old enough to be burdened with the truth; not old enough to understand.

"Who is it? Who is he? Who's the baby's father?" Olivia says, realizing her mother isn't going to say anything, can barely look her in the eye.

"No one. No one you know. It doesn't matter," Gabby says quietly, as her tears start to fall.

"Even better, Mom. You threw away your life for nothing? For no one? You ruined all of our lives for, what? Nothing." Her voice drops, then. "How could you," she says quietly, turning to hide the tears that are starting to fall. She doesn't see Gabby sink to the floor in tears as she goes up to her room to pack, to be with her father, to stay anywhere but under her mother's roof.

Gabby doesn't move, other than to curl up, her body heaving with sobs, for she knows Olivia is absolutely right. She has thrown away her life for no one, for nothing, and no one could be more disgusted with her than she is herself.

She has lost her husband, and she is fairly certain she has lost her best friend, for one always has to choose sides during a marriage split, and given that Claire and Tim have opened their home to Elliott, given that Claire has not been in touch for days, she is pretty certain whom they have chosen. Now she has lost her daughter.

What the hell was she thinking? What had come over her? She doesn't think about Matt at all. They have not been in touch since the emails after the night they slept together. It had been so awkward afterward, her guilt, and remorse, and shame immediate and overwhelming, they had both recognized, without having to say anything, that this was the end.

She will never tell him about the baby. Even thinking of him, seeing his name when she scrolls down her emails, makes her feel physically sick. No matter what the outcome of her life, she will do this without his help, without ever having anything to do with the man whom she now thinks of as having ruined her life.

But it wasn't just him. If he hadn't come along, perhaps there would have been someone else. Gabby still thinks of those weeks of frantic emailing, being up all night thinking about him, messages flying back and forth, their flirtation growing stronger and stronger, as something akin to an out-of-body experience. He came along at a time when she felt invisible, felt that she was growing old and dull, that life would never again be exciting or glamorous.

She became addicted to the thrill, the roller coaster of highs when he emailed, the lows when he didn't. Looking back, which she tries not to do, she can only think of it as an addiction; short-lived, intense, unmanageable. It poured over her, leaving no room for reason or rationale. She couldn't have stopped it even if she'd wanted to. And she did want to; she never wanted it to go as far as it did. She just wanted to feel beautiful for a bit longer, to feel alive, to feel wanted.

Now she is left with nothing but the ability to swim in the soup of remorse and shame she created all by herself.

She doesn't hear the door of the barn open. She is too busy crying, but she feels the hand on her leg, the heat of a small body curled up next to her.

"Don't cry, Mommy." Alanna takes her hand and strokes it. "It's going to be okay." This only makes Gabby cry harder, but eventually she is able to smile at Alanna through her tears, noticing that Alanna's blue eyes are glistening.

"Have you seen your sister?" Gabby strokes Alanna's hair back behind her ears, tracing her fingers along her daughter's cheekbones, noticing the tiny glistening flower earrings she is wearing, that Elliott bought for her the last time they went to Main Street.

Alanna nods. "She left. She told me."

Gabby doesn't say anything. What is left for her to say?

"I still love you," Alanna says. "And it's still my baby brother or sister. I'll be here to look after it even if Olivia isn't."

"You're the best," Gabby whispers. "Do you have any idea how much I love you?"

Alanna nods, and the two of them sit, together, for a very long time.

Twenty

Gabby has texted Claire a few times, receiving responses that are barely responses, their abruptness and detachment supposedly mitigated by an emoticon of a smiley face, or frown.

CAN'T. FRANTIC. :(

MAYBE TOMORROW.

AM GOOD. TALK LATER! :)

But they don't talk later. They don't talk at all. Gabby has left messages on Claire's cell—the only way to get hold of her—which have not been returned. There are other women Gabby could talk to, but none she trusts in the way she trusts Claire.

Never has she felt more alone than now, abandoned by her husband, daughter, and best friend.

She examines her sideways reflection. She might have got away with saying she's just put on weight, but anyone who has been pregnant would know the truth. It isn't just the weight, it's the shape. Her breasts are full and heavy, her stomach extended in a way that can only suggest a baby. Midlife weight gain is often around the belly, she knows, but it is soft, and fleshy, not low and firm as hers is.

Do people know? Gabby has no idea whether people are gossiping, although at times like this, she is aware of living in a very small town. All it takes is one person to tell another. Even though she trusts Claire not to speak, even now, she knows Olivia will not be able to hold it in; she will have told a friend, who will have told her mother, who will have spread it around town.

Her phone has rung more of late. Not her cell—anyone who really wants to get hold of her knows to only call her cell phone for she never picks up her home phone—but the home phone. She always lets it go to the machine, doesn't bother listening, but occasionally scrolls through the caller ID log to see the numbers that have called, noting that various women she knows vaguely are phoning her. These are women who never call her, who are doubtless phoning under some pretext—would she like to help with the bake sale; does she have a piece of furniture she'd like to donate to the upcoming auction—but who, in fact, are itching to find out what's going on, to be able to go to school tomorrow and whisper excitedly that they know something no one else knows.

Gabby has to go to school today. It is the sixth grade Poetry Café, and even though right now, in her current state, she would do almost anything to avoid being there, she needs to make the effort.

When the girls were tiny, in kindergarten, first grade, she made a decision, based largely on the fact she had a mother entirely disinterested in her school life, that she would go to everything.

While not very interested in being a room mother, or volunteering extensively, for years she showed up for every reading, performance, concert.

When they were small, Gabby needed to go, not just to see the girls perform, but to try and make herself part of the community despite never quite feeling that she fit. She did try to make herself fit—has copied the uniform of bootleg jeans and clogs, puffy vests, cute scarves; has entered into conversations about babysitters and sports teams, dance classes and softball coaches—conversation she so often finds mindless—with an enthusiasm she doesn't feel. She has grown accustomed to showing up to Saturday morning games with her collapsible chair and coffee in a portable mug, setting up the chair in a huddle of other mothers, listening to their screams of encouragement when it is their daughter's turn, putting the conversation on pause until the daughter returns to the dugout, at which point the mother will turn back to the gossipy chat and ignore the rest of the game until her daughter is up again.

They take turns, the mothers, pausing for their daughters, and Gabby has had to learn the rules. From the outside, she looks like the others; if you ignore her accent, still so very English, she speaks like the others, uses the same language, the same cadences, but inside she knows she doesn't belong.

Inside she knows she can dress, speak, pretend as much as she wants to, but you cannot take a girl from North West London, drop her in suburban Connecticut, and expect her to fit in.

None of which bothers her. She is used to her life, loves her life, and only ever misses the sophistication and glamour of London when she—very occasionally—goes back there, but today she isn't sure she is up to the pretense. Today she isn't sure she can stand and make small talk about softball, or gossip about coaches, or ask questions about how the house renovation is coming along.

Today she'd much rather stay home and hide. If it weren't for Alanna, forgiving, loving, lovely Alanna, that is exactly what she would do. She is wearing yoga pants that are stretched shinily over her burgeoning bump, covered with a long tunic-style T-shirt and a voluminous scarf that drapes around her neck and falls, covering her torso in swaths of linen.

If they don't know she's pregnant, they might not necessarily guess today. Gabby takes a deep breath. She doesn't have to do anything today other than smile and be polite. And if Claire is there, which she undoubtedly will be, perhaps they can grab a coffee afterward. Perhaps when Claire sees Gabby at the Poetry Café, she will be able to forgive her; she will be able to still be a friend.

Twenty-one

As usual, Gabby is late. She pops in to the school office to sign in, then walks quickly down the hallways to the library. The homeroom teacher is talking, introducing the language arts project, as Gabby waves at the couple of women who look up to see who has come in.

In the front row is Claire. She does not turn around, but Gabby can see her profile and would recognize her anywhere. Next to her is Elliott.

Gabby takes a seat in the back row, her heart pounding. Why is Elliott here? He never comes to school events, is always too busy with work to make it to anything. How did he even organize his schedule to be here, and why? This is her domain; has always been her domain. She looks around the room at the handful of other fathers that are always there, fathers who work from home, who run their own hedge funds in town, or are on "gardening leave," the ironic but oh-so-handy euphemism for being unemployed.

Elliott is not one of those fathers. Had this happened before, she would have been delighted; nothing would have made her happier than Elliott turning up unexpectedly at an event at school, but now this feels like a betrayal. She cannot take her eyes off the back of his head. He is her husband, the man she loves. He shouldn't be sitting there, so far away. If he is here, he should be by her side, but this chasm between them is growing wider and wider, and she still struggles to understand how something so good can fall apart so quickly and so easily.

Claire turns, looks straight at Gabby, who smiles awkwardly and does a muted wave. Claire smiles in return, then turns back. Gabby watches to see if she will tell Elliott, and sure enough, a couple of minutes later, Claire tilts her head to Elliott's and clearly tells him. Gabby knows this because his shoulders tense immediately, as Gabby's sag in dismay.

Elliott has been avoiding her, and Olivia refuses to see her. Gabby drives Alanna back and forth to Claire's house to stay with Elliott, never getting out of the car, texting Alanna from her position of safety if she needs to let her know she is outside. She has asked Alanna if Dad was coming out, but Alanna always says no, and Gabby doesn't want to put her in the middle, doesn't want to ask Alanna to tell Elliott to come outside.

Nor can she walk up the garden path and walk in the house, in the way she has a million times before. This house now has an invisible barrier around it, one that will not allow her to penetrate. Gabby isn't the type to trample boundaries, to walk into homes where she knows she is unwanted. She has already pictured the look of shock and dismay on all of their faces should she have the temerity to walk into the kitchen.

No. That isn't something Gabby will be doing.

Alanna steps up to the front of the class, holding a white piece of paper straight out in front of her. Poised and confident, she reads a poem she has written about fall, as Gabby's heart threatens to burst with pride. Cheering and clapping, she has to physically restrain herself from jumping up and throwing her arms around her little girl, when she turns to see Elliott staring at her.

The look on his face is exactly the same as hers. Pride and love. An acknowledgment of the extraordinary girl they have created.

If only that look were meant for her.

Gabby is standing by the table that has been covered with paper plates of snacks: chocolate chip cookies, cut-up chunks of cantaloupe, cheese sticks, grapes, brownies.

The children have decimated the snack table, but Gabby is helping herself to the brownies. She would never allow herself to eat them were she not pregnant, and never, during her last two pregnancies, did she allow it as an excuse for her to eat whatever she wanted. She remembered being terrified of becoming a whale, never being able to get rid of the excess weight.

This time around, she doesn't care. She's a pregnant single mother, or at least it looks that way. If she can't comfort herself with food, what hope is left?

She turns with a mouthful of brownie to find herself inches from Elliott, so achingly familiar and lovely, it almost makes her burst into tears there and then. His soft, blue twinkling eyes. The stubble that never goes away, even immediately after he shaves. The soft coat she bought him for his fortieth birthday, which smells of waxed cotton and Elliott, that is so lived-in and loved, it is now as soft as silk. All of him is hers. Was hers. His strong, masculine hands. His salt-and-pepper hair, as tousled as ever. She wants to reach up, as she always does, to tuck the stray bits back, but she no longer has that right.

This is her husband, her man, her best friend. The person to whom she has told everything for twenty years, and now she finds herself looking at him with no idea what to say.

Elliott clears his throat. "Hi."

"Hi." There is an awkward silence. "You look good," she lies, for in fact, he looks terrible. His face is gaunt, his clothes hanging off him.

"I look terrible," he says.

"You're right. I'm sorry. You look terrible. Can I just . . ." And she reaches up to tuck back his hair, except when he realizes what she's doing he turns his head sharply, so she brushes the air, withdrawing her hand, embarrassed. "I'm sorry," she says again. "Just . . . your hair."

"Oh. Right." He brushes it back himself. "Alanna was good, wasn't she?"

"I was so proud." Gabby puts her hand on her heart. "Our little girl. Who knew she had such a talent for poetry! And performing!"

"Who knew," echoes Elliott.

"How did you get time off work?"

"Harvey's taking my patients while I'm here. I thought it best, while we figure things out, to be there for the kids. They need both of us. Especially now."

Gabby nods and tries to swallow the lump in her throat. "Elliott, can we talk? I know it's only been a few weeks, and I know you may not be ready, but there's stuff we have to figure out. I can't keep driving Alanna back and forth, and I need to see Olivia."

"She doesn't want to see you."

"I know. But I'm her mother. She and I have to work this out. Please, Elliott. Can we at least have coffee? Can we just sit down and talk about it?"

Elliott thinks, then nods. "Okay. Coffee."

"Do you want to come over after this?"

"No!" He is vehement. Nothing would cause him more pain right now than going back to the house he no longer lives in, back to the life he has been forced to leave. "I'll meet you at Starbucks on the Post Road. In an hour?"

"Okay." Gabby, seeing a glimmer of hope, nods. "An hour." She walks toward the door, turning, surprised, when she feels a hand on her arm. It is Claire.

"How are you?" Claire's face is filled with sadness.

"Pretty terrible. How are you?"

"Okay. Fat. Emotional. Tired."

"How's Elliott?"

"You were just talking to him."

"I know, but Claire, you're with him every night. How is he?"

Claire looks at her for a few seconds before shrugging. "He's pretty terrible, too. He cries at night. A lot. Sometimes I have to take him in my arms and hold him until he stops. Tim has tried to take him out with the boys, drinking, take his mind off it, but he doesn't want to do anything other than sit on the sofa and cry. He pretends to be okay until Olivia goes to bed, but then his pain just fills the house."

"Oh God, Claire. Why are you telling me this?"

"Because you asked, Gabby. I don't know what to say. I'm trying so hard to forgive you, and I love you and Elliott so much, and . . . that's why I'm struggling. I can't see him in this kind of pain and get together with you and pretend I'm okay with all of it."

"I'm not asking you to pretend to be okay with all of it. I don't expect you to be okay with it. God, I'm not okay with it. I'm disgusted with myself. I am ashamed, and if there were anything in the world I could do to change it, I would. Jesus, Claire." Gabby fights to keep her voice low enough that it doesn't project to everyone in the room. "If I could, do you not think I would turn back the clock? I'm twenty weeks' pregnant and there is nothing I can do about it other than feel sick for ruining my life with one mistake. Sick. And disgusted. And the last thing I need is for my best friend to abandon me through this. The last thing I need is to feel judged, and hated, by you." Tears are now streaming down Gabby's cheeks.

"I could never hate you," whispers Claire. "I love you, but I can't be there for both of you. It's too draining. It isn't about my choice, it isn't that I've chosen Elliott over you, but Elliott has chosen us, and I haven't got the strength right now for both of you. I'm sorry. I know you won't understand. . . ."

"You're right," Gabby snaps, whirling as she leaves the room. "I don't understand."

There is a table in the corner of the Starbucks, by the window, which Gabby grabs, cradling her green tea as she looks out on to the Post Road, lulled into calm by the passing cars. She still can't believe the conversation she had with Claire, can't believe that, despite how Claire has decided to reframe it in her mind, Claire has chosen Elliott over Gabby.

And then there were none, she thinks, looking up to see Elliott approaching the table.

"Hi. Sorry I'm a bit late." He sits down as Gabby jumps up.

"Let me get you something," she blurts, in a reversal of their roles, for Elliott would always be the one to get coffee, or food, or anything while Gabby and the girls sat at the table.

"No, I'm fine."

"You must have something. Tea? I'm drinking green tea. It's good. You'll like it."

"Okay," he acquiesces. "Sure."

She gets up to order him tea, knowing this would never happen if they were still a couple. Elliott would automatically order the tea, pulling his wallet from his pocket to pay for it. Back at the table, she sets the tea down and sits.

"Thanks. I just came from the Realtor's office." Elliott takes a sip of his tea. "That's why I was late. They're going to phone you to make an appointment to come and value the house."

Gabby stares at him. "What?"

"I thought it would make sense to sell the house, and even though they don't recommend putting it on the market until the spring, I'd like to have an idea of what it's worth."

"Why would we sell the house?"

Elliott snorts. "Gabby, if we're not together, we each need money for our separate homes, and the only place that money's going to come from is the house. This is the most practical solution."

Gabby's heart is pounding. "If we're not together. But what if we are? What if we are able to work through this? What if we get back together, but we've lost our home? Elliott, you and I both love the house; think of all the work we put into it. We can't sell our house." There is an urgency to her voice.

"Gabby," he says quietly. "I don't think there's anything to work through."

"What do you mean?" She keeps her voice calm, even though her body is filled with flutters of panic.

"I mean, you're pregnant by another man. That's it. It's done."

"You want to divorce me?" Of course she knew this was coming, but they hadn't mentioned the D word before, and she had thought, had hoped, that as long as it wasn't mentioned, their getting back together was always a possibility.

Elliott stares at the table, grimacing with discomfort and pain, unable to believe he is sitting inches from his wife, the woman he thought he would spend the rest of his life with, the woman he imagined growing old with, a woman so perfect for him, he has never, not for a second, even thought about anyone else.

"No," he says, looking up at her, wincing as he speaks. "I don't want to divorce you. But you've left me no other choice."

Gabby holds it in until she is in her car. She holds it in until she turns onto Center Street. She holds it in until she finds a quiet spot on the side of a quiet street, where she parks, hides her head in her hands, and howls.

Putting her head back, she screams toward the ceiling, pounding the steering wheel until, exhausted, she just lays her forehead on the wheel and sobs, moaning in pain.

Her cell phone rings. Maybe it's Elliott. It must be Elliott. He must be phoning to say he made a terrible mistake, he's thought things through, he can't throw away twenty years of marriage like this. Frantically she roots through her handbag, pulling out the crap that mysteriously makes its way into all her bags—tissues, earplugs, leaflets, more leaflets, tampons with torn wrappers, hair bands—until she finds the phone.

It isn't Elliott. It's her mum.

"Darling!" Natasha trills down the phone. "I haven't heard from you for ages. I just turned to your father earlier and said, 'Have you heard from our naughty daughter recently?' and he said, 'Not for months,' so I decided to call! How are you? And how are my gorgeous granddaughters?"

"Hi Mum." Gabby's voice is reedy and thin, despite her attempt to disguise her tears. "We're good."

"You don't sound good, darling. You sound terrible. What's the matter? Do you have a cold?"

Gabby has never turned to her mother in her life. Her mother, who was there for everyone else, who took in strangers and helped them sort out their lives, is the very last person Gabby would ever think to turn to in a crisis.

She rarely thinks to call her parents, and they, she assumes, are too wrapped up in their own worlds to call her. She loves them, naturally, but when people talk of their support systems, their families, Gabby has always known that the only support system to whom she would turn is her family of choice: Elliott, the girls, Claire.

Now that support system has broken down, and the only one that's left is the woman on the end of the phone right now.

"I don't have a cold." Gabby can feel herself start to break down. "Elliott's left me."

Natasha doesn't say a word, just lets her daughter tell her the whole story. She asks questions when necessary, prompts Gabby when needed, but there is no judgment in her voice, only kindness, compassion, and love.

"What am I going to do?" Gabby says, over and over. "What am I going to do?"

"You're going to get the local paper, you're going to go to the notice board in the library, and you're going to go online and Google. You're going to find yourself a divorce support group, with a bloody good therapist leading the group. You're going to find other women going through this, because you cannot be alone through this. You will not be alone. My God, Gabby. What a terrible mess. But if I have to come out there myself and help you through it, I will. Darling girl, you aren't alone. I promise you."

"You'd really come?" Her mother has come to America three times in the last ten years, the last of which was five years ago. It was much easier, she'd taken to saying, if they all came to London. Easier for who? Gabby would think, although she never put up much of a fight as she did so love going home.

"I would. I will. You just say the word and I'll book my flight."

Gabby lies in bed, her hands resting on her belly as she feels the baby do a lazy somersault. She moves her nightshirt aside and watches her stomach undulate, a knee or an elbow pushing her skin out, and despite all that has happened, despite wishing she could go back and do things differently, she cannot help but gasp with the magic of knowing she is carrying another life inside her.

It is as magical today as it was with Olivia—the miracle of a tiny person in her womb, and this time, when the tears roll gently down her cheeks, she smiles, just a little.

This time, they are tears of wonder and joy.

Twenty-two

Gabby has passed the big white church many times, but has never had any reason to go inside. She has always found it easier to say she was not a believer in organized religion than to offer up the truth, which is that she is slightly envious of people who have faith, religion, whatever it is you want to call it.

When she first arrived here, in the suburbs, she looked in astonishment at the smartly dressed people teeming out of their houses on a Sunday.

"Where are they all going?" she'd asked Elliott.

He had been astonished she genuinely didn't know. "To church."

No one she knew in London went to church, other than for weddings and, perhaps, christenings. She knew plenty of Jewish people who went to synagogue, but even then, only for the major holidays, often only Yom Kippur.

Gabby had always wanted somewhere to go. Her parents didn't

believe in organized religion, had decided it was the root of the world's evils.

"The only religion your father follows is that of the liberal intelligentsia," her mother would laugh, if ever Gabby tried to question him. Her mother, having renounced Catholicism, had spent most of Gabby's childhood trying on Buddhism. There were varying kinds. The Nam Myoho Renge Kyo kind, which was said to manifest anything you should want; Zen Buddhism; and finally following the teachings of Thich Nhat Hanh, with his suggestions of daily mindful meditations.

Elliott would admit to being Episcopalian only if pushed. He, too, had religious confusion. It was one of the things they had always shared, always laughed about.

There is a white sign pasted up on the door, an arrow pointing upstairs to the church library. Gabby hesitates in the doorway, wanting suddenly to get back in her car, anxious about what a divorce support group might entail.

Perhaps she can sit quietly, in the back, and listen to the others. Perhaps the therapist who leads the group—Sally, who, incidentally, seemed lovely on the phone—would drop pearls of wisdom from her lips that would instantaneously give Gabby a peace and serenity she has been looking for, enabling her to silently leave, renewed.

She hesitates as another woman walks in, stopping when she sees Gabby.

"Are you here for the . . . support group?" she asks, nervously smoothing her blond ponytail.

"The divorce support group?" As if there would be more than one support group meeting at this time in this church.

The woman nods, and relieved to have found strength in the number two, they both walk up the stairs to push open the library door.

A couple of women who know each other stand at one end, by a large table with some leaflets on it, while others are dotted around the room. One on a soft love seat, the others perched on folding chairs that have been placed in a circle around the room.

Opposite the love seat is a wing chair, in which sits a woman with glasses, grey hair, and a warm smile.

"Welcome." She stands up and comes over to greet the women. "I'm Sally."

The woman Gabby came in with, with whom she feels an instant affinity, is Josephine. They move in unison toward two chairs, heads together as they make small talk, establishing their bond. Where they live, do they have children, is this their first group.

It is a disparate group of women, a group you would never put together. They age from early thirties to terribly sad late sixties. There is one gorgeous, glamorous, high-heeled and sexed-up girl, or woman—it's hard to tell for she is unlined and overly made up—and the rest look much like Gabby: tired, weary, colorless.

The woman with the grey hair, Sally, starts to speak:

"First of all I want to commend each and every one of you"—she looks at each of the women as she talks, her eyes slowly scanning the room—"for coming to this meeting. It is an incredibly brave thing to do, to bring your pain out in public, but sharing that pain with other women who are going through the same thing is ultimately the most healing thing you can do for yourself. So well done. All of you." She starts clapping her hands, as the room slowly joins in, a round of applause for each of them, none of whom feels remotely brave.

"We're going to meet, in this room, for the next eight weeks, and we're going to get to know one another very well. I'd like each of you in this room to take what I call the privacy vow. We need this to be a safe space; a sacred space. We need to be able to trust that we can say anything we want in this room, to express our pain, our fears, our grief, and know that nothing we say will ever leave this room. I'm going to vow that I will not discuss anything in this room with anyone outside this room, ever. Nor will I discuss any of the members of this group with any of the other members. And finally, I will not divulge who the members of this group are. What you see here, what you hear here, when you leave here, let it stay here. Please, one by one, raise your hand after me, and say 'I vow.' "

Gabby turns to Josephine, wide-eyed, to see her expression reflected back at her. They give each other a small smile as Sally looks around the circle.

"I vow."

"I vow."

"I vow," says Josephine.

"I vow," says Gabby.

"Perhaps we can all go around the room telling everyone our names and a little about our divorce. I'd like to start by saying I'm Sally, and I started my first divorce support group eight years ago when I went through my own divorce. I thought I had been very happily married for twenty-three years, except my then-husband claimed I was wrong." She smiles. "It wasn't, as I thought, a happy marriage, but a terrible one." There is a ripple of laughter through the room, this story clearly resonating with more than one woman in here. "It was, without question, the most painful thing I have ever been through. I could not believe that my husband, the man I had loved for most of my adult life, was one day a loving husband, and the next, a stranger." Another ripple as a wave of familiarity washes over the room. "I tried leaning on the women I thought of as my closest friends, but it was as if a chasm had developed between us. They didn't know what to say, or how to help, or, in some cases, how to be there for me in any way, shape, or form, because they'd never been divorced themselves. I tried not to blame them, but I felt abandoned, and betrayed." Several women are now nodding, two leaning forward at exactly the same time to pluck a Kleenex from the box on the coffee table, dabbing at the corners of their eyes.

"As a therapist myself, I am, of course, a huge believer in therapy, but I had been in therapy for years, and therapy alone couldn't help my pain. I knew I needed to talk to other women who were going through what I was going through. I knew I could help them, and in doing so, I could help myself. I started this group not as a therapist, but as a woman in pain, looking for help. The first group met here, in this library, on October tenth, 2004. The women who sat in a circle in this room are today among my closest friends." She smiles. "And finally I have to tell you that there is life after divorce. I got married three years ago to the most wonderful man, a man who is, truly, my soul mate, my partner, in a way my prior husband never could have been. However much you feel your life is ending, I urge you to think of this as a new beginning. It won't always be easy, but there is more joy, and laughter, and love to come, once you have worked through your pain and are open to it. Thank you."

There is silence as the women digest what Sally has said, before Sally catches the eye of the woman sitting next to her, the gorgeous, glamorous, made-up woman, giving her a small nod, indicating she should talk next.

"Hi. I'm Michelle," she says, stretching out her legs, showing off high platform sandals and black toenails, the glimpse of an ankle bracelet as she moves. "Wow. Where to begin." She gives a nervous laugh. "I have three beautiful children. Jason, who's nine; Emily, who's six; and Alex, who's four. My . . . husband and I met in high school. We've been together forever, and he is the love of my life." Her voice cracks. "He has his own business, a chain of retail stores, and for the last few months they've been struggling, so he's had to work like a crazy person to get the business back up and running again. Or at least, that's what he said. While he was at work, I was doing everything. I kept a beautiful home for him, and raised the children. I'm a full-time stay-at-home mom, and proud of it. I loved being a wife, and a mother, and I stepped up to pick up the slack during those months when he wasn't home.

"Two months ago he came home from work and I could see something was wrong. I thought he was losing the business, but he said"—her voice cracks again—"he was leaving me. He was in love with this woman who works for him. Gina." She spits out her name. "His slutty twenty-five-year-old assistant, who I had given jewelry to!" She looks around the room at the women's aghast faces. "She'd babysat our kids when we went away and I gave her jewelry to thank her! On top of money! It turns out they have been having an affair for almost a year, and he wants to reinvent himself with her. We live in a big, beautiful house in Fairfield, which is on the market, and the bastard is refusing to pay for anything. I'm trying to cook for people to make some extra cash, but I have no idea what I'm going to do. The lawyer says he'll have to disclose all his assets, but I know my husband. If there is anything left in the business by the time we get to the divorce courts, he'll have it wrapped and hidden so well even a forensic accountant couldn't find it. So here I am. Crying myself to sleep every night, then waking up two hours later and staying awake the rest of the night, worrying how I'm going to feed my children and where I'm going to live. The only good thing to have come of it is I've lost thirty pounds. Seriously. I've never been this size in my life." She smiles as Gabby mentally berates herself for judging. She had thought this girl one of the wealthy, entitled housewives, the kind of girl she crossed the room to avoid, but how wrong she is.

"Thank you for sharing with us, Michelle," Sally says, looking at the next woman. Four women later, Gabby has heard roughly the same story, four different times, with slightly different scenery. In each story, the husband has unexpectedly left the wife; in each the wives thought they had if not the perfect marriage, then certainly one that was good enough. The women are angry, resentful, upset. They do not understand why this has happened to them. They do not know what they did to deserve this, other than be a wonderful wife, a faithful wife, a wife who bore their husband children and raised them well, kept beautiful homes.

And then it is Gabby's turn.

"I'm Gabby," she says quietly. "And, as you can hear, I'm English. As you can probably see, I'm also five and a half months pregnant. I am married to a wonderful man, the great love of my life. He is the kindest, funniest, greatest guy, and there was never any question in my mind that I would grow old and die with him. And I screwed it up. I made a mistake that threw everything I cared about into jeopardy, and I am so disgusted with myself I can barely even look at myself in the mirror, and I wish I could sit here and say I have no idea why he left, but I know exactly why. And I don't blame him. I just wish I could turn back the clock." The other women wait for her to carry on, want to hear more, wonder what mistake she is talking about, but Gabby is done. She turns her head to Josephine with a half-smile. "There's nothing more I can say right now. Sorry."

"My turn?" Josephine asks as Gabby shrugs apologetically. "Great," she says. "I'm Josephine and I left my husband. I married him seven years ago, thinking I was doing the right thing, even though I knew I didn't love him, not in the way you're supposed to love your husband. But I wanted kids, and love had always been so difficult for me. When he came along and promised to take care of me, it felt like I'd been sent a knight in shining armor. I was a good girl; I was trained to say the right thing. When he asked me to marry him I thought it would be rude to say no. So we got married, and we had kids. Two boys. I adore them. My husband, who had been so incredibly charming, and wonderful, and gentle during the courtship, started to change. He became aggressive, and demanding. And so controlling. He'd tell me what I could and couldn't eat, what I was and wasn't allowed to wear. He'd put me down in front of friends, and scream at me about how incompetent I was. I had been so strong, before I met him, and I started off fighting back, but after a while the fight went out of me and I just . . . gave up. He never hit me, not slapping, or punching, but when his rages were out of control he was terrifying, and often he'd push me into a wall, or shove me across a room." She is dispassionate as she talks, the story made even more powerful by her lack of emotion.

"I used to lie in bed at night and dream about divorce, but I was too terrified to leave. I knew that if I ever said I wanted a divorce, he'd fly into a rage so awful I couldn't even begin to contemplate it. I thought I was stuck. I was terrified of what he would do. I could actually see him spitting with rage, 'You want to leave? You leave. I'm keeping the house. And the boys.' When the boys leave for college, I thought, then I'll go. When they're protected and he has no power over me anymore. But then . . ." A small smile crosses her lips. "I met someone. Not an affair," she quickly explains. "He's a friend. We've become very close. Actually, I don't think I've ever been so close to anyone before. He knows everything about me, and I know it was this friendship that gave me the strength to leave. It made me see that marriages don't have to be filled with rage, and anger, and fear. It made me see that there are men out there who are kind. And gentle. And loving." She sighs. "You know, the truth is I think I am a little bit in love with my friend. And he says he's a little bit in love with me, but nothing's happened. Nothing will happen," she says firmly. "We've agreed we are only ever going to be friends. But it's his love that gave me the strength to leave. I started looking ahead to the future, to a future without my husband, rather than dwelling in the fear of anticipation that was based on the past. So now I'm on my own, and remarkably I am still in the family home, and I thought getting rid of my husband would be fantastic, and some of the time it is.

"But on the weekends . . ." Her voice drops. "When my kids are with him, and I'm in my house without my kids, I have no idea who I'm supposed to be. If I'm not someone's wife, someone's mother, who the hell am I? He's spreading stories about me having an affair, which isn't true, and I've been cut dead by some of the women in school, which shouldn't bother me because it's not like I liked these women anyway, but it does. And I honestly have no idea if I can make it on my own. I'm relieved, and scared, and overwhelmed, and I needed to talk to others who understand."

"Well done," Sally says gently. "You sound like a woman of tremendous courage."

The introductions and personal stories take up the entire hour. Gabby still feels, as she so often does, like a fish out of water, and rather than mill around afterward, talking to strangers, she heads for the door, hoping to make it to the car without getting caught.

But she is caught. By Josephine.

"Do you want to grab some tea?" she asks. Gabby looks at this fresh-faced woman, a woman who in fact looks exactly like someone Gabby would be friends with, and is about to decline, but finds herself, instead, saying yes.

The thing is"—Josephine tears open a packet of sugar and tips it into her tea, stirring it with a plastic spoon—"it isn't the same when you've left your husband. It just isn't the same as having them walk out on you. Those women seem . . . I don't know. I'm sure they're nice, but the only one I felt I had anything in common with is you."

"Do you think that matters, though?" Gabby can't help but feel flattered. "Do we have to like each other? Obviously it's nicer for everyone if we do, but I don't know that it's essential."

"All I know is that if you hadn't been there, I'm not sure I'd be coming back. It just seemed that so many of those other women were angry. I'm not angry. I'm relieved. And terrified."

"Tell me about it," Gabby says. "I still wake up every morning thinking this is a bad dream."

"So what *was* your mistake? How did you screw it up?"

"Isn't it obvious?" Gabby gestures to her stomach.

"You had an affair?"

"I'm not even sure you could call it that. An emotional affair, perhaps. I had a . . . friendship. Probably one just like yours. Lots of flirtatious emails, lots of banter. It made me feel beautiful again. And alive. We slept together once, but once is all you need, it seems. I thought I was going through menopause and pregnancy was the last thing I'd have to worry about."

"I know this sounds deceitful, but didn't you think about telling your husband it was his? If it was just once, couldn't you have just, I don't know, put it behind you and moved on?"

"I could have done. If my husband hadn't had a vasectomy last year."

Josephine claps her hands over her mouth. "Oh shit!"

"Exactly." Even Gabby smiles at the irony. "Oh shit indeed."

"Okay." Josephine leans forward. "Seeing as we're now at secret level, I will confess that my . . . friendship . . ."

"You're sleeping with him," Gabby says matter-of-factly.

Josephine's face falls. "Is it obvious?"

"Only because you left your husband. I don't know that women ever leave their husbands unless there's someone else. I don't think you necessarily have to be sleeping with them, but you have to be emotionally attached to someone other than your husband. A close friendship with an unspoken attraction, maybe. An unfulfilled dream. Or, in my case, a flirtation with an inappropriate man and one night that screws everything up."

"You realize you just got hugely unlucky," Josephine says. "If you hadn't gotten pregnant, you could have gotten away with it."

Gabby nods with a deep sigh. "That's the thing I can't believe. It still would have been wrong, and I would have had to live with the fact that I had betrayed my husband, and honestly? I don't know that I would have been able to do it, but at least he would still be my husband. At least the man I love, the only man I have ever loved, would still be by my side." She looks at Josephine. "Enough about me. Did you sleep with your friend before or after leaving your husband?"

"After!" Josephine looks shocked. "I could never sleep with another man then climb into bed with my husband! Oh Lord." She realizes who she's talking to. "I'm sorry. I'm not judging you. It's just a personal thing. . . ."

"Oh trust me, I'm not offended. I never thought *I* could sleep with another man then climb into bed with my husband either. Amazing the things you end up doing during your midlife crisis. Are you going to run off into the sunset with this other man and live happily ever after?"

Sadness crosses Josephine's face. "That's the thing. It's complicated. He was incredible when I was sharing my unhappiness with him, and then, immediately afterward, when things became physical. I presumed we'd be together. I told everyone else I was leaving

Chris because I was so unhappy and because I'd had enough, and even though that was true, I knew deep down I wouldn't be leaving if James wasn't waiting in the wings."

"And?"

"James now isn't sure we should get involved. Not seriously. He says he loves me but he's worried he's the rebound guy, and I need to heal before he can get involved with me."

"What do you think?"

"I think it's bullshit. I think this is one of the things men say when they're trying to let you down gently. It's like that whole it's not me, it's you thing. I'm on this goddamned roller coaster where I have no idea what's going on. When he calls and says he's coming over I'm flying high as a kite, then when he doesn't respond to a text, or disappears for two days, I sink into the depths of depression and all I can do is lie in bed and cry. You probably think I'm crazy."

Gabby smiles. "I do. But only because I've experienced all kinds of crazy myself. That was me with the guy who got me pregnant. A roller coaster. I was obsessed with him, to the exclusion of everything that was important in my life. My husband, my kids. All I thought about was him. I had no idea how crazy, and how unhealthy, it was. Nor did I have any idea how it would screw up my life."

"Do you think this is unhealthy and crazy?" Josephine's voice is a fearful whisper.

"What do you think?" Gabby asks gently.

"I think it's unhealthy and crazy." She grimaces as she says the words. "I know it is. But I can't help it. I feel like I've jumped into the ocean and he's the only lifeline I have."

"He can't be a lifeline when he's drifting away from you," says Gabby. "Look. I'm not saying you were wrong to leave your husband. Clearly you were terribly unhappy, and he sounds like a terribly abusive and difficult man. You needed to leave, and this man,

James?" Josephine nods. "James saved your life. You should always be grateful to him for getting you out of the marriage, but the ones that get you out are never the ones you end up with."

"You don't think so?"

"I think it can happen but it's rare. He had a specific role in your life: to get you over the fear enough to leave your husband. Of course it's scary. Trust me, I know how terrifying it is to face the prospect of life on your own when you've had a partner for so many years, but you have to face those fears. You can't immediately look to another man to rescue you. That will bring you nothing but pain."

"I know you're right," Josephine says. "It's still pretty shitty to hear. It's a shame you're pregnant. I could do with a glass of wine just about now."

"It's early afternoon!" Gabby laughs. "A bit early, isn't it?"

"Never too early for a glass of wine when you're going through a divorce," Josephine laughs, lifting her mug of tea. "Cheers. I'm glad I met you, and I'm glad I came today. I didn't expect this, but I feel a little bit better already."

Gabby opens the front door, immediately seeing Olivia's Uggs kicked off in the hallway, in just the way that always drives her nuts. Usually she would shout up the stairs, demanding Olivia come down and put her boots away in her cubby, where they belong, but the very fact that Olivia is here is so thrilling, she doesn't want to do anything to destroy whatever peace she may have brought with her.

Should she go upstairs and knock on Olivia's door? Should she bring tea? Olivia has refused to speak to Gabby for weeks, and Gabby wants to make this easy, doesn't want to do anything to further stir up the situation.

Things are not, apparently, easy at Tim and Claire's house. The house really isn't big enough for two extra bodies, and nerves are starting to fracture. Elliott, apparently, is on the sofa bed in the TV room, which is fine during the week, but disastrous on the weekends when Elliott likes to sleep in, but Tim and Claire's kids like to tumble downstairs at the crack of dawn to flop on the sofa in the TV room, where they watch TV for hours, until someone remembers to scream at them to turn the damned TV off.

Olivia is sleeping on a cot in Jolie's room, except Jolie's room is only big enough for one bed, one cot, one nightstand, and one dresser. This means that Olivia's stuff—and teenage girls have a tremendous amount of stuff—is spilling out over everything, which is starting to drive Jolie nuts.

This is all according to Alanna, who sleeps on a blow-up bed in the playroom. She insists on sleeping over at Tim and Claire's because she misses her father so much, wants to spend as much time with him as possible, even though the family is out of beds and the house is clearly overcrowded.

The whole thing sounds like a nightmare. Olivia apparently desperately misses her bedroom at home, her things, but has refused to set foot in the house, blaming her mother for ruining her life.

Gabby tiptoes into the kitchen and makes tea. Being English, she has raised her children in the tradition of tea. Not fancy, herbal, gourmet tea; nothing that blooms like a flower or comes in a triangular gauze tea bag, but proper builder's tea. Strong, sweet, milky. The kind of tea that can lift you out of a depression, warm you to your bones, chase the blues right out the door.

There is nothing as comforting as a proper cup of tea, and Gabby carries Olivia's favorite mug, with a chocolate-wrapped marshmallow, up the stairs, where she raps lightly on the door.

"Who is it?"

"It's me. Mum. Can I come in." There is silence. "I brought you tea."

A rustling, then the door is open, and Olivia, trying so hard to retain her expression of disdain, looks at her mother before bursting into tears.

It's okay," croons Gabby, cradling her daughter's head as they sit on her bed. "Ssssh. It's okay."

"I hate it there," Olivia cries. "I hate not being at home, and sleeping on that shitty bed, and not having any of my stuff."

"So come home," Gabby says. "Come home right now. It's easy."

"I can't," Olivia says, her big brown eyes now smudged with mascara, making them look even bigger, giving her a youthfulness she has almost grown out of.

"Why not?"

Olivia raises her head to look at her mother, her dark eyebrows coming together in a frown. "Because that would be betraying Dad."

"How would that betray Dad?"

"Because that would mean I choose you, and I can't do that to him. He's already hurting so much, and I'm the only one looking after him. I can't leave him, too."

"Oh sweetie." Gabby takes her hand, noticing the chipped blue nail polish, resolving not to point it out. "It's not your job to look after Dad. I know you want to, and I know you feel responsible for him, but you're seventeen. The only person responsible for looking after Dad is Dad."

"And you," Olivia spits. "It should have been you."

Gabby sighs. Olivia really isn't a child anymore, and there doesn't seem any point in protecting her. She has a sense that if she has any hope at all of rebuilding her relationship with Olivia, she needs to be honest with her. However much that might hurt, and however wrong it may feel, to tell your child the truth, a truth that paints you in a terrible light.

"You're right," Gabby says. "It was my job to look after your dad, and I spent many years doing that. I would like to still be doing that, but I screwed up. I was feeling old, and unattractive, and that my life and my youth were slipping away from me. A man came along, someone younger, who told me I was beautiful, who made me feel young again. I swear to you, Olivia, I never meant for anything to happen, but something did, just once, and as soon as it was over I knew I'd made a terrible mistake, and that it would never happen again. Except I became pregnant. And now I have ruined not only my life, but Dad's, and yours and Alanna's. I will never be able to apologize enough, and I will never be able to make you understand how ashamed I am. But I will have to live with my mistake for the rest of my life. As will we all, and we have to find a way to forgive and move on because Olivia, you are still my daughter. My firstborn. And I love you today as much as I did the day you emerged from my body. Do you understand that, Olivia? *Can* you understand that?"

Olivia, staring silently at the floor, reluctantly nods.

Twenty-three

Gabby had no idea how hard it was to be a single mother. She remembers looking around at women she knew, newly separated or divorced, not understanding why they kept complaining.

Now she understands. There is no Elliott to take out the trash, or deal with the bills, or phone whoever you're supposed to phone when the sump pump isn't working and the basement floor is one large and growing puddle.

There is no Elliott to take the girls to softball, to break up a fight, to get up at the crack of dawn, leaving her to sleep in, because one of the girls has a game in New Haven and has to be there by eight. There is no one for her to discuss her growing concerns about Alanna's unhappiness in middle school with; no partner to sit by her side and try and figure out what is wrong with their daughter, and what to do about it.

There is no one, in short, to take the flack, to ease the burden, to give Gabby a break.

In the beginning, she hated the weekends when the girls went to stay with Elliott. He has rented a small house off Green's Farms Road, a cape with three bedrooms and one bathroom.

He had been back to Gabby's house a couple of times to pick up his things, some furniture he needed. The bed from the guest room, the sofa from the den, a couple of tables. It wasn't much, yet the house feels strangely empty. Gabby has not been able to go into the den, with its two beanbags and coffee table, a large space where the sofa once was.

The house felt emptiest, of course, on the weekends the girls were with their father. Gabby had no idea what to do with herself, often staying in bed for most of the weekend, counting the hours until the girls, with their laughter, and shouting, and messiness and energy, came back to bring the house, and Gabby, to life again.

A couple of months into their separation, Gabby now counts off the days until the girls go to Elliott's. No fighting. No getting up long before her body's natural wake-up time. No meals to worry about, no chauffeuring back and forth to friends' houses or sports events.

She has come to treasure the weekends she is on her own. She now welcomes the peace, the serenity, the quiet. She welcomes padding down to the kitchen in the morning, at whatever time she wakes up, making herself coffee and sitting in the easy chair by the window with the paper, or a book.

She has started painting again; sitting on a stool for her poor legs and feet are swollen, and she cannot handle standing for the hours necessary for the works she is doing. She has no models, but has files of pictures of pregnant women, is painting vast canvases of burgeoning bellies, glowing faces.

The heartache and discord that marked the beginning of this

pregnancy have given way to a beauteous glow, a constant marveling at the miracle of life, an appreciation of what a blessing it is to be lucky enough to have a child at her age.

Even if it isn't Elliott's child.

At the beginning she was so scared she'd never feel connected to this child; so scared she wouldn't feel maternal, wouldn't want the child that had changed her life so irreparably.

She did all the right things, despite wishing she could turn back the clock; took her prenatal vitamins, turned up to her doctor's appointments. She did the genetic counseling, does the blood work, gives the urine samples. She smiles when strangers stop her and ask her when she's due, congratulate her, tell her, with great conviction, that they can tell it is a girl. Or boy. *And they have never been wrong.*

The minute she saw the tiny black and white body on the sonographer's screen, that very first time, her bonding began. That was the last thing she had to worry about.

The alarm on her iPhone goes off at three p.m. She was fast asleep, is sleeping away most of the days of this pregnancy, but is determined to be there when Alanna comes home, is convinced that Alanna's veering off into unknown territory is because of her own lack of presence, is certain Alanna's unhappiness in middle school is partly due to Gabby not being there for her, too caught up in her separation.

Poor Alanna. Her new friends continue, none of them lasting. Each week there is another "new best friend," each girl with long, straightened hair—straightened! At twelve!—each in designer clothes, with nonchalant shrugs and no eye contact. Gabby may not have approved of the last crowd of popular girls, but they were, at least, known to her; she knew their mothers, knew she could phone a mother when one girl labeled her Instagram picture with: *You wouldn't believe the shit I had to put up with when I was best friends with Alanna*; she knew the mother would hear.

These new girls have mothers as terrifyingly blasé and disconnected as the girls themselves. Alanna needs her mother more than ever. Gabby forces herself out of bed, blinking until she starts to swim back into consciousness, going downstairs to heat up scones she had made earlier. Alanna's favorite.

The back door slams, followed by the sound of footsteps going upstairs.

"Alanna? I have scones!" Gabby shouts up the stairs, sighing at the lack of response as the phone starts to ring.

"This is Lisa Cooperville, principal of the middle school."

Gabby freezes, forcing her voice to sound normal. "Yes?" She can't hide her hesitancy, even with the politeness that follows. "How are you?"

"I'm fine, and I'm sorry to call with this news, but there has been an incident at school involving your daughter Alanna, and we would like you to come in as soon as possible."

"What kind of incident?"

"Alanna has been involved in a bullying incident. As you know we have a zero-tolerance policy, and we need to gather all the parents involved to let you know procedures for the next step."

Oh God. That explains so much. Alanna has been bullied. Sweet, loving Alanna has been a target for those vicious bitches. No wonder she has been so quiet of late; no wonder she is withdrawn.

"I had no idea," Gabby whispers. "My poor baby. Do you know what happened? She hasn't said anything, but she's been so quiet. It never occurred to me she was being bullied."

There is an awkward silence.

"Your daughter is the antagonist, Mrs. Cartwright. She tackled

Josh Gordon to the ground, with the help of three of the other girls, then Alanna cut his hair off. She is the bully. I know this may not be easy for you to hear, but there were numerous witnesses, and the boy, Josh, is extremely upset."

Gabby gasped, but has no words. There is nothing she can say, her mind a jumble of thoughts, feelings, denial, defensiveness, acceptance: all mixed up together.

"When shall I come in?" Her voice is a whisper.

"If you and your husband could come in tomorrow morning at nine. Alanna and the two other girls are on suspension until we decide how to progress so she will be at home tomorrow. I will make sure her teachers send you the work so she doesn't miss out."

Gabby and Elliott sit outside the principal's office, Gabby occasionally letting out a deep sigh, Elliott pretending to be engrossed in vital emails on his iPhone.

"Why do you think she did it?" Gabby asks, again. "Do you really think there hasn't been some kind of mistake?"

"She said there were witnesses." Elliott keeps his voice low, aware of the hustle and bustle of people passing them on the corridor, all looking at them curiously, doubtless already having heard of the story, wanting to see the terrible creatures that spawned this girl that committed the terrible act. "I have no idea why she did it. She was with you last night. What did she say?"

"I already told you. She screamed at me, telling me I didn't understand anything and that she hates me. She refused to even talk about it. I still have no idea."

The door to the principal's office opens, Gabby and Elliott looking up at the same time to see one of Alanna's new "friends," eyes downcast as she is ushered out by her parents, both grave-faced.

Gabby has met the mother once—she was frosty and disinterested—and their unwanted link today brings them no closer together. The mother deliberately avoids looking at them, although Gabby knows there is also a distinct possibility that the mother, who didn't openly acknowledge her when they did meet, has no idea who she is.

The principal walks them to the end of the corridor, nodding an acknowledgment at Gabby and Elliott, but not officially greeting them until the other parents are gone, the other parents of one of the other girls who was quite clearly involved.

On the bench opposite, another couple appears, with their son. She does not know Josh Gordon, but knows of him, and this must surely be him, with his new buzz cut. She knows who he is for the last time Alanna had these girls over, they spent the time prank calling a boy called Josh, a boy she overheard them describing disdainfully as "so gay."

Gabby is mortified, remembering that. Would her daughter, whom she has raised to be accepting of all, truly do this to a child just because he is slight, effeminate, unlike the other boys?

She is grateful she does not know the family, that they don't know her. The principal ushers them in, without mentioning their names, and Gabby attempts to ignore the couple's searching looks as it dawns on them who they might be.

"This is enormously distressing to all concerned, as you can imagine," Mrs. Cooperville says. "Josh has been the target of some mean behavior already this year. He is a sensitive and sweet child, but those are not qualities that necessarily serve you well in middle school. Your daughter, and others, physically pinned him down while Alanna cut off his hair. We gather it was a dare, and I understand some of the unique pressures involved in middle school, particularly for girls who are struggling to fit in, but on no level is this behavior acceptable. I have spoken to the Board of Education, and we believe that after a period of suspension, Alanna must be transferred to the other middle school." Her face suddenly softens. "I know Alanna," she says. "And I don't believe she's a bad kid. Unfortunately she's got in with a crowd here that is . . . challenging. I don't believe she would ever have entertained doing anything like this had she not felt pressure. I understand from two of the girls involved that they threatened to turn the entire grade against her if she didn't do this."

"So why are you punishing her?" Gabby blurts out. "She was blackmailed."

"I understand that, but they are all culpable. Each one is being punished, and you have to understand, Alanna may not have felt she had a choice when she picked up those scissors, but she did, and that she made the wrong choice is terrible, but she has to have consequences for making the wrong choice."

"But it's not right that our daughter was blackmailed into doing something she clearly didn't want to do, and is now being forced to change schools. What's happening to the other girls? Are they being punished in the same way?"

Gabby has never been more grateful that Elliott is by her side. Just a few days ago she thought things couldn't possibly get any worse. Until they did. At least, for this, Elliott has been able to step up and be the parent, coparent with her to ease some of the burden.

She is bordering on hysteria, but Elliott is reassuringly calm. She knows it is not the case, for his jaw is clenched, the muscle in his cheek twitching, but his exterior has, as it has always had, the effect of calming her down.

"The other girls are having a different punishment; we are still figuring it out."

Gabby says nothing. What are they supposed to do with Alanna?

• • •

"How dare you!" the built-up stress flies out in a rage when they get home, Elliott standing in the doorway as Gabby screams for Alanna to come down from her room. "What the hell were you thinking? What kind of monster did I raise for you to do that? How dare you? Who do you think you are?"

"Gabby. Stop." Elliott lays a hand on her arm, jolting her out of her fury slightly.

"You're going to apologize," she spits. "I'm disgusted. You're going to apologize to him, and to his parents. How could you? How could any child of mine do this?" Gabby is appalled she is breaking into sobs as she shouts.

Alanna is already crying. "Sophie said I could be part of the Populars if I did it," she blurts out. "If I didn't, she said she'd make everyone in sixth grade hate me. I didn't want to do it. I knew it was mean, but I didn't know what else to do. I didn't want everyone else to hate me." Her voice turns into a wail as she collapses on the stairs. Gabby instantly switches from fury to remorse.

"Oh darling." She gathers Alanna in her arms. "I'm sorry. I didn't mean to say the things I said and I love you so much. I'm just so upset. And I don't understand. I don't know what we're going to do, how we're going to manage school." She looks up then, eyes filled with tears, knowing that Elliott will say something like, "Don't worry, we'll get through it together," or, "We're a family and we love each other, and we'll find a way." But he doesn't. He merely looks at the floor.

Twenty-four

It is early December and most of her Christmas shopping has been done, courtesy of Amazon. Giant boxes are piled in the closet in the barn, waiting to be unpacked and rewrapped in brightly colored paper.

She isn't yet sure what they will do about Christmas. It has always been their favorite holiday. They have never been a family to vacation at Christmas, choosing instead to huddle up indoors, decorating the tree, praying for snow.

Gabby always cooks a turkey, English style, on Christmas eve. She lays bacon on the breast, makes a sage and chestnut stuffing, brussels sprouts, roasted potatoes. They have Christmas pudding and brandy butter her mother sends over from Fortnum & Mason, and when they are all stuffed and sleepy, they build a fire in the family room and decorate the tree.

The lights—miles of white lights, plugged together—are wrapped around the tree, pushed carefully in to the center of the branches, as far as they can go, so the tree appears to glow from the inside. The decorations, collected for years, each of them choosing a new one to add every year, others that have been in their respective families for decades, are carefully unwrapped and placed on the branches.

The girls decorate while Gabby and Elliott sit on the sofa, a giant bowl of popcorn between them, stringing the corn with cranberries on dental floss to make a garland for the tree.

Stockings are hung, and quietly filled in the early hours of the morning when the house is asleep, to be discovered with shrieks of joy on Christmas day, unpacked during a breakfast of blueberry pancakes, scrambled eggs, and extra-crispy bacon.

But this Christmas? It hasn't been discussed. Alanna has not been back to school, and the homeschooling is adding yet another stress to Gabby's life, but in January she will start at the other middle school. Neither Elliott nor Gabby wants this, preferring to send her to a small private school instead, but they cannot afford to do so, and are hopeful this other school, which has less of a reputation than the one from which she has been suspended, might be better.

Either way, Alanna has been encouraged to find friends outside of school: the lovely girl from gymnastics who lives in Fairfield; the daughter of people they know who live in Norwalk: girls who have no connection to the scandal, children not connected to her school.

The scandal, as Gabby thinks of it, has changed her Christmas plans. Initially they thought perhaps they would split it up—Christmas eve with one parent, Christmas day with another—but the very thought of having Christmas without Elliott is heartbreaking, particularly given recent events. They need to be together as one family, if only over a holiday. How could it be Christmas if they are not all together as a family, exchanging gifts over bacon and eggs?

Alanna has been wanting a parka she has seen in a store in town for ages, and Olivia is desperate for the Uggs with sweater-style cuffs and buttons, Uggs that Gabby has point-blank refused to buy, for what seventeen-year-old deserves a pair of two-hundred-dollar boots? Particularly when those boots are likely to be ruined or lost within the month.

That was before the separation. Now she wants the girls to be happy, wants to make up for the pain she is forcing on them. It may be material, and superficial, and oh-so-very-clichéd, but if buying them nice things will make them feel better, make them love her more, forgive her for what she has done, then buy them nice things is what she will do.

Gabby pulls into the parking plaza behind Main Street, frustrated at leaving this until now. From Thanksgiving onward, Main Street turns into an outdoor mall, hundreds of people descending for their holiday shopping, most from out of town, huddling en masse on street corners, waiting for the seasonal traffic cops to wave them across from Tiffany to Pottery Barn.

Each time she thinks she sees a spot, she pulls up, excitement building, to discover a little car in the spot, its shadow hidden by the SUVs sandwiching it.

"Bloody little cars," she mutters. "I *hate* those little cars." Then she lights up, seeing a Land Rover's reversing lights come on.

At eight months pregnant, she is grateful to have found a spot at the right end of Main Street. The two stores she wants are next to each other, and after buying most of the products in Benefit for Olivia, she moves next door for the parka.

As she reaches for it, so too does another hand, and she turns, with an apologetic smile, for she is sure she reached it first, to see Elliott.

"Oh." She drops the parka.

"Ah." He drops the parka. They both stand there, looking at each other, until he clears his throat.

"I was Christmas shopping. For the girls."

"Tell me you haven't just cleared the shelves at Benefit," she says, looking down with relief to see he is carrying bags from Jack Wills and J.Crew.

"I just have Alanna left," he says. "And I know she wanted this parka."

"Could that be because it's all she's been talking about for the past month?"

Elliott laughs.

"We could buy it together," Gabby says carefully. "It could be from both of us. I have small things to give her from me, and a load of junky stuff for her stocking, but there's a craft set I know she's been looking at that you could get her."

"Stockings," Elliott says thoughtfully, nodding his head. "I hadn't thought about stockings. I'm going to have to get stockings for my house. Where do I even get stockings?"

"I don't know," Gabby says, for she has had their stockings for years, each of them finely needlepointed with Christmas scenes, their names embroidered above. She has no idea where they came from, only that they appear to have been there forever. "Do you think it would be weird for Santa to do two stockings each? I think it might be . . . overkill. Which raises the point, how are we going to do Christmas this year?"

Elliott shrugs sadly. "Split up Christmas eve and Christmas day?"

"We could," Gabby grudgingly admits, "but I think the girls would hate it. And honestly? I'd hate it. I know we aren't a family anymore, but don't you think, for something like this, we could come together? Not for us, Elliott, and I know the last thing you probably want to do is spend Christmas with me, but this is a holiday for the girls; this has always been a holiday about the girls, and nothing would make them happier."

"I don't know." Elliott frowns. "I think it might confuse them."

"What do you mean?"

"I don't want to give them false hope; make them think this means we're getting back together."

"Oh no, no," Gabby says quickly, pushing aside the pictures that were already invading her head: the four of them laughing over eggnog and spiced apple cider, Elliott and she meeting eyes in a meaningfully soulful manner as they string popcorn and Elliott realizes what a terrible mistake he made in leaving, as he starts to plot his way back into Gabby's heart. "They wouldn't think that at all, not if we made it quite clear. We both love them, and Christmas is a time for children to be with their parents. We didn't want to force them to make a choice, so we have all come together for the love of the children. . . ." She trails off. "Something like that."

Elliott doesn't say anything for a while. Eventually he nods, with a half-smile. "Okay," he says, as a huge smile spreads on Gabby's face. "Christmas eve. Your place. The parka?" He turns back to the coat. "Shall we do it together then?"

"Absolutely." Gabby is beaming. "I'll wrap it and it will be from us both."

Twenty-five

So how do you feel about all being together at Christmas?" Josephine says, leaning down to look at the handles on the chest Gabby had been restoring before leaning down became too cumbersome.

"Honestly?" Gabby squeezes herself. "Thrilled. Excited. Nervous. I know Elliott. All he ever wanted was a family, and nothing makes him happier than when we're all together. Add in all the Christmas joy, and I think he'll realize how much he misses us. I think he'll see how much happier he is when we're all together and he'll come home."

"And you'll all live happily ever after?"

"Something like that."

"Gabby. I hope you're right, but I'm worried you're getting your hopes up too much. What if it just means he's thinking about the children? What if it doesn't mean anything at all? Then you'll be left feeling horrible at Christmas."

"I don't think I'm wrong," Gabby says. "But even if I am, so what? I have a couple of depressed days before I pull myself together and life carries on exactly as it had before? I'm a big girl. Growing bigger." She gestures unhappily to her stomach. "I can deal with it. It just might be an opportunity. I kind of told myself, mentally, that if he said no, there'd be no hope, but if he said yes, it meant we'd get back together again."

Josephine laughs. "That's about as random as telling yourself if the lights stay green something will happen."

"I do that all the time!" Gabby says. "And they almost always do!"

"So you're convinced you and Elliott are going to get back together?"

"I wouldn't say that, but we have been getting on well recently, better than we have done in ages. It was a little awkward when I ran into him Christmas shopping, but that was only because neither of us expected to see each other. I really think he might be forgiving me, and I can't believe he has stopped loving me. I don't think you can switch off like that. I really don't."

"Do you still love him?"

"Oh my God! Yes!" Gabby looks at her friend in horror. "As if there could be any doubt. What are you doing for Christmas? Is James here?"

Josephine sighs as she sits next to Gabby on the sofa. "I don't know. It's all up in the air again. He went AWOL last weekend and now he says he loves me but he's not ready. The thing is"—she shakes her head—"I know he's going to be on the phone again next week saying how much he misses me and that he can't live without me. I love him, but this is exhausting. I don't know how much longer I can do this."

"I've told you before, many, many times, you shouldn't be doing this. It's time to move on, and you need to be the one to say it because James clearly doesn't have the strength to do it himself."

"I know, I know," sighs Josephine. "I wish you weren't pregnant."

"Me too," says Gabby, as Josephine laughs.

"No, seriously. If you weren't pregnant we could go out and do the singles scene together. I keep hearing that if you're single and our age you need to be out at the Spotted Horse, or the Grey Goose, or Artisan, but I don't have anyone to go with. Michelle from the divorce support group apparently goes there all the time, but I can't go with her or no one will even look at me."

"She is gorgeous," murmurs Gabby.

"Exactly."

"And I am hugely fat and swollen, so everyone would look at you."

"Exactly," Josephine says, in exactly the same tone, as they both laugh. "Are you sure you won't come with me?"

"Not only will I not come with you, I don't think you should be going. Trust me, you're not going to meet the sort of man who's going to take your mind off James in a bar of all places."

"So where am I going to meet him?"

"Where you're least expecting it. You'll probably meet him when you've forgotten all about men and you've decided to swear off relationships completely."

"But that's never going to happen. What about you? If you and Elliott don't get back together, what will you do?"

Gabby grimaces. "God only knows. I can hardly bear to think about it. Thank God he hasn't started divorce proceedings yet, which, naturally, gives me more hope. But if that were to happen? Lord. I'd have to get a job, I suppose. And one that pays enough to cover childcare for the baby." She shudders in horror as she shakes her head. "This was not how my life was supposed to turn out, let me tell you."

"Why don't you sell your furniture?" Josephine gestures around at the unfinished pieces dotted around the barn. "You could turn this into a store and sell from here. Imagine, you'd keep the overhead down, get to do something you love, and make money doing it. These pieces cost you nothing, right? Don't you find most of them in Dumpsters?"

Gabby laughs. "Not most, but it's true, I have found some of my best pieces in Dumpsters or at the dump."

"So? Isn't that the obvious thing to do?"

"Funny. Claire always said the same thing. Exactly that, that I should clean this place up and give it a great name, and open it to friends. I couldn't open it to the public as we're not zoned for commercial use, but I could do open house sales, and invite everyone on the mailing list."

"That's a great idea! And you should take advantage of the fact that everyone's probably talking about you, so if you managed to do it soon a ton of people would show up."

Gabby's face falls. "Do you really think everyone's talking about me?"

"I do. Sorry. It's part schadenfreude, delighting in someone else's misfortune, and part relief that their marriage is okay. I think that's why everyone abandons you when you get divorced. Your crumbling marriage, when they thought you two were so perfect together, reminds them of the fragility of their own marriage, and each time they see you they feel a sliver of fear that this too could so easily happen to them."

"How do you deal with it?"

"Same way as you. By becoming more of a hermit, and by keeping my cards very close to my chest. You wouldn't believe the number of people who have phoned expressing sympathy and concern because they heard Chris and I have split up, who then get angry and resentful because I don't fall apart on their shoulder, or confide my pain to them."

"That's why you decided to make me your new best friend." Gabby grins. "I'm safe because I don't know anyone you know."

"True. And because you fucked up as badly as I did. Not that leaving Chris was a fuckup, but James and all the drama around that. I know how dysfunctional this relationship is, and I'm desperate to get out, but I'm terrified of being on my own."

"Okay, I'll make you a promise. Once the baby comes, once I get my figure back, I'll consider coming to a bar with you. Just once, just to prove that a bar is not where you will find your future love. But I will come, and we will drink martinis, and we will have fun. How's that?"

"Good enough for now. And in return"—Josephine surveys the barn—"I'll help you get this place together."

Gabby's face lights up. "Really? You'd do that for me?"

"Of course. That's what friends are for."

Gabby endures the stores one more time before Christmas. Elliott has long been in love with watches. He has an ancient Patek Philippe that was passed down to him by his grandfather, and a couple of other watches that he loves. He always said to Gabby that if he had the money, he would collect watches. One year she bought him a box in which to house his future collection, mahogany, with automatic turners so the watches never stop.

Gabby had sold a couple of pieces, back before the size of her stomach and general feeling of crappiness stopped her from further restoration, and she had put the money aside. Walking into Mitchells, she goes straight to the display of watches, knowing exactly which one to get. It is still there, in the same spot as when she and Elliott were here, six months ago, when Elliott insisted on trying it on, gazing at it in awe, wanting so badly to buy it.

"In the future," Gabby had whispered, wishing their expenses weren't so great, or they lived in a part of the country where the cost of living was lower than it is here.

She hadn't remembered the price of the watch, only that it was beyond her wildest dreams, and when the salesman takes it out, tells her of the history of the company, how special this particular watch is, she flinches as she turns the price tag over and sees it is so very much more than she had thought.

So very much more than she had brought.

But there are credit cards. And future earnings. Josephine has been as good as her word, and has been at the barn every morning, filling her car with useless junk and driving it to the dump, sweeping out the dust, whitewashing the walls and thereby turning the barn into a space clean and bright, a space in which you'd want to linger. Gabby wanted to call it the Dumpster Dive, but Josephine wouldn't hear of it.

"I know you find stuff in Dumpsters, but you don't want anyone else to know it. How do you expect people to pay eight hundred dollars for something if they know you got it for free?"

"Because I broke my back stripping, restoring, and painting it?" grumbled Gabby.

"Doesn't matter. You have to have a story. Tell them you import faded antique pieces from England, restoring them in your New England barn."

"It's not really New England," Gabby says, impressed. "It's Westport."

"Still counts. From old England to New England," Josephine declares dramatically. "A piece of the old country."

"That's what we should call it! The Old Country!"

"I love it!" Josephine says. "Perfect!"

They haven't opened yet, but they will, and Josephine, who seems to have become an official partner, is convinced they will sell everything. Living in New Canaan, she has access to a whole new crowd of girls, all of whom, she says, will love it.

"I thought no one was talking to you?"

"No. I'm not talking to them. They're all dying to find out what's going on. Trust me, they'll come."

Gabby turns the watch over in her hands, mentally doing the calculations. If she put it on the credit card and sold five more pieces, that would cover it. And if she didn't sell the pieces? She could sell her engagement ring. She hasn't worn it for years anyway, never comfortable with the large solitaire diamond that seemed so essential at the time.

What if none of this worked out? What if she and Elliott got divorced? Did she really want to be spending this kind of money? Yes, she decided. She loves him, has always loved him, and doubtlessly will always love him. This watch is her way of letting him know that, of letting him know how sorry she is, and how despite whatever transgression and mistakes she made, he was loved.

"I'll take it," she says, her heart pounding, unable to believe she is spending quite so much money.

"An excellent choice," he says. "Your husband will love it. He's a lucky man."

Gabby smiles sadly. There is nothing else to say.

Twenty-six

Each year Gabby, Elliott, and the girls get their Christmas tree at Maple Row Farm, where they insist on traipsing through the fields in search of the perfect uncut tree, despite the fact that there are lines of perfect trees, trees that would, indeed, suit them just fine, cut and stacked up on the side of the parking lot.

It never takes less than two hours, the girls darting around calling, "Over here! What about this one?" Elliott tramping over with saw in hand, Gabby yet again cursing the fact that she didn't bring extra gloves, because Olivia always forgets hers and ends up wearing Gabby's, while Gabby tucks her freezing hands under her armpits, convinced she will have frostbite by the end of the day.

They buy apple cider and doughnuts at the stand, and sit on low benches around the roaring fire to warm up, while Alanna darts over to the two giant cows lazily munching hay in a small paddock next to the barn.

They haul the tree up to the roof rack, Gabby on one side of the car, Elliott on the other as they loop orange twine around and around, Elliott saying next year they'll get a smaller tree, as Gabby agrees, although each year the tree gets bigger and bigger.

There will be no Maple Row Farm this year. Not without Elliott. It wouldn't be the same, and Gabby could never manage to cut down and haul up a tree by herself, and certainly not in her condition.

She drives instead to the Audubon Society, where there are precut trees that are perfectly fine, and they tie it to the roof of her car, and she runs next door to her neighbor, whose husband comes out to bring it in to the house.

Gabby has become increasingly reliant on the kindness of neighbors. And strangers. She hadn't realized how much she needed Elliott around, until there was no Elliott.

There was the night she heard a rustling coming from downstairs, and came down to find a frantic and terrified squirrel, that had somehow fallen down the chimney, tearing up the living room. Squirrels, which she had always adored as a child, when crouching down to feed them peanuts in Regent's Park, were, she discovered, infinitely terrifying when trapped inside your home.

A neighbor's husband—different neighbor—came to help, swiftly accompanied by two other husbands as word of the rampaging squirrel spread around the neighborhood.

As a thank-you, Gabby baked mince pies and chocolate florentines, delivering them, beautifully wrapped in cellophane and plaid ribbon, to her neighbors, with wishes for a wonderful holiday season.

The mince pies and florentines, Elliott's favorite, are laid out now, on a white platter, on the dining-room table. The turkey is roasting, and Frank Sinatra has been replaced—at Olivia's insistence—with the Christmas album from *Glee*.

Swags of spruce, garlanded with burlap, drape the fireplace and banister in the front hall, where the theme is white and silver: thick pillar candles wrapped in silver birch glisten on the mantelpiece, wreaths of white feathers hang on either side, silver glittery deer traipse along the hearth.

On into the family room, where all is red, and green, and tartan. Plaid throws adorn the sofas, making them cozy and warm. More spruce is draped along the mantelpiece, this time with red velvet ribbons. A fire is blazing, the stockings hung high, out of reach of the licking flames.

The tiny electric model ice rink has been dug out, with its twinkling lights and miniature skaters who do endless magnetic figure eights. They found this together in Boston one year. The girls were fascinated by the little skaters, and delighted that Elliott and Gabby bought it. Still, today, Alanna will sit and watch the skaters, lulled into a zombielike state by the repetitive motion. Flicking a switch turns on tinny Christmas carols, but none of them flicks the switch, preferring to watch the skaters in silence.

The gifts are piled high under the tree. Large for the girls, and, in the back, where no one can see it, a beautifully wrapped bronze box, with a striped gold ribbon, for Elliott.

Elliott will be here soon. The turkey will be ready soon. But there is just time for a phone call. Gabby ladles some eggnog into a cup and takes the phone into the hallway, where she sits on the stairs and dials home.

"Darling!" her mother answers. "I was just saying to your father, I wondered where you were! Where are you? What are you doing this year for Christmas?"

"The same as always," Gabby says. "I invited Elliott to come and he said yes, so we're all together again. Like a proper family."

"Oh. That sounds . . . cozy."

"Why do you say it like that?" Gabby feels herself bristle.

"I'm sorry. I didn't mean anything. I just don't want you to get your hopes up."

Gabby remembers how Josephine had said the same thing. Her hopes were up, it was true, but why was everyone so worried about it? The worst that could happen was nothing, in which case life would carry on. There really was no greater hurt that could occur, nothing that could happen that would make things worse than they already were. And would she have wanted the excitement and anticipation of the last few days to have been different? No! They have been the single bright spots in her life of late. Even if that is all there is, those moments of joy at prospects that do not occur, it will, surely, have been worth it.

"What's the worst that can happen?" Gabby says lightly. "That my hopes are dashed? So what. Mum, he's my husband. I love him. I never wanted us to be apart, and please don't say I should have thought of that before I was unfaithful, because I already know."

"I wasn't going to say that, darling. I know you love him. We love him, too. Nothing would make me happier than for the two of you to get back together, and I can't bear seeing you in pain."

"You haven't seen me."

"Ah. Yes. I know. But I am planning on coming when the baby's born."

"You'd better, because the only thing I'm certain of is I won't be able to do it all by myself."

"Actually, I beg to differ," her mother says. "I will come, and I will do everything you need me to do, but Gabby, you have always been the most independent and self-sufficient of children. I so wanted you to need me when you were little, but you never did; you were always perfectly happy off on your own."

But that's not true, Gabby wants to say. I did need you. I just couldn't tell you because you never wanted to hear me.

She doesn't say that. It's Christmas. Why rock the boat now?

Twenty-seven

"Elliott? Will you carve the turkey?" Gabby frowns, wishing she didn't have to call him in to the kitchen to help in such a formal way. Wishing it were the old days, when he automatically assumed certain roles, turkey carving being one of them.

"Coming!" he calls from the dining room, where he has been laughing with the girls, who are giddy with delight at their family being back together again. Elliott has been in fine form. He looks wonderful, thinks Gabby, much more . . . handsome . . . than he used to. He has lost weight and looks younger.

He is wearing his old cords tonight, his loafers, but the shirt is new, and it galls Gabby slightly to see him in something she doesn't know, something she has not bought him, for Gabby has always been in charge of Elliott's wardrobe, Elliott professing to hate nothing more than buying clothes.

"That's nice," she said when he walked in and took off his

Barbour, fingering the sleeve of the shirt. "It brings out the blue of your eyes."

"Oh this?" He looked down, as if surprised to see himself wearing that particular shirt on this particular day. "I got it a couple of days ago. Glad you like it."

Gabby smiled, attempting to keep her voice light, wanting to know more. "You hate shopping for clothes. Where did you get it?"

"Somewhere on Main Street," he said nonchalantly, turning away as Gabby wondered why he seemed reluctant to pursue the conversation.

"Here." Gabby pulls open a drawer and withdraws Elliott's apron. "You don't want to stain your new shirt."

"Oh. Thanks." He smiles a smile of genuine gratitude as he ties the apron around himself, the eggnog finally taking the edge off the awkwardness as he falls into routines unchanged for many years.

"Honey? Can you bring me the board with the ridge?" Gabby's heart skips a beat. Honey. He called her honey. This meaningless word seems loaded, has more meaning than anything else Elliott has said in months.

His warmth, how relaxed he is, eases Gabby's anxiety, makes her see a burning light at the end of the tunnel. Were you to peep through the window, were you not to know otherwise, you would look at the family sitting around this table and think them unutterably happy. No, more than that. You would think them unequivocally *right*. They all look right together. The two pretty girls, one brunette, one strawberry blonde, the proud father, and the expectant mother, glowing with happiness and pride.

Gabby looks around the table with gratitude, joy, and overflowing hope. Her family is back together again. When she smiles at Elliott, love in her eyes, he smiles back, as the girls look from one to the other with delight. And hope.

Elliott pours the brandy over the Christmas pudding and sets it alight, he and Gabby cheering as the girls roll their eyes, neither of them liking Christmas pudding, both of them loving the tradition of doing the same thing every year; doing the same thing this year.

The mince pies follow, and the chocolate log Gabby made for the girls; the chocolate log she always makes for the girls.

Then, stuffed, they retire to the family room, where Elliott builds up the fire while Gabby pops popcorn, the girls excitedly unwrapping the decorations, catching each other's eye from time to time as they make secretive gestures at the sofa, where their parents are sitting together, gestures that are filled with certainty and hope.

Gabby is waiting until the girls go up to bed before giving Elliott his gift. After they send Olivia and Alanna upstairs, amidst much grumbling, Elliott stands up, announcing he'd better make a move.

Gabby's heart plummets. "I thought you were staying." She wishes her voice hadn't emerged in a whine.

"I can't," he says. "I need to go home."

"But I bought a bed for the spare room. It's an inflatable bed but it's really comfortable. I made it up. . . ." She stops, not wanting to sound desperate. "The girls want you to stay." She tries a new tack. "They've been talking about waking you up in the morning. It's Christmas, Elliott. Why not stay? Think of all the drunk drivers you'll be avoiding. I promise I won't try and seduce you." This last is an attempt at a joke, which falls flat to both their ears.

"I'm not worried about that," Elliott says gently. "It's just better if I go. I'll be back early and we'll make breakfast. I won't miss anything. I promise."

"Wait." Gabby reaches down toward the back of the tree, fumbles until she finds his gift. "I got you something. I wanted to give it to you when we were alone."

Elliott's face falls. "Oh Gabby. You didn't have to. I don't have anything for you."

"That's okay," she lies. There is nothing material Elliott could give her that she would want, other than the fact he had thought of her at all. Still, she reminds herself. He is a man. They don't think in the way women do.

He stands for a while tapping the box in the palm of his other hand, looking as if he doesn't quite know what to do with it.

"Open it," she encourages, no longer certain this is the right thing to have done, to have spent quite as much money as she did on a watch for her soon-to-be ex-husband.

Reluctantly, slowly, Elliott unwraps the paper. He folds the wrapping paper into a neat parcel, and insists on rolling up the ribbon as Gabby refrains from tapping her fingers with impatience.

He stares at the box, the watch company's lettering on the top, looking bewildered and sad.

"Open it," Gabby says again softly, wishing the ground could open up and swallow her shame, for it is blindingly obvious now, what she was trying to do, even though she couldn't see it at the time. This is her guilt gift. Like the men who have affairs, leaving their mistresses and stopping to buy glittering bracelets for their wives, a wordless apology, an expunction of their guilt.

Elliott says nothing, opening the box, staring at the watch.

"It's the watch you loved," whispers Gabby. "Remember?"

He doesn't gasp with pleasure, or amazement, or joy. He doesn't take the watch out of its box and try it on, as he did all those months ago in the store, gazing at it in awe.

Elliott closes the box and looks at Gabby. "Thank you. It's beautiful. But I'm not going to accept it."

Gabby feels the prick of tears. "What do you mean? It's just a gift. It's a thank-you for . . . I don't know. For being such a good husband. A good father. It's an apology for everything I put you through. I want you to have it. . . ." She's babbling now and trails off, as Elliott gently places the watch on the hall table.

"There's something I have to tell you," he says quietly.

A million things go through her head. Cancer. He has cancer. Oh God, that's why he's got so thin. Or he's being transferred. He's moving to Alaska. Or Canada. Somewhere far, far away. He's—oh God, please no—he's seen a lawyer and he's started divorce proceedings.

Gabby looks up at him with fearful eyes as Elliott swallows.

"I'm seeing someone," he says, not looking at her as he says the words.

"Seeing someone? What do you mean? *Dating?*"

He gives an embarrassed smile. "Yes. I suppose dating. I wanted you to hear it from me rather than from anyone else."

"Anyone else? Why would I hear it from anyone else?" Gabby narrows her eyes as it dawns on her. "Do I know her?"

Elliott nods. "It's Trish."

Gabby sucks in her breath. Trish. Perfect, blond Trish. Trish who is doubtless a millionaire several times over. Trish who has always made Gabby feel inadequate in every way.

Afterward, Gabby thinks back to the moment Elliott uttered the word "Trish" and sees herself physically deflate, like a character in a cartoon. She sees her shoulders slump and her chin cave in onto her chest, her legs giving way as she wobbles to the ground.

Of course that doesn't happen. Not externally. Externally her shoulders slump just a little, her eyes widen to a startled understanding, a disappointment, but nothing gives Elliott any indication of the pain and grief she actually feels.

Gabby doesn't say much after that. Forces a smile to acknowledge his thanks for a lovely evening, and nods when he says he'll be back in the morning. Of course he has to leave. Of course he can't stay the night. He has to go and curl up with Trish. He has to make love to Trish. He has to take her in his arms and kiss the tip of her nose, just as he used to with her, and tell her how much he loves her.

She waits until she can no longer hear his car driving off down the road, then she slowly sinks on to the bottom step of the stairs.

Twenty-eight

Trish is upstairs in bed as Elliott quietly lets himself in her house, still feeling a little awkward about having a key, although Trish had insisted.

He walks through the hallway admiring her Christmas decorations, how perfect everything looks, beautiful enough for a magazine, which in fact, it is, a huge interiors magazine having just been to take photographs for next year's edition.

The house smells of pine, and cinnamon, and winter warmth. Nothing is out of place here—the sofas are white, with turquoise accents, everything bright, and shiny, and new, a huge white porcelain Buddha casting a benevolent smile over the living room, turquoise gourd lamps, the Christmas decorations matching the decor.

Even the books have been covered with white parchment paper, the odd book covered in turquoise alligator. It is the most beautiful house Elliott has ever been in. He just wishes it were a little more comfortable, for the sofas are modern and hard, and he is terrified of spilling a drink, of crumbs being ground into the rug. He teases Trish that he'll move a La-Z-Boy in while she's not looking, and although he is joking, he misses his comfortable chair at home.

The place he used to call home.

Trish is wearing a silk nightgown. He had never met anyone who wore a nightgown before, unless it was cotton, short, and printed with a whimsical design. Trish wears nightgowns every night; always ivory, silky, strappy; this is, to her, what flannel pajamas are to Gabby. He didn't think women like Trish existed anymore, and he certainly didn't think, given the fact of their existence, a woman like Trish would be interested in a man like him.

It was Tim's idea. Elliott didn't know this until afterward. Tim and Claire invited Trish to join them for dinner one night, Trish having broken up with her boyfriend some time before.

"What was the matter with him? He seemed like a great guy," Elliott remembered asking.

"I think he was. But not the guy for her. She needs someone older. More stable. Honestly? I think he was probably just about sex."

"That's a problem?" Elliott had asked. Tim laughed.

The dinner had been perfectly lovely. There certainly hadn't been any flirting, the four of them sitting round the kitchen table, but there had been lots of laughing, and Trish had been very interested in Elliott, genuinely interested in his work, asking him thoughtful questions. He missed being heard, being thought of as interesting, rather than being taken for granted. At the end of the night, as Trish got up to leave, Tim suggested Elliott walk her to her car.

"I really enjoyed getting to know you," she said. "We should do this again."

Elliott just stared at her, having no idea what to say. He had been married forever, had dated a hundred years ago as a very young man, had no idea how to pursue, or whether this meant something, or what he was supposed to do next.

Trish made the move for him. She leaned forward and kissed him, very softly, and not for very long, on the lips. When she stepped back she was smiling. "You should call me," she said, before getting into her car, beaming a smile at him, and reversing out of the driveway.

Elliott walked back in to the house in a state of shock.

"She kissed me!" he muttered to Tim, who high-fived him. "What do I do now?"

"Now you call her. Not now; I mean tomorrow. Ask her for dinner. Damn. Claire was right. I can't believe she kissed you on the first date. It wasn't even a date, and she kissed you! Was it hot?"

"Claire was right about what?"

"She said she thought Trish was interested in you. Apparently she's been asking about you for a while. The only reason Claire hadn't set anything up was because she feels she's betraying Gabby."

"Even though they're not speaking?"

"She misses her, you know? But we made our choice." He gives Elliott a rueful smile, as if the choice wasn't made willingly, as if the friendship had suffered from their having been put in the position of making a choice, even though Elliott had never asked it of them.

There were so many things Elliott hadn't asked for, Trish being one of them.

During the first few dates, Elliott felt as if he were in some surreal version of his life. This was him. Elliott. Married with children. He didn't go to smart restaurants with gorgeous women and charm them with his stories. Hell, he didn't even have any stories. Except, he found he did. He found his stories, and his humor, and his charm. He asked lots of questions, and relaxed under the gaze of a gorgeous, intelligent woman.

The first time they slept together was strange. Fantastic. Overwhelming. Terrifying. He and Gabby had a routine. It was comfortable, and quick, and it suited them both. Here he found himself with new territory to explore. Trish didn't like being touched like that, she wanted it softer, but harder there. . . .

They both moved over and under, excited by the discovery, flipping like slippery fish until they exploded, first Trish, then Elliott, in unexpected delight.

Afterward they hadn't, as he and Gabby had done for so long, rolled onto their respective sides of the bed, picked up their books, or turned on the television and said only a handful of words to each other before one gave the other a quick peck on the lips, switching off the bedside lamp and going to sleep.

He lay, Trish in his arms, talking softly for hours, murmuring, punctuated by the tinkle of her laughter, until she fell asleep, actually in his arms. It was desperately uncomfortable, but he didn't want to move and disturb the perfection of this moment. This exquisite, tiny blonde, in her rustle of silk, sleeping so prettily on his dead arm. Eventually he had to move, and Trish just burrowed under the sheet without waking up, as Elliott gazed at her, unable to believe they had just made love.

Trish is, he thinks, as he walks up the stairs to her room, completely selfless. She makes him feel like the most important man in the world. She creates a beautiful home, cooks like a dream, runs a hugely successful business, is a loving and present mother. She is the woman who has it all, the domestic goddess personified. She is the opposite of Gabby.

Why did Gabby have to buy him the watch? It was so . . . *sad*. So desperate. So heartbreaking. The hope in her eyes and the disappointment when he couldn't take it. There was no question of him taking it. He knew exactly what it was, and he knew too that he couldn't *not* tell her about Trish. Not when Gabby's need for him was so evident.

He never wanted to hurt her. However much she has hurt him—and my God, the pain these last few months has been, at times, unbearable—he would never want to cause her pain. He did, tonight, telling her about Trish; he had no choice.

Things with Trish seem to be serious. Elliott walks in the bedroom, marveling at how beautiful she looks, her legs crossed, not a patch of stubble on them, her nail polish always perfectly, prettily pink, her hair slicked back behind her ears.

"How was it?" she asks, craning up for a kiss.

"It was good. Good for the kids. A little awkward."

She reaches up and caresses his cheek. "You're a good man, Elliott. You did the right thing."

"This is what I love about you," he says, careful not to say he loves her, for he is not there yet, even though he suspects he may be well on the way. "You give me room to do the things I have to do."

"I'm not the jealous type." She smiles.

"I know. And it makes it possible for me to be the man I want to be. To show up for my kids. To be a father to them, and to give them a Christmas they couldn't have otherwise had. Thank you." He lifts her hand, brings it to his lips, and kisses it. "Honestly. Thank you for never being threatened by Gabby or the relationship I have to have with her for the sake of the children."

"I'm not threatened by Gabby." Trish smiles, pulling him in for a kiss. "I'm not threatened by anyone."

Elliott likes being married. He likes being a father. He likes familiarity, and comfort, and knowing where he stands. These past few months, first staying with Claire and Tim, then the loneliness of the little house close to the railroad tracks that never felt like home, have thrown him.

Nothing felt right. Elliott would wake up in the morning feeling out of sorts, wasn't able to regain his equilibrium, no matter what he did. His equilibrium had always come from having a partner; waking up next to a woman you love; raising your children together; phoning each other a couple of times during the day just to check in, or remind the other of a dinner date they may have forgotten about. His equilibrium came from being able to go down to the boatyard on the weekends and chat with the men there about the old boats for sale, knowing his wife was at home, taking care of the kids, getting lunch ready, keeping everything balanced and even.

Until Trish, nothing had felt balanced and even for a while, and Elliott wasn't a man able to deal with his life being off-kilter. If it hadn't been Trish, it might have been someone else.

Yet if it hadn't been Trish, it is entirely possible Elliott would have found himself staying in the spare room tonight.

If it hadn't been for Trish, it is entirely possible Elliott would have lain under the blanket on the new bed in the spare room, listening to his soon-to-be ex-wife getting the kitchen cleaned up.

It is entirely possible he would have fallen asleep, thinking about the years they were married, how happy they were, how she looked when she lay underneath him, gazing into his eyes with love. He would have been woken up in the early hours of the morning by the creaking of the stairs, would have emerged from his bedroom to find Gabby creeping down to fill the stockings while the girls are fast asleep, no danger of them waking up and seeing that there is no Santa Claus, even though they both know there is no Santa Claus.

He would have crept down alongside her, smiling in the darkness, to help with the stockings, and while they were filling them perhaps their hands would meet, in the soft illumination of the Christmas tree, and then they wouldn't be smiling, and he would be kissing her, melting in the familiarity of her lips, the smell of her, the feel of her hair.

If it hadn't been for Trish, perhaps he would have gone home. But then he remembers the bump; the baby. Then he remembers the betrayal that ruined his life, that will never go away, that will be a daily reminder of how his wife screwed him, screwed someone other than him, and his heart closes down, and he is thankful, so thankful, that Trish came along when she did.

Gabby is weighed down with dread in the morning. Elliott and Trish. Trish and Elliott. She slept terribly, waking up all night with visions of her husband and Trish playing in her mind. She hadn't prepared for this, hadn't imagined, for a second, that Elliott would even be thinking about dating anyone else.

Don't they say that men take far longer to get over things because they can't process them emotionally in the way women can? Why isn't Elliott taking longer to get over her? How is it possible that he has moved on so quickly? Jesus. It's hardly been any time at all.

With Trish of all people. She groans out loud. "I hate her," she says, suddenly.

"Who do you hate?" Alanna stands in the doorway, arms filled with goodies from her stocking.

"What? No one," she says quickly. "I was just thinking of the lyrics to a song."

"I hate her?" Alanna gives her a strange look. "Are you sure?"

"Yes," Gabby snaps, heaving herself out of bed and stumbling to the bathroom.

"Wow, Mom," Alanna says. "You're huge."

"Thanks, Alanna," Gabby snaps. "Way to make your mom feel good at Christmas."

"Sorry." Alanna follows her into the doorway. "It's just . . . you look like you're about to give birth."

"I hope not," Gabby sighs. "Actually I wish. But it's still a little early. I have to tell you, I feel ready. I cannot wait to hold this little baby in my arms." She looks up at her daughter. "I can't believe I'm going to have a little one again. Oh Alanna. You were both so gorgeous when you were tiny."

"Don't cry, Mom. You should be happy."

Gabby starts to laugh. "I am! I'm just sentimental. I'm so crazy about babies, and I never thought I'd have another one. These are tears of joy."

"Mom? Can I ask you something? The baby's father. Are you still in touch with him?"

Gabby sighs. This is so hard. She didn't want the girls to know, but in the end she can't protect them. But how does she explain this, when she isn't even sure she's doing the right thing?

"I'm not, and I honestly don't know what I'm going to do. He's young, and not ready for children. I don't want to impose upon his life. I think at some point I might let him know, but I have no expectations, and I think it's better this way."

Alanna thinks for a while. "But don't you think the baby deserves to know who his father is?"

Yes, thinks Gabby. But she always hoped Elliott would step up to fill the role, still hopes Elliott will step up to fill the role. "I think," she says, "we'll cross that bridge when we come to it."

Alanna says nothing, leaving the room to take her stash of goodies back downstairs.

Today, Elliott's presence is getting on Gabby's nerves. Gone are the fantasies of all of them playing a happy family, the fake perfection and coziness of last night long gone. Gabby watches him, frying up bacon, pretending that everything's fine, feeling a surge of anger. His happiness has nothing to do with her, and everything to do with that bitch Trish.

How she blames Trish. It doesn't matter that it could have been anyone, that Elliott is free to date given that they are officially separated; it doesn't matter that Gabby was unfaithful to him, is pregnant with another man's child; all that matters is that Trish is the woman who stole her husband, and Gabby will never be able to say her name without gnashing her teeth in rage.

I bet Claire set this up, she thinks, in a flash of fury. For years she called herself my best friend, then couldn't wait to set my husband up with Trish, the one woman guaranteed to make me nuts. Claire, who emailed her a while back, out of the blue, who now sends her emails on a fairly regular basis, as if nothing is wrong between them, as if they are still great friends.

Claire, who filled those emails with funny stories about her child, the horrors of being the oldest mother in the mommy and me group, the bags under her eyes large enough to carry groceries in, thanks to the endless sleepless nights.

Initially flabbergasted to receive a chatty, warm, information-filled email from her former best friend, speaking to Gabby as if she hadn't dropped her like a dirty shirt at a time when Gabby needed her most, after a while she couldn't help but enjoy Claire's emails.

Gabby wanted to write back telling her how disgusted she was, but as she read through that first email, she realized how much she missed Claire's voice, her point of view, her guidance and wisdom.

She grew to look forward to the emails, even though she didn't respond. She wasn't ready to forgive Claire for not being there for her, but at the same time she couldn't help but laugh at the things Claire wrote; couldn't help but miss having a friend like her.

However much she missed her, she wasn't able to forget Claire's betrayal by choosing Elliott, when Gabby didn't see a choice had to be made.

And Elliott? He is trying, oh how he is trying, to make things right, to re-create last night, but their easy camaraderie is gone, Gabby looking grim as she takes the strawberries out of the fridge and pours hot chocolate for the girls.

She closes her eyes for a second as she stands by the fridge, so tired, so desperately wanting her life to be something, anything, other than the life she has.

"Mom? Are you okay?" Olivia is watching her.

"I'm fine. I'm just really tired suddenly."

"Why don't you go upstairs and lie down?" Elliott is concerned. "The girls will bring you up breakfast in bed."

What do you care, she wants to say, but she doesn't. She nods and goes upstairs, relieved as soon as she lies on her bed, cradled in the heap of pillows. Elliott telling her about his girlfriend—the word is snarled nastily in her head—has thrown her. She hasn't felt right since then. Sick and tired. Ha! She is, indeed, sick and tired. And terrified, now, of what this means.

All this time, she has harbored the hope they will get back together. More than hoped. Known. She had presumed Elliott would come home, because this is where he belongs. This is where he has always belonged. She has been able to stay away, to give him space, only because she has always known that at some point he is going to take her face in his hands and gently kiss her, telling her how sorry he is, asking her to give things another chance.

But she was wrong. Which means she is on her own. Which means that life will never be the same again. And despite what Sally at the divorce support group says, despite her assurances that there would be love, and possibility, and joy again, Gabby knows that's not true.

Not without Elliott.

After breakfast, brought up by the girls, Gabby falls asleep. When she awakes, the house is quiet. She crawls out of the covers and takes the tray downstairs, finding Elliott asleep on the sofa in the family room, Olivia and Alanna on either side of him, both of them avidly watching some movie as a fire dies down in the fireplace.

Gabby stands watching them for a while. Alanna notices her and waves, Olivia doing the same, neither of them talking.

"What are you watching?" she asks, finally.

"*Love, Actually*," mumbles Alanna. "Then we're opening presents. Ssshh."

"Do you want any popcorn?" Gabby asks, as she feels a warm whoosh run down her legs. "Oh God," she says, reaching out a hand to steady herself, trying to make sense of what just happened. Could she have had an accident? Has her bladder been rendered so weak by pregnancy that she could just stand and wet herself?

"What's the matter?" Both girls look scared. "What is it?"

Gabby reaches down to swipe her legs and inspects the liquid. It's clear. Has no color, no scent.

"I think," she moans, "my water just broke."

. . .

Elliott keeps turning to her. "Are you okay? Are you sure you're okay?"

Gabby clutches the handle of the door, furiously breathing in and out, nodding with wide, scared eyes.

"Mom?" Olivia, excited and terrified, leans over the backseat. "I saw some counting in a movie. Do you want me to count?"

"I don't know," Gabby puffs, exhaling as the contraction passes, leaning her head back on the headrest with a groan. "Oh God. I should have gone to Lamaze classes."

"I remember Lamaze classes," Elliott says. "We did them before."

"Yes, but that was for Olivia. That was almost eighteen years ago. I don't remember anything."

"You're doing great." Alanna reaches a hand forward and rubs her mother's arm, before turning to Olivia. "I can't believe we get to watch!"

"No!" Gabby turns her head in horror. "You're not watching!"

"Aw, Mom!" Alanna grumbles. "It's natural. Childbirth. What could be more beautiful?"

"Ew," says Olivia with a grimace. "I do not want to watch. No thank you. Call me in when it's all over."

"I'll call you both in when it's all over," says Gabby. "Oh God. Here comes another one. Elliott? Can you drive faster? Fuck!" And she's breathing hard again, trying to ease the pain, looking not unlike a terrified blowfish.

Elliott says nothing. He doesn't want to be here. He can't believe he *is* here, his bad luck in Gabby's water breaking when he happened to be in the house. And yet, there is a part of him grateful to be here, for what the hell would Gabby have done were she on her own with the girls?

All he has to do is get her safely to the hospital, deliver her into the arms of a waiting doctor. Perhaps he'll go with her to the room, make sure the girls are okay, leave just before they put the epidural in.

That would be the perfect time to leave. The one thing he's certain of is he doesn't want to be anywhere near the place when the baby arrives.

Twenty-nine

"Come on, nearly there, you can do it. Keep pushing, Gabby, one last time."

Gabby leans her head back in exhaustion, summoning all her strength to push the baby out, certain that if it doesn't come out with this push, it's not coming out at all.

With a long grunt, Gabby pushes hard, feeling the release as the slick of life leaves her body, slithering into the waiting hands.

"Congratulations!" The doctor smiles. "You have a beautiful baby boy."

The baby is placed gently in Gabby's arms as tears of wonder roll down her face.

"A boy!" she whispers, her face lit with a beatific smile. "He's perfect!" The tiniest of features, scrunched up, he is still the most beautiful baby she has ever seen, more beautiful perhaps because he was so unexpected. Whatever misgivings she may have had, whatever regrets, she knows she wouldn't change this moment for anything.

The surge of love is instant and all-consuming. She would do anything for this baby; this baby will make everything okay; this baby is the only thing that matters in the world.

A nurse catches Elliott's eye. "Congratulations, Dr. Cartwright." She smiles. "Or should I say, *Dad*." Elliott smiles awkwardly, nodding in acknowledgment. How can he tell her, tell anyone here, that he is not the father; that he is overwhelmed by the miracle of birth, by the fact of this new life, squalling in Gabby's arms, but that it has nothing to do with him?

He wasn't able to leave. He tried, many times, but each time a nurse, or a doctor, would come in and address him as "Dad," or give him instructions—not to let Gabby have too many ice chips—or simply speak to him as if he were supposed to be there, and he didn't know how to just walk away.

The truth was he didn't feel angry at Gabby anymore. Not since his relationship with Trish. He felt, mostly, sad. Sad for her, for her predicament, for what she had done to her life. He, after all, was in a relationship, and could, at times, see it becoming serious. This had little to do with Trish, and everything to do with Elliott liking being married, needing the security, the routine, the comfort of having someone to come home to.

Here at the hospital, with Gabby, he feels at once connected and curiously detached. She is the mother of his children, the woman he knows better than anyone in the world, but there is a barrier between them now that can never be removed.

In the hospital, being treated like the father of this baby, Elliott feels like an imposter. Few of his colleagues, and certainly not the staff of different departments, know he is separated from his wife. Why would they think he was not the father?

As for who the baby looks like? The baby looks like . . . a baby. Elliott has never been able to see familial likenesses in newborns.

When both Olivia and Alanna were born, everyone said they looked exactly like Elliott, but he could never see it. Now, when he looks at Olivia, he only sees Gabby. Alanna looks like her grandmother. Clearly Gabby's genes are stronger than his.

The baby is a week early, but six pounds, and healthy. Back in the room he is placed in a crib next to Gabby's bed, the girls, who were waiting in the room, crowing over their new brother.

"Look how tiny his fingers are!" Olivia whispers, grinning as she places her finger against his, as he wraps his minuscule fingers around hers, squeezing tight. "Oh Mom! He loves me!"

"Look at his teeny nose!" Alanna, not to be outdone by her sister, reaches down to brush his other hand, for him to wrap her fingers, too. "He's perfect!" she whispers in awe. "Can we hold him?"

Elliott is about to say they can hold him later, but it is not his place to say that. This has nothing to do with him. It is time for him to leave.

"Congratulations." He walks to the side of the bed, leaning down to kiss Gabby's cheek. She tears her eyes away from the baby to look up at him.

"What am I supposed to do with a boy?" she says. "I have no idea what boys are like."

Elliott smiles. "You'll have to fill the house with Tonka trucks and Legos. It will be a disaster area."

"Oh God," she groans. "I hadn't thought of that. No more pink tutus and fairy castles." They share a smile of remembrance.

"I have to go," he says gently.

"Thank you for staying. For being with me. It means the world to me."

"You're welcome," Elliott says automatically. "Have you thought of a name for him?"

"Henry. Henry William Cartwright."

Elliott starts. Hearing the baby with his last name is strange.

He hadn't thought about what the baby would be called, but realizes now he had subconsciously assumed the baby would have his father's last name. Not Elliott's.

"Isn't his last name something else?"

Gabby shakes her head. "It's the same as mine."

Elliott can't find the words for an argument. He suspects he is being petty, or would be accused of being ungracious were he to voice his discomfort. It is true, Cartwright is Gabby's last name, but not by birth. He isn't sure she has the right to convey it to another, but doesn't know how to voice that, doesn't know if he wants to be the kind of man who is so ungracious, so ungenerous.

He kisses his daughters, smiles at the baby—fair! Long and thin! So unlike the dark chubby girls when they were born—and takes the elevator downstairs. His cell phone starts buzzing as soon as he switches it on. Texts and texts, missed calls from Trish. He should call her, but he doesn't know how to explain that he was present at the birth of his soon-to-be ex-wife's baby.

As understanding as Trish has been, as encouraging as she has been for him to be present in his daughters' lives, as willing as she is to accept that with the daughters comes his ex, this is not something he can easily explain.

Nor that Gabby is still his soon-to-be ex-wife; that he hasn't yet summoned the courage to speak to a divorce lawyer. Trish emailed him last week an article she had "stumbled upon" online recommending the ten best divorce lawyers in Connecticut.

He had thanked her, and when pushed, agreed to start making calls, but he hadn't. The thought of a trial, of the expense, of having to paint Gabby as the wicked witch—he knew the lawyers would encourage him to think of her that way, knew it behooved them to stir up the acrimony and bad feeling—filled him with dread.

He knew he couldn't put it off forever, but hadn't been able to stomach the stress of making it official.

He doesn't call Trish. Instead, he scrolls through his emails and finds the one Trish has sent, reading it carefully as he sits in his car, in his reserved spot, in the parking lot of the hospital. He picks the one referred to as the Divorce Lawyer's Lawyer: the lawyer the others choose to steer them safely through their own divorces. He likes that they refer to him as clean, quick, thorough. They say he is "no-nonsense," gets the job done "painlessly."

He waits until the next day to phone, when the office is open again after Christmas. On the phone with the receptionist he is asked for his children's names and dates of birth, then left on hold while the receptionist checks a computer. She comes back saying they are fine to set up an appointment, and he realizes only afterward that she had gone to check if Gabby had already been to see them.

The appointment is made, and he puts down the phone feeling none of the relief Trish had said he would feel once he had taken the first step toward the second part of his life.

How *does* he feel? Guilty.

Thirty

The girls have been in a buzz of excitement for days. First, the baby has come home, and it is like having their very own breathing, crying living doll. They fight over who gets to change him, who gets to hold him, who gets to dress him.

Gabby knows this won't last, that they will be bored of doing everything for their brother once this becomes routine, and has wondered whether, while it lasts, she might be able to let them take over the night duty so she can catch up on sleep, but as tempting as it is in theory, she would never let the girls have that much responsibility.

Her mother is flying in. This afternoon. Gabby has arranged a car service to pick her up from JFK, and the girls keep appearing in the kitchen, asking if Grasha will be here soon.

This may not be a good idea, but it's too late to do anything about it now. Gabby has always got into trouble when she has expected more from her parents than they have been able to give.

Each time it happens, she berates herself for behaving like a child, but still the disappointment comes.

Even now, knowing what she knows, she harbors a hope her mother will actually be of help with the baby. It's not that she has to do much, but it would be wonderful if her mother helped drive Alanna to her practices, or took the baby for a couple of hours during the day so that Gabby could shower or nap.

She has been exhausted these past two weeks since the baby was born. A tiredness unlike any she experienced with the girls. A tiredness doubtless born of age, and lack of a partner.

I had no idea, she thinks. But this wasn't something she wanted. Or planned. A baby on her own, at her age. Yet, clutching the tiny Henry to her breast as he suckles on her nipple, she loves him. Despite the circumstances in which he came to be, she feels a fierce, binding, all-encompassing love quite unlike the love she remembers feeling for her daughters. The girls were always shared between her and Elliott, but this little boy is hers alone, and there is something different about having a son. She had always dismissed the old wives' tale that every father needs a daughter, every mother a son, but the love she feels for him is so all-consuming, she wonders if it might be right.

Gabby places Henry down in the bassinet at the end of her bed and tiptoes out of the room. He is fed, full, happy. Perhaps, if she is lucky, she will get a couple of hours to herself before he wakes up, shrieking in fury that he is on his own.

She dumps a pile of baby clothes and burp cloths in the washing machine before heading downstairs to make some tea, just as a town car pulls into the driveway.

Gabby watches out the window as the driver opens the rear door, and there is her mother, draped in asymmetrical oatmeal fabrics, her neck swathed in cashmere, her feet clad in beige suede slippers that, Gabby is certain, cost a small fortune. She is dressed as haute hippie by way of North West London. Her hair, now a dark shade of auburn, is clasped back in a clip. She looks chic. Comfortable. She has always seemed to Gabby to be beautiful, but now, aging, she has an elegance that eluded her when she was young. The lines on her face only add to her grace, and Gabby smiles as she watches her mother extend her arms to give the driver a warm hug, knowing she will have extracted his life story during the drive from the airport.

In the driveway, Grasha's face lights up when she sees Gabby, her arms extending yet again before she holds her out at arm's length, inspecting her delightedly from head to toe.

"You don't look like you just had a baby. You look fabulous! How did you get your figure back so quickly?"

"Oh Mum," Gabby tuts. "I'm still a stone overweight. But separating from your husband while you're pregnant does wonders for keeping the weight gain down. I highly recommend it." She reaches down for her mother's suitcase as she shoots her an ironic grin. "The girls are at school and the baby's asleep. I just put the kettle on. Do you want some tea?"

"I'll do it," her mother says, taking the suitcase out of Gabby's hands and going inside. "You go upstairs and have a rest. I'm here to take the strain off you, not have you running after me making me cups of tea. I'll make the tea. Milk, one sweetener, yes?"

A wave of relief washes over Gabby. "Perfect," she says, as she goes upstairs.

A boy!" her mother keeps whispering, looking from the bassinet to Gabby, who is lying in bed with—oh the bliss!—a stack of trashy magazines by her side. "Look how different he is! How lean! And my goodness, so long! Is his father tall?"

Gabby had deliberately pushed aside all thoughts of Matt leading up to the birth. She used to shudder with disdain when she pictured him, how he had caused her life to fall apart, but now he has unknowingly redeemed himself by giving her this beautiful child; now she finds herself softening, looking at Henry's face and seeing Matt's features.

Wondering if she ought to let him know.

"His father is tall," Gabby says, hesitating for a second before reaching for her MacBook. "Do you want to see a picture?"

"I would." Her mother nods. "Because he certainly doesn't look anything like our side of the family."

Gabby goes to Google and types in his name, finding a picture of him at a tech conference. She turns the screen around as her mother fishes inside her drapey cardigan for her reading glasses, peering at the screen.

"My God, he's a hunk!" She sounds astonished, before picking up the screen and holding it closer. "And a child. Good Lord, darling. How old is he?"

"Older than he looks," Gabby says. "Thirty-four."

"Well that's a relief. I was worried someone might call the police on you. He's so handsome, isn't he? No wonder you weren't able to resist."

"It wasn't really like that," Gabby says. "We became friends. It was all on email, and I was still harboring resentment at Elliott, I suppose, about the vasectomy. Here was this, as you see, gorgeous young man who seemed to find me irresistible. It was less about him, and more about how he made me feel."

Her mother gives a small laugh. "It so often is," she says. "Especially at your age."

Gabby frowns. "Why my age?"

"Because you are entering the afternoon of life, and all is different. There is a wonderful quote by Jung. Let me see if I can remember it correctly." Her mother takes her glasses off as she thinks, before speaking slowly.

" 'Thoroughly unprepared, we take the step into the afternoon of life. Worse still, we take this step with the false presupposition that our truths and ideals will serve us as hitherto. But we cannot live the afternoon of life according to the program of life's morning, for what was great in the morning will be little at evening, and what in the morning was true, at evening will have become a lie'." She stops with a smile. "Marriage is hard, my darling. You and Elliott always had a charmed life, but even those with charmed lives hit bumps in the road from time to time."

"What about you and Dad? You never seemed to hit bumps in the road. You've been happy forever. You managed to enter into the afternoon of your life pretty unscathed."

Her mother smiles. "That's how it appeared, yes."

"What does that mean?"

A smile. "It means that when I was forty-six I fell in love."

"With someone other than Dad, you mean?" Gabby is part fascinated, part horrified, not at all sure she wants to hear the story; she also knows she cannot live without hearing it.

Natasha laughs. "Oh yes. Someone other than Dad."

"So? What happened? You had an affair."

"I had . . ." She trails off, thinking. "An awakening. An earthquake. A seismic shift in who I thought I was."

"Mum? I have no idea what you're talking about."

Her mother raises her eyes and looks at her with a sad smile. "Remember Joanie?"

Gabby does remember Joanie. One of the waifs and strays her mother collected, Joanie had recently divorced her husband, and was, Gabby remembers, something of an emotional wreck. She became part of their family for a while; longer than the others. She moved in with them, her mother's new project, her mother's new best friend.

She recovered quickly. Those first few weeks of sobbing at the kitchen table gave way to peals of laughter. She made Gabby's mother laugh more than Gabby had ever heard. Gabby would come home from school and find them cooking together, both of them giggling at something unspoken. Joanie made her mother seem younger, happier, softer.

One morning she was gone. There was no goodbye, no warning, just a stripped bed and an empty wardrobe. Natasha refused to answer any questions Gabby had, stonewalling her and asking her not to mention her name. It was clear to Gabby there had been a betrayal, but she knew not to ask.

Gabby frowns. Of course she remembers Joanie. What did that have to do with anything?

"I fell in love with Joanie," her mother says simply, as Gabby's eyes open in shock.

"You had an affair with *Joanie*?" But that's not what she's thinking. My mother is a *lesbian*? How is this possible? How is it possible that I do not know my mother at all?

"I did. Oh don't look so shocked. I didn't plan to have an affair with anyone, and I certainly never thought I'd fall in love with a woman of all things, but there it is. Joanie was utterly compelling. I wasn't just in love with her, I was obsessed."

"Mum, I'm not sure I want to know all this."

"Oh darling, I'm not going to give you any gory details. The point is, I fell in love with her, at an age not dissimilar to yours now, and part of it, so much of it, was me desperately trying to run away from the dreadful specter of middle age. Joanie was much younger than me, and she made me laugh more than anyone had in years. And she made me feel young. Alive."

This time Gabby nods silently. She knows what her mother's talking about.

"I was happily married, but this was something I couldn't resist. I told myself it didn't count, her being a woman, but of course it did."

"Did Dad know?"

"He knew I was infatuated with her, but he didn't think, of course he didn't think it was anything more than a strong friendship. He didn't know until afterward, when I was so floored by grief I couldn't get out of bed. Even then, I'm not sure he knew for certain."

"And he never confronted you, or said he was leaving?"

"The thing is, I love your father. I have always loved your father. Of all the gifts he has given me, this was the greatest. I think he understood that I needed to have one final fling before settling into the afternoon of life. To be honest, I think the fact that it was a woman probably made things easier. I'm not sure he would have been so quietly circumspect had Joanie been Johnny."

"I'm sorry, Mum. I still can't quite get over my mother revealing her secret lesbian tendencies. I'm a bit freaked out right now."

"Get over it," Natasha says matter-of-factly. "And stop thinking about the sex stuff. I fell in love with a person who happened to be a woman, end of story."

"So, do you regret it?"

"I regretted causing pain to your father. When it ended and he was so sweet and solicitous to me, as I lay there sobbing in my pillows for weeks, I felt awful. You know your father. He went very quiet. Well, he's always quiet, but for those weeks he barely said anything at all, and I regretted that. But I think he understood. We never spoke of her again."

"Do you know what happened to her?"

"She left me for a young man she'd met at the bookstore. I know they split up after a couple of years and I lost track of her after that. I get cards from her, from time to time, on my birthday. She never says anything other than wishing me a happy birthday, and I tend to put them in the bin. It was . . . a moment of madness. I'm lucky your father is the sort of man he is."

"The sort of man Elliott is not."

"I think Elliott might have handled things in much the same way had this little bundle of joy not come along. It's very difficult for men to handle betrayal when they are forced to look at the evidence every day. It is, for them, a daily reminder that they somehow fell short, they weren't able to make their wives happy, or happy enough."

"Do you really think that's true?"

"I do. But how about the father of delicious Henry? What does he have to say about all of this?"

Gabby turns her computer around so she can see the screen, Matt in his golden loveliness, smiling into her bedroom. "He doesn't know."

Natasha is shocked. "But you must tell him."

"Mum. Please. I've made a decision. This is my baby, and I don't want him to feel obligated to be involved, or feel pressured, or think I'm coming after him for money, or anything else. I made a decision, recently, that he would never know. I thought I wanted him to be involved, but no."

"But what if he *wants* to be involved? What if he wants a child?"

"Even worse!" sputters Gabby. "The last thing I could handle is a custody battle right now. And he has money. Enough to pay for the best lawyers in the world. It would be a disaster. Anyway, I haven't spoken to him in . . . nine months. It was one night. Nothing. I need to move on."

"Then what will you tell Henry about his father?"

"I'll cross that bridge when I come to it."

"I can't tell you what to do, but I urge you to reconsider. Henry has a right to know his father, and his father has a right, certainly, to know about Henry. The biggest mistake any of us can make is to keep secrets. They always come out in the end, and it is the unspoken that causes the most problems. I truly believe that what is called for here is absolute clarity. You need to give his father the opportunity to step up. If he doesn't, you will always know you have done the right thing."

Gabby just stares at her mother. Everything she has told herself, every argument she has used to convince herself she is doing the right thing now falls flat. Her mother is right.

She has to get in touch with Matt.

Gabby!

I can't believe I heard from you! It's been, what, a year? Feels like forever since you and I were in touch. I always meant to get in touch after I came to visit, but everything got really awkward and I could tell you were uncomfortable, and I thought it best to just keep my distance and give you some space. I figured you'd get in touch when you were ready, and this morning there you were! Bringing a huge smile to my face. But you told me nothing—I don't know anything about your life these past few months and I'm dying to hear your news. Did you finish the barn? Are you now a furniture-restoring and selling mogul? Are you happy?

Life here is as crazy busy as ever. Remarkably, I'm in a relationship! Yes, you heard me right. A real relationship.

Monroe is her name—I know, so LA :)—and she's truly a great girl. She's a model, but completely unlike so many of the airhead models I've come across out here. She has a degree in physics, and is very precise, and organized, and competent. I suppose I would describe her as a woman of substance. She reminds me of you in a lot of ways. She's warm, and fun, and wickedly clever. She's also the most secure woman I've ever met, other than you. She inhabits her skin comfortably and easily. I hope the two of you can meet—I know you'd get along.

So what's the cryptic message about wanting to talk to me? We could chat on Skype, but I'm coming to New York next week and it would be easy to come out to Connecticut for lunch. Are you around next week? Does that work? Tuesday?

Am sending you a big hug, and I want to hear all your news. I'm so happy you got back in touch!

Matt xoxoxoxox

Gabby reads the email over and over, a large smile on her face. She has felt nothing but anger and resentment toward Matt for months, all of which dissipated as soon as she read this email.

Her own, to him, was stilted and short. She never expected such warmth, and, dare she say it, even love, in his email. But there is undoubtedly affection in every line, and the prospect of seeing him, of telling him about Henry, is suddenly far less frightening.

She sends him back an email, managing to fill it with fluff—books she has read that she loves, her happiness at him having found someone, her life being busier than ever.

She resists the temptation to even drop a hint during the email.

Such life-changing information needs to be delivered in person, even during these digital times, and she phones Le Farm to book a quiet table so she can break the news.

The jeans are nowhere near ready to be done up, so it is the ubiquitous yoga pants for her today, teamed with a flowing sweater and scarf, cute white sneakers.

I look like my mother, she thinks with a smile, as she checks her reflection before going downstairs.

"You look like me!" her mother exclaims, as Gabby walks in the kitchen to find Henry in a bouncing chair on the table, Grasha having warmed up a prepumped bottle of breast milk that was left in the fridge.

"Mum!" Gabby warns. "It's not time. He's not supposed to eat for another twenty minutes."

"But he was hungry!" complains her mother, who still does not understand Gabby's need to follow a routine, particularly since Gabby was fed on demand and slept in the family bed long before the concept of the family bed even had a name.

"Okay, okay." Gabby can't be bothered to argue. She has little tolerance for the screaming of a hungry newborn baby either. When Olivia and Alanna used to scream, Elliott would take them in his arms and walk them endlessly up and down the stairs until they stopped screaming. With no Elliott, it is far easier to just give the bottle to Henry when he wants it.

Perhaps her mother is right after all.

"You look beautiful," her mother says. "In all seriousness. You really ought to wear makeup more often."

"Thank you." Gabby leans down to give her a kiss, before planting a kiss on Henry. "Wish me luck."

Natasha raises her free hand to show her fingers are crossed, before blowing Gabby a kiss as she heads out the door.

She wasn't nervous in the slightest before she pulled into the parking space outside the restaurant, but as soon as she parks she starts to feel slightly sick. How is she supposed to tell him? And when? Does she make small talk throughout lunch and drop the news like a bombshell over coffee? Would she even be able to do that? To pretend everything was fine, knowing she was about to change his life forever?

Or does she blurt it out in the beginning, risking him storming out of the restaurant, leaving her alone and embarrassed to pay the bill? What if there's someone she knows in there? What if there are women who overhear, who then spread rumors, or pass her pitying looks as she stumbles out in a fog of humiliation?

She pushes open the door, passes the heavy curtain, and scans the tiny restaurant to see Matt already there, in the corner, his face lighting up as he sees her. There is something so familiar about him, so reassuring about seeing him, and yet all the attraction she once felt has disappeared. It is like seeing a long-lost brother, not a man with whom she was once obsessed.

"Gabby!" He holds out his arms, giving her a huge hug, and she allows herself to be held, relieved not to have seen disappointment in his eyes. She no longer wants him, not in that way, but for him to be so instantly comfortable, so warm, so clearly pleased to see her, gives her confidence, sets her at ease.

"You look beautiful," he says, and it is clear he means it. "This has obviously been a good year for you."

"It has been . . . a tumultuous year," she says, seeing the opportunity, wishing it hadn't presented itself quite so early on in the lunch. "You look handsome. And happy. I love your hair longer. It suits you."

He blushes. "You won't believe this but I think I've finally met the girl to . . . tame me. I've actually fallen in love, and she, Monroe, likes my hair longer." He is bashful telling Gabby this. "This is all her doing, I'm afraid." He runs his fingers through his hair with a self-conscious grin.

"You're in love!" Gabby teases. "Oh Matt. I'm so happy for you. You deserve it." She is astonished to find she means these words, that there is not a hint of jealousy in her being, only pleasure that he has found happiness. "What's she like?"

"Funny. Smart as a whip. No-nonsense. She's a little like you—she can make anything, and she's far better with a screwdriver than I am."

"And beautiful, I'm sure."

"She does some modeling." He shrugs as if to apologize. "But enough about me. You said you've had a tumultuous year. What does that mean?"

"Oh God. It's a very long story. One that needs a drink." She smiles. "Will you join me?"

"Martinis at lunchtime? How decadent!" He grins. "I'd forgotten what a good drinking partner you were."

"No martinis for me at the moment. But a weak white wine spritzer would be lovely."

They order drinks and chat about the restaurant, the menu, the deliciousness of the dishes that pass them, until there is a pause.

"You still haven't told me about the tumultuous year."

Gabby nods slowly. "That's because I'm not sure where to start." She takes a deep breath. "I separated from my husband."

Matt's eyes fill with sympathy as he reaches across the table for her hand. "Oh Gabby. I'm so sorry."

"Thank you. It's been devastating. Oh God." She starts to laugh, raising her eyes to the ceiling, unable to believe how like a bad movie this is feeling. "I just don't know how to say this, so I'll come out with it. I had a baby."

"Are you serious?" Matt's smile contains astonishment and confusion. "My God. That was quick! You look amazing."

"Matt. My husband had a vasectomy. The baby isn't his."

Matt just stares at her, uncomprehending, until the expression on his face conveys that he understands what she means; what she is saying by saying nothing at all.

Thirty-one

Grateful he didn't ask whether she was sure, Gabby steers the car up the Post Road, checking in her rearview mirror that Matt, in his rental car, is still behind her. She thought about offering him a ride, but didn't know what they would talk about, needed some time alone to think about what just happened, instead quietly offering to lead him back to her house to meet Henry.

Of all the scenarios, she hadn't imagined him to be so . . . calm. He was, he said, "blown away," but not unhappily so. "A son," he kept repeating. "A *son*!"

Instinctively, Gabby knew he wouldn't fight her for custody, try and steal Henry. He was boyishly bewildered, incredulous that he had managed to create another life. She also knew that her mother was absolutely right in advising her to do this, and she had a feeling that Matt would play a part in Henry's life, that it wouldn't be a bad thing.

She had been so terrified of having anything to do with him, with this man she had turned into a powerful demonic figure, capable of breaking up a marriage, she hadn't thought she would be able to give anything up.

Seeing Matt in her rearview mirror, concentrating on following her, she has a sudden vision of Henry as a small boy, holding Matt's hand, splashing in the water and learning to surf.

She is there, watching, as the matriarch. Perhaps his girlfriend will be there, too, in the water with them, but she will not be threatened by Gabby. Gabby has no designs on Matt. Seeing him today, without the rose-colored glasses of obsession and intoxication she once wore whenever he was around, she is able to enjoy his youthful enthusiasm, his boyish charm.

Quite how they will figure this out, with her on the East Coast, him on the West, remains to be seen, but Gabby is curiously content with his reaction, with the knowledge that he wants to be involved.

You're back so soon!" Her mother's voice comes from the kitchen. "Henry's upstairs sleeping. How was it? How did he—"

"Mum! We're here. He, Matt, is here." Gabby shoots Matt an apologetic grin as she leads him through to the kitchen.

"Oh!" Natasha stands up. "Gosh. You are tall. I'm Gabby's mother. Natasha de Roth. How do you do?" She extends a hand as Matt smiles awkwardly.

"It's nice to meet you, Mrs. de Roth. Are you staying here for long?"

"Call me Natasha," she says. "And you don't have to make small talk with me. Questions like that always make me think of the Queen. Do you know, at her garden parties she's always reported to ask people, "Have you traveled far?" over and over again. Can you imagine? I'd rather kill myself. I'd much rather ask someone what's their favorite car, or what their movie star name would be."

"1956 Porsche Speedster. George Lazenby."

"You can't have George Lazenby." Natasha is twinkling with delight. "It's taken."

"I know. But you have to admit it's the perfect name. Most people my age have no idea there ever was a George Lazenby, so I could easily steal it."

"True. And a 1956 Porsche Speedster. Sounds glamorous. And expensive."

Matt grins. "It is. Both."

"Okay you two," Gabby says. "We're going to go upstairs. How long has Henry been asleep?"

"Almost two hours. Go on up."

Matt leaves the room as her mother grabs her arm and pulls her back to whisper furiously in her ear. "He's adorable!"

Gabby just smiles and shakes her head, detaching herself as she and Matt go upstairs.

I'm so scared I'll drop him." Matt has a look of terror on his face when Gabby offers him Henry.

"You'll be fine." She shows him how to support the baby's head, sitting down next to him on the bed as they both gaze at their son.

"Wow," whispers Matt. "I think he looks like me. Don't you think he has my eyes?" Henry is staring up at his father. "I think he knows me. Hi little dude. Do you know who I am? I'm your daddy." His whispers are filled with awe, bringing back memories of when Olivia was born.

Each of her children's births was awesome, but none quite so magical or overwhelming as the first; the first time she held Olivia she couldn't tear her eyes from her, wanting to drink her in, unable to believe this mysterious, magnificent creature had grown inside her body, had been created by her.

Matt feels it, too. The awe at the life he has created, and when he finally turns his head to look at Gabby, there are tears in his eyes, and a lump in her throat.

"He's amazing," he whispers. "I can't believe it."

"I know," she says, as the front door bangs open, and with shock she hears the girls come in from school, their footsteps stomping up the stairs as they scramble up to see their brother.

Olivia is first, pulling up short, the smile wiped off her face as she stares at this strange man holding her baby brother, Alanna coming up next, still smiling, but curious as to who this man is, in her mother's bedroom, cradling Henry.

"Hi?" Olivia's greeting is a question, as Gabby thinks of her mother saying absolute clarity was called for. What was she supposed to do here? Lie?

"Hi girls," she says warily. "I'd like you to meet someone. This is Matt." She takes a deep breath. "This is Henry's father."

"Wow. Hi!" Alanna comes in, bending down to inspect her brother, completely unfazed by this information, but Olivia stays in the doorway, her eyes narrowed as she glares at Matt.

"Olivia?" Gabby prompts. "Please come in and say hello properly."

But Olivia says nothing. She whirls around and stalks down the hallway, and the next thing to be heard is the slamming of her bedroom door.

Gabby is mortified. "I'm so sorry." She turns to Matt. "I don't know why she was so rude."

"Yes you do," Matt says, for he got the remainder of the story about her marriage breaking up due to the pregnancy as lunch progressed. "It's understandable. She blames me."

"I'll go talk to her. Are you okay being here with the baby?"

His face lights up. "You don't mind leaving me with him?"

"Can you handle it?"

"If you can." He looks nervous. "What do I do if he cries?"

"I'm two rooms away. If he cries, cuddle him. He loves being rocked and going up and down stairs." She lays a hand on his arm just as she leaves. "Relax," she says. "You're going to be great."

There is not a peep from Henry as Gabby walks down the hallway to Olivia's room, knocking tentatively on the door. She waits, but there is no response.

"Olivia? Let me come in."

She turns the handle and opens the door, seeing Olivia sitting at her desk, pretending to be immersed in work, but her back and shoulders are tense, and she won't turn around and look at her mother, won't respond.

"I talked to your grandmother last week about what to do, whether or not to tell Henry's father he has a son, because I wasn't going to. She pointed out, and I agree, that the father has a right to know Henry; that Henry has a right to know his father. He flew in from California today and I told him at lunch, and I honestly didn't know what his reaction would be, but he wants to be involved."

"Involved how?" Olivia spits, finally. "Involved with you?"

"No. Not with me. There is nothing between us anymore." Gabby doesn't know if it is her imagination but she is certain she sees a slight relaxation of Olivia's shoulders. "Involved with Henry."

"But he's in your bedroom. And he's the man responsible for

Dad leaving. If it wasn't for him, you and Dad would still be together. We'd still be a real family."

"Oh Olivia. We are still a real family. If you're going to blame anyone at all for what happened, blame me. I know you do, *have* blamed me, but don't blame Matt. He had no idea of the circumstances of my life, and he's a nice man."

"I just . . ." Olivia's voice chokes. "I just wish things were how they used to be. I wish you and Dad were still together. I wish he wasn't with that horrible Trish. I wish everything was like the old days." She dissolves in tears as Gabby rushes to comfort her.

"I know," she croons. "I wish that, too, but we have to accept things are different now. This is our life now. We can't keep looking into the past and wishing for something that no longer exists. We have to move forward. You have to find a way to accept Henry's father because like it or not, he's a part of this family."

"He's not a part of *my* family."

There is little point in saying anything else, in trying to persuade Olivia otherwise when she is in a mood like this. Gabby kisses her daughter on the top of her head and leaves her, knowing that she needs some time on her own, that she will reemerge in an hour or so, pretending to still be grumpy, but will in fact be fine.

She closes Olivia's bedroom door softly, standing and thinking about what Olivia said in there, her description of "that horrible Trish." Thank God, she thinks, feeling ever so slightly guilty. But thank God it isn't just me.

In her bedroom Matt is now standing, walking around, gently rocking Henry and singing him nursery rhymes, while Alanna lies on her bed, heels up in the air, laughing each time Matt gets the words wrong, which he is clearly doing deliberately to make Alanna laugh.

Gabby smiles and goes downstairs to her mother, who smiles

broadly at her as she finishes topping a cottage pie with grated cheese.

"Well!" She turns, folding her arms and beaming. "What a wonderful man. Boy. I'm not sure which, but he's wonderful. What does he think of his son?"

"I think he thinks he's pretty amazing." Gabby tears up, sitting at the table and running her fingers through her hair. "God. I feel emotionally exhausted. All the pent-up dread and anticipation, but it couldn't feel more right. I think Matt's fallen in love."

"Who wouldn't fall in love with that delicious little baby, who is, by the way, the best baby ever. Hardly a peep out of him. Makes me wish I'd had more."

"Except they would undoubtedly have been screamers like me," Gabby reminds her.

"True." Natasha pops the cottage pie into the oven and sets the timer. "Now. Is there any laundry to be done? I'll go upstairs and check, shall I?"

"No. Mum, it's fine. Sit." Gabby gestures to the chair, not wanting to overtire her mother, who is turning out to have surpassed all expectations, however deeply hidden, Gabby had had. Natasha hasn't stopped looking after all of them, making Gabby wonder if in fact part of the problem was that Gabby was an only child. Natasha needs a crowd, needs to be needed by a large number of people, not one independent, self-sufficient child.

Perhaps she could see Gabby never needed her, which is why she pulled in all the waifs and strays in the first place. Now she is needed. By Gabby. By the girls. By Henry, and now, perhaps, by Matt.

Natasha is in her element, cooking, doing laundry, and Gabby wants to tell her how grateful she is, but doesn't know how to say the words. Instead she reaches out and squeezes her mother's hand, as her mother squeezes back, for she knows what Gabby would say if she were able to say the words.

They both turn as Matt comes into the room, Henry starting to fuss in his arms. Matt holds him out, panicked, as Gabby takes her son, who instantly calms down when his mother holds him.

"Do you want to stay for supper?" Natasha asks with a bright smile. "It's cottage pie."

"What's cottage pie?"

"Shepherd's pie," explains Gabby. "In England shepherd's pie is made with lamb, and cottage pie with beef, but here I know everyone just calls it shepherd's pie."

Matt looks at Natasha as he shakes his head slowly. "I have no idea how you knew this, but that happens to be my favorite."

"There are those who have called me something of a witch." Natasha twinkles.

"No, I think it was a 'b,'" Gabby says. "Bitch. They said you were a bitch." She and her mother crack up as Matt watches.

"Well? Are you staying?" Natasha directs her attention back to Matt.

"Let me talk to Gabby," he says, for which she is entirely grateful. It is so like her mother to invite all and sundry to stay, and she cannot blame her for inviting Matt, whom she has clearly taken an immediate shine to.

There is Olivia to think of, and Alanna, although Alanna seems fine. And there is Gabby, who is delighted, but unprepared for Matt to suddenly be a part of this family. She thinks it is probably the right thing to do, but needs to take it slowly.

"Do you want to go for a walk?" Matt says. Gabby hesitates, but her mother takes the baby and waves her off. She grabs her coat and gloves, slips her feet into snow boots, and they set off down the road.

"I feel completely overwhelmed," Matt confesses, as they reach the corner. "I have no idea what to feel about this. I'm thrilled, and awed. And scared. I don't know if I'm ready to be a father."

Gabby says nothing, gives him room to try and sort his thoughts out, imagining how hard this must be for him, dealing with such unexpected news.

"When you told me, at lunch, I was freaking out inside, but then I thought, okay, so I made you pregnant, but it didn't mean my life would have to change. I hadn't thought about kids, other than to assume I'd have them at some point, but I figured that was all down the road. I guess I came back to meet him because it felt like something I had to do, but I didn't expect to feel . . ." He shakes his head. "I didn't expect to *love* him. *Instantly*. To feel this . . . this, bond. Like I would do anything for him, would throw myself off a bridge for him. I know, it sounds dramatic, but I just have never felt anything like this, and I've spent, what? half an hour with him? Nothing!"

"He's your son," Gabby says simply. "You're *supposed* to feel that way. That's what parenthood is. It's utterly selfless. You put your own thoughts and feelings and desires aside, without even being aware of doing it, and you put your children first."

"So what do we do now? How do we do this? I have to be a part of his life, but I don't want to get in the way of yours, or do anything that would make you uncomfortable."

"Thank you." Gabby stops, and turns to him, tears in her eyes. "Thank you for saying that."

"Gabby, I didn't expect this. But now that he's here, I couldn't hope for a better mother for my son. I know you're an amazing mother, and I know how much you do for your kids. I don't want to do anything other than be there for Henry when he needs me. Listen, your mom is awesome, and I love that she invited me for dinner, but I don't know that I should stay. I was thinking that maybe, if I go back to the hotel tonight, I could change my flights and stick around for a few days. I could spend time with Henry, and you and I could maybe figure out some kind of schedule. Maybe I can fly over here a couple of times a month to see him."

"That sounds perfect," Gabby says. And it does.

Thirty-two

"Are you nearly ready?" Trish calls out from the bathroom, where she is finishing her makeup, as Elliott sifts through the handful of clothes he now keeps in her closet.

This is all moving very fast. A little too fast, he thinks, pulling out another new shirt Trish insisted on buying him. He looks at himself in the mirror, not quite recognizing the man who stares back at him.

It wasn't that Trish was trying to change him, she teased him gently, she was just trying to gently propel him from old New England WASP of the eighteenth century to modern man.

She had bought him Italian suede driving loafers to replace his old loafers and deck shoes; fine cashmere shirts; Ermenegildo Zegna jeans, which, he had to admit, did fit him beautifully.

"See how elegant you are now?" she'd said, in the dressing room of the store where she insisted he come out to show her every new outfit.

"But I can't let you buy this for me," he'd said, fishing in his wallet for his credit card, terrified of the thousands of dollars this little spree was going to cost, but feeling like he'd traveled too far down the road to get out of it now.

"You absolutely can!" Trish insisted, before leaning forward and whispering her annual turnover the year before. Elliott put his wallet back in his pocket as she instructed the sales assistant to put it on the house account.

Tonight they are having dinner with friends of Trish's she has wanted him to meet. Jennifer and Colin. He is a hedge fund something, and she is an aspiring photographer and fellow yoga addict—she and Trish do yoga together several times a week.

Elliott rarely went out for dinner when he was with Gabby. When they did, it was a treat, but they were far more likely to cook dinner themselves, have people over, or go to friends' houses.

He had no idea, prior to dating Trish, that there was a whole other world that existed in his town; a world where couples got together to "couple date." They would dress up in their finest clothes and go to the newest restaurants, striding through with an air of authority, if only because they were the most beautiful people in the room, the people everyone else in there watched with envy.

He has had, now, a number of these evenings with Trish, as she brings him deeper into her world. They have eaten at all the trendiest restaurants in the area, stretching three towns over. She has worn a selection of ever-changing chiffon tops, chunky long necklaces, high platform heels that make her almost as tall as he.

She looks gorgeous. Exquisite. Together, with his new, fashionable wardrobe, they look gorgeous. Exquisite.

Yet it all feels like so much effort for so little return.

Tonight, as he walks into the bathroom, seeing Trish in yet another diaphanous top, large diamond hoops in her ears, skin-tight pants, and high silver pumps—ridiculous given the snow outside—he is hit with a sense of dread.

He doesn't want to sip a cocktail in a trendy restaurant and think of things to say to a man with whom he has nothing in common, while the women chatter animatedly between themselves. He doesn't want to pretend to be interested in sports—which he couldn't care less about—or ask questions about derivatives, and acquisitions, and futures, none of which he understands, nor wants to understand.

He doesn't want to have yet another conversation about house values, or the new mansions going up, or how much value for money there is in town now, and how, if they had spare cash, they should really be buying up the teardowns and building for under two hundred a square foot.

Trish is wonderful, but her lifestyle is tiring. Elliott is longing for a home-cooked meal. Trish is a beautiful cook, but it is all about show; she only cooks if she entertains, or seduces. The rest of the time she expects to go out, or perhaps, at a push, get takeout sushi.

And the house is so damned quiet. The children, Skylar and Greyson, are usually down in their basement kingdom, playing Xbox or watching TV. He hears them laughing, and shouting when they are with their friends, but around him they are the most well-mannered children Elliott has ever encountered. He misses the squabbling and fighting of his girls. He misses even their screaming and chasing each other through the house, flinging accusations of having stolen clothes, or hairbrushes, or makeup.

Trish has said he must make himself at home, but how is he supposed to make himself at home when it doesn't *feel* like home? Where are the piles of papers and magazines next to the computer in the kitchen? Where are the shoes and boots, kicked off and left strewn about the mudroom floor? Where is the clutter, the art, the knickknacks that you have collected over the years, that tell the story of your life?

The objects in Trish's house have all been bought since she renovated a year ago, and chosen to match the rest of the decor. What little clutter there might be is swept away by the housekeeper, artfully arranged in paneled closets you would never know existed.

Elliott looks at the soap dish, thinking of the soap dish in his old bathroom, at Gabby's house. The soap was green, and there was always mushed-up green slush in the soap dish. The soap dish would never stay clean longer than one use. Once you picked up the soap, it was all over. Here, the soap is white, and however much you use it, there is never residue left in the bowl. He walks over to the sink and picks up the soap, looking at the dry, shiny dish.

"What are you doing?" Trish finishes pushing bangles onto her wrist before swiveling with a smile, watching him finger the dish.

He shakes his head. "Nothing."

"How do I look?" she says, knowing she looks beautiful.

"Perfect." He sees her face fall. "Beautiful. Stunning."

She smiles, as she approaches him for a kiss. "You look very handsome, too," she says, admiring the shirt she bought him to turn him into the man she needs him to be in order to go out with him.

The evening is exactly as Elliott expects. Every head turns to inspect them as they walk in, and of course they should, for Trish is now, certainly among their age group, the most famous woman in town. Regularly profiled in magazine articles, written about in the papers, she is the woman everyone wants to be seen with.

And she wants Elliott. Which should make him the happiest man in the world. What must it say about Elliott that this beautiful, accomplished woman, this woman who could, let's face it, have pretty much any man she could want, has chosen Elliott? How lucky he must be. He can see it in the faces of the people as they walk through the restaurants, the cocktail receptions.

They scan Trish first, checking out her clothes, her jewelry—she is famous for her sense of style—before their eyes alight on Elliott. Ah. This must be her partner. What kind of a man is it that Trish would choose?

Sometimes he wishes he could pull Trish away from all this. Away from this house, this world, these places where she feels pressure to see and be seen, to dress, and act, and look the part.

A cottage in the country would be perfect. Perhaps they could live somewhere remote by the ocean. A place where neither of them had to dress, where they could wear shorts and flip-flops all summer, wrap up in fleece and down when the weather gets cold.

They could cook together over a big range in the kitchen, their children—in the fantasy all the children would be there together, both hers and his—would run through the house squabbling, as he and Trish laughed about how wonderful it was to have this chaotic blended family.

"How about we go to the country?" he says to Trish on the way home after he has lied and said how much he liked her friends. "A friend of mine has a place in Vermont that he barely uses, and he loves friends going to stay. I thought maybe you and I could go up there one weekend. Maybe take the kids."

"What kind of a place?" Trish asks.

"It's wonderful." He remembers the couple of times he and Gabby had taken the kids. "It's a big sprawling farmhouse. Not fancy, very basic, but comfortable. There are big squishy sofas and huge fireplaces, plus board games going back centuries. It's on a large pond with a swimming deck, and it's just the most peaceful place on earth. It's really a place where you get back to your roots."

"I'm not sure I'd ever get my kids in a swimming pond," Trish laughs. "Particularly not at this time of year! I'm afraid they're chlorine addicts at any time of year. I took them to a hotel in Greece that had a saltwater pool and they were horrified."

"I can understand them not liking saltwater in a pool, but this is a beautiful clear-water pond. They'd love it."

"With green slimy things underneath them?" She looks at him doubtfully. "I'm not so sure."

Elliott remembers going one summer when Olivia and Alanna were much younger, and they'd spent hours throwing themselves off the swimming deck, shrieking with laughter.

The four of them took the kayaks onto the lake, saying they were going on a bear hunt, whipping the girls into a frenzy of excitement and fear. Everything was quiet, then the air was filled with a deafening snap of branches as the girls shrieked with terror. It was probably, almost certainly, a deer, but to this day whenever they talk about that day, it was the day they got away from the bear.

They had been to the farm a few times in winter. Gabby was not a skier—her skiing experience was limited to school trips to Austria and Switzerland, where she spent all her time mooning over the ski instructors, too busy lost in the fantasy to really bother to improve her skiing beyond a green run.

At the farm Elliott would take the girls to the local ski mountain, while Gabby stayed home and made huge pots of soup, stews, warming casseroles. One night she produced fondue, proudly drawing out the fondue pot she had discovered nestled in the back of the dusty pantry, and they sat by the fire skewering chunks of baguette and swirling them round the melted garlicky Gruyère and Emmental.

The house was dusty and basic, lived-in and loved. It was a house that held nothing but happy memories for Elliott, a house in which he wanted to create new memories with Trish. A house in which, surely, Trish would be able to let down her guard and be her true, natural self.

"When you say the word 'basic,'" Trish says slowly, "what does that mean?"

He describes the house in more detail, trying to impart the magic of the property, the surrounding woods, the beauty.

"I don't know." She shakes her head with a smile. "If we're going to do Vermont, I'm thinking Twin Farms."

"Twin Farms?"

"Oh it's *fabulous*!" she says. "*That's* what we'll do! I'll book Twin Farms for the weekend. It's the most fantastic, quiet, beautiful, luxurious place in the world. You'll go nuts! What a great idea!" She draws out her iPhone to punch in a note to herself to have her assistant book Twin Farms, as Elliott stares stonily ahead.

That is not what he had in mind at all.

He can't shake the feeling of things not being right. It isn't that this relationship isn't working—he is determined to make this work with Trish—but is aware that he is being shoehorned into a life, a lifestyle, into which he doesn't quite fit, and isn't sure what to do about it. The deeper into their relationship he goes, the stronger the feeling he has of trying to be something he is not.

Elliott has never been a man who is uncomfortable in his skin. He has always known exactly who he is, where he is going, and what he wants. Yet here he is, nearing fifty, for the first time in his life feeling uncomfortable in his skin. It is a new feeling, and not one he enjoys.

Pulling into the driveway at Trish's, he doesn't make a move to get out of the car.

"Are you coming?" Her door already open, Trish is ready to get out, pausing only when she sees Elliott is not moving.

"You know," he says. "I realize I have a very early start tomorrow, and I need some equipment I've left at home. I think I'm going to go home now so I won't have to stop off in the morning." He looks at her. "Is that okay?"

"Of course." She smiles brightly, and he thinks again how much he loves this aspect of her; that she is never jealous, or insecure; that she never thinks his desire to go home means he doesn't want to be with her.

Even when that is the case.

He doesn't go home, though. He drives around town for a while, then down to the beach. He parks his car and sits on the low stone wall by the beach and looks out toward Long Island, where the lights from the lighthouse glitter on the black water. He wishes he smoked. Now would be a perfect time for a cigarette, but he has never indulged in that particular habit.

Back in the car, he drives aimlessly, until he finds himself drawing up outside the house that was once his. He smiles at the only light left on, in Alanna's room; she is too old to be scared of the dark, and allows her light to be turned off by her parents when they say goodnight, but always climbs out of bed when she knows they are safely in their bedroom to turn her light back on.

The privet in front is overgrown and straggly. Even without leaves; you can tell it needs shaping. He is tempted to creep into the garage for the clippers and prune it right now, as a surprise, for it has always been his job, and Gabby has enough to do with the new baby.

He doesn't. He sits in his car, staring at his house, thinking of his old life, trying not to think about his new one, until there is nothing else to do but drive back to his new life.

Thirty-three

Josephine and Gabby's mother have become new best friends. Since Natasha has been here, Josephine has started coming over every day, dropping in to see how Gabby is doing, bringing something for the baby, carrying an extra pumpkin pie she made, but Gabby is convinced she's only coming to sit at the kitchen table and chat to her mother.

As a child, Gabby found her mother incomprehensible. As an adult, on Gabby's home turf, Gabby finds her magical. With no one to distract her, nothing to disturb her, no stream of people walking through the front door—and Josephine could never qualify as a stream—Natasha is warm, loving, engaged. Gabby is terrified of what she will do when her mother leaves.

Already it has been three weeks, and her mum is talking of leaving at the end of next, filling Gabby with dread. Being on her own and pregnant was one thing, but being on her own with a newborn baby is quite another entirely.

She comes downstairs knowing Josephine is here, having heard her car pull up earlier, and walks in the kitchen to find Josephine and Natasha sipping big mugs of tea, Natasha in peals of laughter over a story Josephine is telling her.

"Why do I always feel like the gooseberry around you two?" Gabby walks in and pulls a mug down from the cupboard, dropping in a tea bag as she puts the kettle back on.

" 'Gooseberry'?" Josephine looks at her.

"Odd man out."

"That's because your mother and I have fallen in love." Josephine grins as Gabby looks at her in alarm. She is joking.

If only you knew, thinks Gabby.

"Josephine has an excellent idea. She wants you and her to go on a girls' night out tonight. Olivia and Alanna are with their father this weekend, so you have no excuse not to go. I think it's exactly what you need."

"It's not what I need," Gabby says. "It's what Josephine needs. She's been desperately trying to get me to go to some ghastly singles bar with her, and now you're press-ganging me into going, too. I know I said I'd go, but not yet. I'm not ready to go out in public yet."

"I think going out will do you good. You go nowhere," her mother says.

" 'Nowhere,' " echoes Josephine, with a grin. "You're turning into a dusty old maid. Let's go out and have fun! You look great, Gabby. Come on, let's flirt!"

Gabby peers at her. "Have you seen the men in those bars? Are you seriously suggesting we put our energies into flirting with those creepy professional singles?"

"Yes!" Josephine laughs. "Maybe tonight will be our lucky night and the two most gorgeous single men in Fairfield County will decide to be there. You're coming, whether you like it or not." She sits up then, looks out the window. "Speaking of gorgeous men, a car just pulled up and someone extremely interesting is getting out. He's coming here!" She turns to Gabby. "Please don't tell me that's your ex-husband or I may have to slap you."

Gabby cranes up to see Matt walking up the path.

"Not ex-husband," she explains. "Father of my child."

"What? And he's *here*? I thought he wasn't going to have anything to do with Henry."

The bell rings.

"It's a long story." Gabby gets up to open the door. "Saved by the bell."

Josephine does not, thankfully, flirt with Matt, but she cannot take her eyes off him. When he goes upstairs to get Henry from his nap, she leans forward and says with a hiss, "How did I not know how adorable he is?"

Gabby laughs. "Don't look so surprised. I'm not that awful."

"No! That's not what I mean, but I'm wondering why I'm dragging you out to hit the singles scene when you have the perfect man right here in your house. Why aren't you up there with him? Why aren't you seducing him right now?"

"Because you and my mother are sitting around the kitchen table making my devious plan impossible?" jokes Gabby.

Josephine's face falls. "Oh God. I'm sorry. I'll go." She stands up before Gabby, laughing, tells her how ridiculous she is being.

"I'm not interested in Matt."

Josephine frowns. "But he's the father of your baby."

"Yes. And I was interested, obviously. But . . ." She thinks. "It's as if there was an internal light switch inside me, which was on for a while, and then suddenly it switched off, and nothing will get it to go back on."

Josephine is skeptical. "Nothing?"

"Truly. Nothing. He's adorable, and brilliant, and handsome, and funny, but he's a child, and beyond that, he's just not for me. I don't want to be anyone's mother unless I've given birth to them. We had a . . . dalliance. It was utterly all-consuming, and it changed my life. I can't say any longer I wish it had never happened because I have Henry, and he is amazing, but it turned my life upside down in ways I didn't want."

"You know," her mother says thoughtfully, "it may not have been what you wanted, but, as you pointed out, you have Henry, and you wouldn't change that. I always think that we are exactly where we need to be. There is a greater plan for you, and Henry is part of that plan. Perhaps Matt needed to come into your life. Perhaps, as painful as it has been, you and Elliott needed to be apart."

Gabby says nothing. Her mother's words sound so wise, except when they refer to her.

"Meanwhile, I'm perfectly happy to babysit Henry. I imagine Matt will stay here too to keep me company. You two go out and have fun."

Gabby rolls her eyes, the last thing she wants to be doing tonight being to hit a bar, but she checks her watch. "I give in." She turns to Josephine. "I have to drop the girls at their dad's at five. Shall I pick you up at seven?"

"Perfect," trills Josephine. "I'm going to run down to Main Street and get something to wear."

I like him," Alanna announces, from the backseat of the car, as Olivia rolls her eyes and glares out the window. Gabby doesn't ask to whom she's referring.

"Good," says Gabby. "He's a nice man. What's not to like?"

"How about, he's young enough to be your son, and he's forcing himself into our family when he's not wanted," mutters Olivia.

"*I* want him," says Alanna.

"Henry wants him," says Gabby.

"What about you?" spits Olivia. "You definitely want him."

Gabby sighs. "Only as Henry's father. I don't want him for me. Listen, Olivia. I know this is hard, to have another man around who isn't your father, but I promise you, if there were anything going on between us, or if I thought there might ever be anything going on between us, I'd tell you. I'm not going to keep any secrets from my family ever again. Whatever happened between us happened, and I can't change that, but nothing's ever going to happen between us again." She laughs. "Quite apart from the fact that there's no chemistry whatsoever, Matt has a girlfriend."

"I bet she's pretty," Alanna pipes up. "I mean, I know Matt's old, but he's very cute."

"I'm sure she is. She's a model. And she has the coolest name. Monroe."

Olivia turns her head slowly toward her mother. "He's going out with *Monroe*?"

Gabby stares at her daughter. "Yes. Why? Do you know her?"

"Monroe the model?"

"Is there more than one?"

"No! There's only one Monroe. She's gorgeous. She's going out with him? Our brother's father?"

"Apparently so." Gabby keeps her eyes on the road as Olivia whips out her iPhone and starts Googling.

"Oh. My. God. Mom! You didn't tell us who he is!"

"Who is he? Who is he?" Alanna bounces up and down in the backseat, stretching through the middle to try and see Olivia's phone.

"He's, like, a *gazillionaire*. He invented Fourforsight and sold it for *bajillions*. And he dates Monroe! And he's part of our family! Oh my *God*. I have to tell *everyone*." She starts furiously texting.

"Not so bad anymore, is it?" mutters Gabby, who can't resist a small smile.

Usually the girls climb out of the car and Gabby drives off without seeing Elliott, or, heaven forbid, the dreaded Trish, although according to the girls Trish rarely comes to their dad's house—"It's far too small and pokey for her," Olivia said—and if they do see her on their weekends with their dad, it's either going to her house where they tumble into their amazing basement to play Ping-Pong or air hockey or watch movies on the giant TV, or going out to an event.

This time, Gabby has to retrieve clothes. The clothes in the girls' closets are dwindling, and she has no idea what has happened to them. They aren't in the laundry, and unless the girls have lent them to friends—which they swear they haven't—they must be at their father's house.

Before Trish, she would have just called him, but things have been strained since he embarked upon a relationship with a woman Gabby has never liked, the dislike now having turned into full-on hatred. Gabby wishes she could let it go, but every time she imagines him with Trish, she starts gnashing her teeth together in fury.

For a few days, she was obsessed with Googling her. She found out everything about her, unable to tear her eyes away from Trish beaming her perfect white smile at the camera. There was even one picture of Trish and Elliott together, taken at a charity gala two weeks ago, that popped up on a local website. Elliott looked dapper and sophisticated in a way he never had when he was married to Gabby.

Trish, who had been, for Gabby, a figure of envy and secret derision, is now a full-blown monster. Gabby has found herself barely able to communicate with Elliott, barely able to look him in the eye, since this began.

They pull up outside the house, and Gabby gets out of the car, forcing a smile on her face, as if everything is fine, as if she isn't consumed by hatred of her soon-to-be ex-husband's girlfriend, consumed by the overwhelming fear that she is not good enough, that Trish knows she's not good enough, that now Elliott knows it, too.

The girls push open the front door. "Dad? We're here!" Gabby is somewhat gratified to hear them say "we're here," rather than "we're home," but remains on the doorstep, waiting to be invited in by Elliott. "Dad?" They walk through the silent house. "Dad?" Olivia turns to Gabby. "I don't think he's here."

Gabby is relieved. "Can you just run upstairs and get the clothes you think are from my house and bring them down?"

"Mom!" Olivia pouts. "I don't know which is which. I keep telling you. You come up and take the stuff that's yours."

Gabby frowns. She has never been inside this house, but peering through the doorway, she has to admit she is curious. There is the old sofa from the family room, but she has never seen those pillows before. They're stunning. Why didn't she think of putting pillows like that on the sofa? It completely transforms it.

She steps in gingerly, her eyes scanning the rooms as she walks through. I remember that rug, she thinks. Looked better in our house. And that painting! She looks up at the huge oil cityscape that she had never liked but Elliott had fallen in love with and insisted on buying, despite it costing a small fortune. Thank God that bloody painting's finally out of my house, she thinks. I hate it even more here.

She doesn't touch anything for that would be too much of a

trespass, but tiptoes up the stairs, peeking in to Elliott's bedroom. The bedspread and sheets are new. Crisp white, with a matelassé cover and matching shams. Two small armchairs by the fireplace, chocolate brown velour. Gorgeous. She can't help but walk in, notice the medical journals on Elliott's nightstand, his spare reading glasses. Her eyes flick over to the other side of the bed, *her* side of the bed, and she takes a sharp intake of breath.

On the left nightstand are two glossy magazines, an eye mask, and a novel with a pink cover. The girls are wrong. Trish does sleep here after all. Gabby suddenly wants to get out as quickly as possible, her nosy exploration bringing her nothing but pain.

Thirty-four

Her mother told her she looked beautiful. Matt told her she looked beautiful. Why is she feeling so . . . wrong?

Gabby is well aware of the uniform of the newly single middle-aged woman. She is well aware she should have, like Josephine, found the time to run down to Main Street and buy the requisite diaphanous top, or brightly colored little dress, the chunky jewelry, the platform heels, but she is too depressed by the memory of the nightstand on the left that won't leave her mind, and anyway, it's not like anyone would be the slightest bit interested in a woman who has a month-old baby and a postpregnancy paunch that doesn't seem to want to go away. Not that, Gabby has to admit, she's the slightest bit interested in anyone anyway. The last thing she wants to be doing is flirting and having fun. She'd much rather be curled up in her bathrobe, watching Apple TV, eating popcorn.

The outfit she is wearing was chosen deliberately for its lack of sex appeal. No hint of cleavage, no flash of thigh. Nothing that would make anyone think she might possibly be interested in picking up a man. She is—thank you, God—finally able to get into her "fat" jeans. She may have a substantial roll over the top, and it is entirely possible that she will not be breathing by the end of the evening, but she got them on and got them done up, and frankly that is all that matters. The substantial roll is covered by a thin grey sweater that is simple and, to her mind, elegant. She is wearing the chunky necklace she bought, once upon a time, to impress Matt, and the high-heeled boots she also bought, once upon a time, to impress Matt, but both choices are largely to prove to Josephine that she is not the dowdy housewife she appears, and can scrub up rather well when forced.

She couldn't be bothered to blow out her hair. It feels like years since she visited the hairdresser, and her hair is now past her shoulders. She isn't sure how appropriate it is for a forty-three-year-old mother of three—three! she still can't get over that it's now three!—to have a tumbling mane of long, curly tresses, which is why she usually clips it back. But tonight she did as she used to do when she was a teenager: scrunch mousse into the curls, tip her head upside down, and dry it, flipping her head back at the mane to produce a cloud.

She wears a touch of makeup and carries a clutch purse that Elliott bought her once upon a time, but walking through this place, with its crowds of people, all busily chatting away, their eyes scouring the room to check out each new person that enters, makes her seize up with anxiety, makes her feel out of place; wrong. She resists the urge to grab Josephine and run, instead following Josephine to the bar, her eyes cast down to the floor, terrified to make eye contact lest one of these men—and oh Lord, how lascivious these men seem to her, with their flashing smiles and appreciative looks—lest one of these men think she might be available.

They are there less than five minutes before they are surrounded. I wonder if we give off the scent of fresh meat? thinks Gabby, smiling politely but coldly while Josephine giggles prettily and tells the men what they will be drinking.

"I haven't seen you ladies here before," one of the men says, handsome, but a drinker, thinks Gabby, staring at the broken veins on his nose.

"We're fresh meat," Gabby says with a bold grin.

He raises an eyebrow. "English fresh meat!" He seems delighted. "Does it taste different over there?"

Gabby gives him a withering look as he laughs and throws his hands up with a boyish shrug, as if he couldn't help himself, as if he's a naughty boy. Oh *God*, she thinks. This is exactly why I didn't want to come.

She glances at Josephine, who is already in an animated discussion with one of the other men. It is hard to tell whether she is genuinely interested, or whether she is just enjoying the attention. Either way, her body language is open and flirtatious; the pair of them both laughing. Gabby sighs, wondering if she might be able to call a cab, leave early.

The professional singles have, it seems, claimed the bar. As long as she perches on a stool by the bar, she will have men like this chatting her up all night. Would it be worse, she wonders, if men like this didn't chat her up? Would she feel inadequate? Less than? She looks around at the women, at their high, high heels, their midwinter tans, their straightened hair and heavy makeup. It isn't about being less than, she realizes. It is about being entirely different. She isn't one of these women, nor does she want to be. She should have trusted her instincts and not agreed to come. As wise as her mother has been of late, she is not always right. This was not a good idea.

A couple gets up from a table in the bar area, and Gabby swoops in. She will sit there and lose herself in her iPhone until it is time to go, or until she feels she is able to make her escape. Her Kindle app is on the phone, and even though she doesn't find it particularly easy to read on such a small screen, it's better than being the fresh meat at the bar.

She orders a cup of tea from a passing waiter, ignoring his surprise at the unusual request in the bar that is famous for its singles' night on this particular night, then gets stuck in the novel she has been meaning to read for weeks.

"Is this seat taken?"

She wasn't sure she heard it properly as she looks up. Oh God. She should have got rid of the other chair. Why didn't she anticipate this was going to happen? She hesitates, looking at the man standing by the table, not wanting to be rude, but if she says yes, he will see there is no one to join her, and if she says no, she will have to fend off yet another awful man.

He doesn't look awful. He is wearing a Barbour, and how could she not warm to a man in the coat that always reminds her of home? He is rugged, and has kind eyes. How is she supposed to be so rude as to say no?

"I'm sorry?"

"Is this seat taken? May I sit here?"

"You're English!"

He smiles. "So are you."

Gabby puts her cell phone back in her purse. "Where are you from?"

"London."

She looks at him. She has met a lot of people since living here who are English and say they are from London. "Where?" she used to ask excitedly, always hoping they would be from her "village";

hoping they might say Belsize Park, or Primrose Hill, or Camden Town.

Invariably they'd say "Guildford." She has no idea why, but it seemed everyone she'd met who said they came from London ended up coming from Guildford. "Right," she'd say, covering her disappointment. "Surrey."

"Where in London?" she asks, dubiously awaiting the Guildford reply.

"Maida Vale."

"No!" She is delighted. "I'm from Belsize Park!"

He grins from ear to ear before doing what any good Londoner does when far from home and connecting with someone from their village: declare their school. "City of London."

"South Hampstead!"

"Oh my God!" he laughs. "I think I went out with the whole of your year."

"Who? Who!" It is an unspoken language, an immediate familiarity, as Gabby leans across the table toward him.

"Sarah Diamond."

"She was in the year above me!"

"Emma Montgomery."

"My year!"

"Daisy Luckwell."

"My God, you were busy!"

"What can I say? I was very charming when I was at school. Didn't you know City boys?"

"Not really." She shakes her head. "I was too busy falling in love with the boys at UCS."

"Oh please!" He waves a hand dismissively. "How could you possibly have fallen in love with boys from that school! Maroon-and-black-striped blazers! What little taste you must have had. You should have looked farther afield to us, where the real men were. We played rugby. And tennis. Very manly."

"Oh yes. And cricket. Very manly."

"What's the matter with cricket?" He feigns hurt. "I'll have you know I'm an excellent bowler."

"You're certainly bowling me over." She grins, before her hands fly up to her mouth. "Oh my God. I didn't mean that. I was just making a double entendre, I didn't mean for that to sound like a come-on."

He grins. "First of all, I'm just thrilled to hear someone pronounce '*doobl ontond*' correctly, and secondly, I haven't had such a nice come-on in years. Even if it wasn't one. What are you drinking? Sorry, I can see you're drinking tea but that's completely ridiculous. You can't sit in a bar on this ghastly singles' night and drink tea and think that's okay. You need something far stronger to give you the fortitude to get through this evening."

Gabby cannot stop smiling at the banter. "Why? Are you that bad?"

"Oh I'm much worse." He grins. "Let me guess. Cosmopolitan."

She grimaces. "Do I really strike you as a Cosmopolitan kind of girl?"

"Good point. Pint of scrumpy?"

"If I knew you better I'd tell you where to go."

"Vodka and tonic, lots of lime?"

"Perfect." She grins, watching him as he heads over to the bar, knowing this isn't going to be such a bad night after all.

"Excuse me?"

She looks up into the face of a leering, perma-tanned man.

"Is anyone sitting here?"

"Yes." She smiles at him. "I'm afraid someone is."

. . .

I'm Julian." He extends his hand over the table and they shake hands, formally.

"Gabby."

"I hate to ask the obvious question, but do you come here often? Know that if you say yes I may have to get up and leave, but no pressure."

Gabby laughs. "I have been here before, but for dinner. This is the first time I've been to the singles scene, and it is, as you said earlier, ghastly, as I knew it would be, and the only reason I'm here is because my girlfriend has been begging me for weeks to accompany her, and I did promise. In the end I ran out of excuses. I also thought, it's one night. How bad can it be?"

"Worse," Julian says.

"Clearly." They chink glasses in a silent toast.

"So what brings you here, in your Barbour and brogues? Are you looking for a glamorous divorcée to tuck you in at night?"

His face grows serious as he studies his glass before looking up at her. "Actually, I'm here in much the same way you are. I'm newly separated and my mates at work have been trying to get me out for a night's drinking for weeks. I kept trying to put them off, but in the end I ran out of excuses and thought I'd just get pissed and get it over with."

"Pissed as in English pissed?"

"Yes. Drunk. Not angry."

"God it's nice to meet someone who speaks the same language," Gabby says. "I've been here forever, I'm an American citizen, I love this country more than I could ever imagine, but when I'm with someone English, I just feel I've come home."

"I have that effect on all women," Julian says. "Seriously, it isn't meeting someone English, though. At least, I don't think so. It's meeting someone from your 'village.' We probably went to the same parties. I'm sure if we tried we'd come up with a ton of people in common. Were you hanging out at the Dome?"

"Yes!" she says in delight. "The Mud Club? Quiet Storm?"

"Yes!"

"Hang on." She peers at him. "Didn't I snog you on New Year's Eve 1985?"

"Oh my God! That was you? I've been looking for you forever!" They both laugh. "So what's your story, Gabby. Husband? Kids? What brought you here. . . ."

"I had a husband," Gabby starts, leaning forward so he can hear.

"What?" He cups his ear, the music having just been turned up. "Can you speak up?"

"Not really!" she yells, as he leans forward again and speaks loudly, his lips up against her ear.

"Have you eaten? This place is too damn noisy for me. Do you want to leave and grab something to eat?"

She beams up at him. "That would be lovely!" she says.

Josephine turns to see Julian before gaping at Gabby, open-mouthed.

"What? How is it that you've met a cute guy already?"

"It's not a romantic prospect," Gabby assures her. "He's from the same place as me. We have friends in common. To be honest, it's getting a bit loud in here. Would you mind terribly if I left?"

"You're going to get in a car with him? A stranger?"

"No! We're just going across the street. I'll be back."

"Oh. Okay."

"You're sure? Because I won't go if you're not okay with it."

"It's fine." Josephine leans forward. "This guy Rich is really nice. I'm more than fine," she says, and winks.

"Be back later," Gabby says, giving Josephine a kiss on the cheek.

She told Josephine he wasn't a romantic prospect, and the truth is she was enjoying herself too much to even think about whether he was a romantic prospect or not. There was certainly banter, perhaps one might call it chemistry, but Gabby suspects it's from familiarity, rather than any sexual attraction. He feels like a brother, like someone she has known forever, for while she does not know him, she has known a million men, boys, like him, and is completely safe and comfortable in a way she rarely is with people she has just met.

They walk across the street, both chattering nineteen to the dozen, and walk in to the restaurant there. Julian guides her in through the door, one hand on the small of her back, then helps her off with her coat, hanging it on the rack by the door.

How lovely it is, Gabby thinks, to be with a man who knows what to do. He pulls the chair out for her before sitting down himself, and shakes out his napkin as soon as he sits down, smiling over the table at his new friend.

"This is so much better," Gabby sighs. "Thank you for suggesting this. I felt like my ears were going to pop."

"I haven't forgotten you were about to give me your life story," Julian says. "I think you were at the part where you had a husband."

"Ah yes. I was." Gabby is quiet for a moment, for she is not sure how to edit her story to make it palatable. He may feel like someone she has known forever, but what would he think if she were to tell him the truth? Is it necessary to tell anyone the truth?

Would it not be better just to say she and her husband split up and she has a baby? But she has tried that before, and everyone gasps in horror at how disgusting her husband is, that he could leave her when pregnant.

She may be furious with Elliott now, but he is not the bad guy here. He does not deserve to be castigated for something he did not do.

"I had a husband," she starts, her eyes flicking to the door as she stops, abruptly. "Oh shit," she says. "And there he is."

She looks at Julian like a rabbit trapped in the headlights.

"Do you need to hide?" he leans forward and whispers.

"I don't want to see him," she whispers back. "Or his ghastly girlfriend."

"I like that you like the word 'ghastly,'" he whispers. "It's my favorite word. I've made a pact to myself to use it at least five times a day."

"This is ghastly," she says. "Seriously. I don't want to see them."

"Stop being a baby," he commands. "I can't throw my Barbour over your head and pretend to be dining with the incredible shrouded woman."

Gabby, despite herself, laughs, just as Elliott spots her, and stops in his tracks.

"Don't look now," Julian mutters, "but the ex has seen you."

"If you had thrown your Barbour over my head I wouldn't be able to look now," she mutters, wishing she could stop smiling. "I wish you had."

"Don't be silly," he says gently. "If I had then we'd have to cut a hole in it so you could eat, and that wouldn't be very practical, would it."

Gabby bursts out laughing before sinking her head in her hand.

"Oh God. This is awful. I don't mind saying hello to Elliott, but the smug ghastly girlfriend? Ghastly!"

Julian peers over. "She does look rather smug. Very American perfect. Not my type at all."

"Oh no? What's your type?" Gabby couldn't help the question, but Julian says nothing, merely smiles and raises an eyebrow, lifting his water glass in a silent toast.

"Touché," he says. "Here they come."

"Elliott!" Gabby summons every ounce of graciousness she has ever possessed, flashing a charming smile at them both. "Trish! What a small world!"

"Lovely to see you." Trish smiles, without stopping, continuing through the restaurant to their table, shooting a look at Elliott as if he should follow her. Which he doesn't. "Elliott?" she says.

"Be there in a minute," he says, looking at Julian. "Hi," he says, and extends a hand. "I'm Elliott."

"Julian. How do you do?"

"Oh. You're English. Are you a friend from home?"

"No," Julian says pleasantly, not offering anything else. An awkward silence descends.

"Where are the girls?" Gabby asks, annoyed that on his weekend with the girls he is out for dinner with Trish.

"They both made plans," he said. "I asked them to cancel but apparently they were long-standing, so we're picking up Alanna after dinner, and Olivia's sleeping over at Gemma's." Nice, thinks Gabby. On your weekend you farm them out at friends' houses. She says nothing, merely nods.

"I think some of the clothes from my house are at yours," she says eventually. "Maybe you can bring them back on Sunday?"

"Do you know what they are?"

"Some leggings. Long-sleeved T-shirts. And socks. We seem to have run out of socks."

"I'll look," he says, standing awkwardly a bit longer. "Well, I'd better get going. Nice to meet you." He looks at Julian.

"Enjoy your evening," Gabby says, watching him walk toward Trish, reminding her so much of an unhappy little boy. She turns back to Julian, an apology already on her lips.

"Well," he says, settling back in his chair. "*That* wasn't awkward."

Thirty-five

Usually Elliott is a sound sleeper. Gabby used to tease him because he could sleep anywhere, in any position, asleep almost before his head hit the pillow.

Lately, though, he has found himself waking up in the early hours of the morning, anxious, with no idea why. He has tried lying in bed, counting sheep, deep breathing, meditating on ocean scenes, but nothing is able to send him back to sleep.

He turns his head and raises himself slightly, better able to see the digital clock on Trish's nightstand. She is fast asleep, her cream silk nightgown bunched up, almost to her waist. He looks at her perfectly rounded naked bottom, with no desire to touch her. He is admiring, but dispassionate; as if he were marveling at the cool white perfection of a marble Michelangelo statue.

4:33. He knows he won't go back to sleep now. Occasionally, if he wakes up at two, or even sometimes three, he can get back to sleep, but after four he knows it's all over; there's little point even trying.

He climbs out of bed, not worrying about making noise for Trish is dead to the world until morning. In his own house, he would lie back in his recliner and flick through the channels until he found something that caught his interest; he might catch up on his reading, or find himself playing one of the kids' mindless computer games.

Here, in Trish's house, he is a little stuck. He hovers in the doorway of the living room, negatively anticipating the feel of the hard, modern sofa. It looks beautiful, but it is not a sofa on which to lie, cushioned by down pillows, feet up on a large wide armrest as you read a book, or watch TV.

Wait, there *is* no TV in here.

The sofas in the family room are not much better, for this is not a room where anyone ever lounges, or relaxes. There is a television; for want of something better, Elliott makes himself as comfortable as he is able and starts to flick.

He isn't looking for anything in particular. His thoughts are far away from anything on the television set, and little, at this point, could bring his thoughts back.

Ever since he saw Gabby with that Englishman, he has felt out of sorts; wrong; ill at ease. They separated with Gabby having already slept with, having been impregnated by, another man. They were getting divorced, even though he had to cancel the initial appointment with the lawyer because something at work came up—he doesn't remember what—and he is supposed to have found happiness with Trish. What right does he have to feel uncomfortable seeing his wife with another man?

He stares blindly at the television screen and pictures Gabby with that man. Elliott was facing their table, looking directly at the pair of them, had to focus hard so as not to stare all evening. Even then, his eyes kept involuntarily landing on them. It wasn't so much that she was with another man—she had the right to be with anyone; they were separated, after all—it was that she looked so happy; happier than she has looked in months.

And he wasn't just any other man. He was English. He sounded just like her. He had that rugged English, Bear Grylls-ish quality. If you threw him in the middle of a jungle, by the end of the first day he would have built a two-story hut out of banana leaves and twigs, would have caught a few fish with a stick he'd whittled into a spear, and would have a wild boar merrily roasting over a fire. He looked, he realizes with shock, exactly like the sort of man Gabby should be with. They looked good together.

Better than good. *Right*.

"Hey," he hears behind him, turning in surprise to see a sleepy Trish, running her fingers through her hair as she pads into the room, sitting next to him on the sofa and kissing his cheek. "What's up? Bad night's sleep?"

Elliott shrugs. "You know how it is. My body's exhausted but my mind's racing."

"Which is stress," she says. "What are you stressed about?"

"Who knows. Everything. Life." His voice is light, but his expression is not.

"And Gabby," Trish says after a pause. "Being with another man."

"What?" He feigns innocence, his eyes open wide. "That? Oh no. That's no big deal."

"Elliott." Trish gives an ironic laugh, leaning back from him, as if her body is getting ready for the distancing that she knows is about to come. "I'm not stupid. I was there with you all night. You couldn't take your eyes off the two of them, and you were frowning every time you looked at them. Just like you are now."

Elliott quickly corrects his features. "It was just a shock," he says. "I didn't know she was dating anyone."

"It was more than that," Trish says sadly. "It was that she was dating someone appropriate. You know what I saw tonight?" Her voice is quiet. "I saw that you still love her."

"Of course I still love her!" Elliott says. "I was married to her for twenty years! We have two children together. You don't just stop loving someone overnight."

"I did," she says.

"That's different."

"Not much. Here's the thing. You may still love her, but what I saw tonight was that you are *in* love with her. I saw love, and loss, and all the things you're going to admit to if I push you, but I saw something else that you may not even realize. I saw *yearning*. You didn't want Gabby sitting there with some other man, and you didn't want to be sitting there with me. You wanted to be with her."

Elliott says nothing, just looks at his hands.

"I have no idea what the future holds," Trish says. "I don't know if this thing she has is serious, or how she feels about you, but the one thing I'm absolutely sure about is that you're still in love with her. Which means, you're not ready for a relationship with me, or anyone else."

Still, there is nothing for Elliott to say.

"I think you're wonderful," she says, blinking back the tears that are threatening to spring. "I wish things were different. Who knows, maybe in a year's time you and I will circle back to each other again, when you're more ready, but I think we need to call it a day."

She reaches out and takes his hand, squeezing it gently as Elliott just nods, ignoring the tears in his own eyes, which slowly trickle down his cheeks.

Thirty-six

Elliot doesn't do anything for a while. He sits, and thinks, and yearns, and finally he goes back to his old house.

"Natasha!" Elliott stumbles on the doorstep. "I had no idea you were here." He has always got on very well with his soon-to-be ex-mother-in-law, and has no idea how he should greet her.

"Elliott!" With her trademark warmth, she flings her arms around him, enveloping him in gauzy scarves and a squeezing hug. Stepping back, she holds him at arm's length and examines him. "You look incredibly dapper and handsome. I hate to say it, but separation suits you."

"Only you could say that," Elliott laughs. "And not have me think you were crazy."

"Some might say I am crazy," she laughs. "Which is why I can get away with it. It is true, though. I haven't seen you look so good in years. And yet . . ." She peers at him. "You don't look terribly happy. You look tired."

"I didn't sleep last night. No idea what happened. Recently I've started waking up in the early hours of the morning, and once I'm up, that's it. No more sleep."

"Sounds like you're going through menopause," Natasha says. "Maybe you should go and see a doctor."

"Ha!"

"Are you coming in?" she says after an awkward silence. "Gabby's out but the girls are here. Are they expecting you?"

"No . . . I brought some clothes that Gabby said were missing."

"Good. Come in. Do you still take your coffee with half and half and one sugar?"

Elliott smiles in relief as he shrugs off his coat. "Good memory."

"It *has* been twenty years," she says.

"True."

Footsteps come running down the hallway as Alanna runs into the room. "*Daddy!*" She flings herself onto his lap, giving him a reception far better than the usual grunts hello when they are dropped off at his house.

"Unexpected visits can bring unexpected pleasures." Natasha smiles, putting a steaming coffee in front of him, just as Olivia walks in, Henry leaning against her shoulder, gently burping as she pats his back.

Her face lights up as she blows her father a kiss, then sits down, careful to sit far away from coffee, or anything that could spill and hurt Henry.

"You look scarily proficient with that baby," Elliott says, looking for Gabby in the baby's face, but not finding much. The eyebrows? Perhaps. Ears? Maybe. The baby is blond, and lean, and bouncy, as different from the girls as he could possibly be. They were dark, chubby, and so obviously girl-like, with tiny delicate features.

Alanna takes Henry from Olivia and bounces him up and down.

"Look, Dad!" she says. "You have to see this!" She puts him in a bouncer in the corner of the room, then crouches in front of him.

"Achoo!" she says, pretending to sneeze, as a huge smile comes across Henry's face.

"Achoo! Achoo!" Henry starts chuckling, as both girls continue sneezing, his chuckling becoming full-on hysteria. Everyone starts laughing. Even Elliott, for this baby, with his delighted giggling, is adorable enough to spellbind everyone who lays eyes upon him.

"Isn't he *amazing*?" Alanna looks at her dad, laughing. "Don't you *love* him?"

"He's definitely amazing," Elliott says, astonished that he doesn't feel more of the animosity he had expected to feel. He had been dreading meeting this child. He had seen him, vaguely bundled, in Gabby's arms, but to her credit she had never offered up the child for him to approve of, and he had always tried not to look.

This was painful enough, he had always felt, without having the physical reminder forced upon him.

But here was the physical reminder, and it wasn't painful. It was adorable.

"Can I hold him?" Elliott has no idea where the words come from as he nervously looks at Natasha, knowing he has no right to this child, has nothing, in fact, to do with this child, but she just smiles approvingly as Alanna lifts him up and hands him to Elliott.

"What a good boy!" Elliott bounces him on his knee as Henry giggles, bringing him forward and holding him, burying his nose in the baby's neck and inhaling that sweet, powdery baby smell, immediately sweeping back to when the girls were little.

"Isn't he so delicious?" Olivia says. "Don't you just want to eat him?"

"He is delicious," Elliott croons. "You're delicious! Yes you are! You're delicious."

"Wow, Dad." Alanna watches him. "You're really good with babies."

Elliott fixes her with a fake hard glare. "You would think so, given that I've had two of them myself. Hard as it is to believe the two of you were ever babies."

"That's not what she means." Olivia is watching. "She means you're really good with *this* baby."

Unseen by the girls, Natasha silently raises her eyebrows before taking a sip of tea.

"I like all babies," Elliott says. "When they're not screaming."

"Henry never screams," Alanna says. "He's the best-behaved baby ever. He doesn't wake up at night either. He's been sleeping right through until five. You'd love him if you lived here again."

"Don't be stupid," Olivia says. "Dad's not going to live here again. Are you?" She didn't mean for the note of hope to creep into her voice for the last two words, but nevertheless, it was heard by everyone in the room.

Elliott doesn't know what to say. He'd been thinking all night about what Trish had said, and as much as it pained him to admit it, she was right. It was all true. He did still love Gabby, but things were different now; they could never go back to how it was before, and he couldn't see a way forward.

Gabby was dating, and she had a new baby with another man. He had to move on. It was definitely too soon for him to have another relationship, and perhaps time would heal the wound; perhaps acknowledging that he was still in love with Gabby, instead of pretending that he pitied her, would allow him to move on properly, rather than attempting to project feelings he doesn't have onto the first woman who steps in his path.

But he didn't expect this: to like this baby. Any baby. He, after all, was the one who continued with the vasectomy despite knowing how much Gabby wanted a baby; he was the one who told her, in no uncertain terms, he was done. He didn't want to get up for night feeds; he didn't want to show up to preschool events when he was old enough to be a grandfather; he didn't want to give up his life for another eighteen years when the light at the end of the tunnel was just starting to become visible.

Yet here he is, holding this adorable, chuckling boy, and all he wants to do is continue burying his nose in his neck; blowing raspberries on his tummy; bouncing him up and down to make him laugh.

And he isn't even his.

The front door opens as all of them start. There's a jingle of keys down the hallway, and Gabby stops, stunned to see her baby in the arms of her husband. Soon-to-be ex-husband.

"Elliott. What are you doing here?"

"I brought the clothes you were looking for. I couldn't find all of them, but I'll check the laundry when the wash is done."

"Oh. Great. Thanks." She's speaking slowly, carefully, unable to believe he has Henry in his arms and is clearly comfortable. More than comfortable—loving it.

"Girls? Go tidy the mudroom, please," she commands. "Your shoes are everywhere."

Reluctantly, for they can tell something interesting is going to happen and don't want to leave, the girls sidle out of the room.

"I just made Elliott a coffee," says her mother. "Would you like tea? If not, I'll go upstairs and do some laundry of my own."

"I'm fine," Gabby says, as her mother walks past her, giving her arm a discreet, supportive squeeze. She sits down at the table, opposite Elliott and Henry, and fixes a cool gaze upon him.

"I thought you didn't like babies," she says.

"What? Of course I like babies. We had babies. I love babies. I just didn't want one of my own at this stage in our life." He pauses, knowing he has to tread carefully. "I have to say, though, I'd forgotten how completely delicious they are. This little guy especially. He's so different from the girls. Remember how chubby they were?"

Gabby laughs. "Oh God. Remember Alanna? She came out with a full head of thick black hair. It was terrifying. I thought I'd given birth to a three-year-old."

"And remember how Olivia screamed all night long? For months. That goddamned colic. Alanna was the same. Oh God. I just remember whenever the pacifier fell out there was hell to pay."

"I remember you walking both of them up and down the stairs all night long to get them back to sleep."

"Yes." Elliott smiles. "And the minute they fell back to sleep and I'd try to oh-so-gently lay them back down in their cribs, they'd start screaming again. It was hell."

"It was," agrees Gabby.

"I knew I couldn't go through that again."

"Luckily"—Gabby holds her arms out for Henry as Elliott reluctantly gives him back—"we don't have to with this one, do we, mister? Aren't you the best baby in the whole world? Yes you are! You are! Because you know Mummy might off herself if you weren't."

"No up all night?"

"None. Sleeps all night."

"No screaming for no reason?"

"None."

"No sleepwalking through your life with exhaustion wondering how you're going to make it through the day, let alone the rest of your life?"

"None. He truly is the best baby I've ever known."

There is a silence as they both watch Henry, his mouth opening over a rattle he is grasping as he mouths silently on it, looking up at each of them and breaking into a large grin.

"I better go." Elliott drains his coffee before standing up. "Did you have fun the other night? He seems like a nice guy."

"He is," says Gabby simply, as she shows him out of the door.

Thirty-seven

Gabby doesn't remember laughing this much, nor feeling this comfortable, in years. She and Julian are tucked into the corner of a cozy, tiny pub, the likes of which she didn't think even existed in this country, while a fire blazes and they sit and talk, over pints and half-pints of lager, because Julian refuses to let her drink anything else in a pub.

They have had bangers and mash for dinner, and toad in the hole, Julian expressing concern that there was no steak and kidney pie. The waitress, from Birmingham, grabbed the chef (from Guildford, naturally), who said he'd absolutely put it on the menu, and if they came back the following week, they'd have steak and kidney pie.

They have ordered spotted dick and treacle tart for dessert, and Gabby, who is no longer the slightest bit concerned about portraying herself as a waiflike creature who doesn't actually eat anything, has cleaned her plate.

"So." Julian leans back against the banquette. "Your husband. Seems like a good guy. Not wankerish in the slightest."

"He isn't. He is a good guy. He really didn't deserve the way I treated him."

"We all fuck up," Julian says simply. "Men find it harder to get over. Lack of support systems, Neanderthal mentality, blah blah blah. You've heard it all before, and it's all true. But I realize, going through it myself, there's another factor. I think women are more detached from the ending of a marriage; they see it as the marriage having failed, whereas men see it as a personal failure."

"You see your marriage as a personal failure?"

Julian nods, sadly. "If I had been a better husband, had been home more, been more engaged, more present, I truly don't believe this would have happened. I don't believe Stacy would have looked to someone else to provide her with what I wasn't."

"I don't know that that's true," Gabby says. "Elliott was an amazing husband. I honestly can't say he was at fault, but when temptation presented itself, I was . . . I don't know, powerless. It was like something came over me and all reasonable and rational thought went out the window. I threw everything away for nothing."

"So there was absolutely no tension between you? No resentments? Nothing?"

Gabby thinks about Elliott's vasectomy, knowing that was the moment a part of her shut down, a part of her felt she would never be able to forgive him for making such a momentous decision, one that impacted her so hugely.

"There were," she says quietly. "I think there usually are. Ooh goody. Dessert." She is grateful for the distraction that allows her to change the subject. The waitress puts down enormous plates of treacle tart and spotted dick, with a jug of custard on the side.

"Mmmm!" Gabby moans in delight. "You know what I've never seen anywhere since I was a child? Do you remember those huge trays of chocolate cake? The school dinner ladies would cut them into massive squares and pour over this gloppy chocolate sauce. It was disgusting, but I've never seen it since."

"I loved that pudding! That was my favorite!" Julian says, knocking Gabby's spoon out of the way to attack her treacle tart, as both of them start to laugh.

It has been a glorious evening. When Julian stops by his house to grab a book he wants Gabby to read about an uncomplicated divorce, she steps out of the car, curious as to how he lives, intrigued by this man who feels like someone she has known forever.

He is handsome, and clever, and fun, and funny. He feels exactly as she imagines a brother to feel; like those friendships she had, lifetimes ago, with men just like him, when they were all young and single in London.

She hasn't thought of him in a romantic context, except she recognizes that he has all the qualities she should be looking for, if she were looking. Which she isn't.

When she feels his hands on her waist in the kitchen, she jumps, in surprise, turning to tell him she doesn't think this is such a good idea, but before she has a chance to say anything, he is kissing her, and it is so lovely to be held in someone's arms, so lovely to be kissed in just the way she remembers the English boys kissing—softer, more gently, anticipation building with desire, that she relaxes, seconds later snaking her hands into his hair, gasping as an unexpected wave of desire sweeps over her.

When finally they pull away, Julian leans his forehead on hers and smiles into her eyes. "Can we go somewhere more comfortable?"

He leads her by the hand into his bedroom, where they fall on the bed, laughing, playfully teasing each other before the kissing starts again, swiftly moving into unknown territory.

Julian's hands start to unbutton her shirt, as she stops him, suddenly horrified, because she is lactating and this wouldn't be right.

His hands move down, stroking her urgently between her legs, on top of the fabric of her pants, before moving up to undo the button, only for Gabby to move his hand gently away.

"I shouldn't be doing this," she whispers. "I just had a baby. I don't know that this is . . . right."

She waits for him to ask why she came back to his house, knowing there was nothing to say, knowing he would think her ridiculous if she told him she just wanted to cuddle, wanted to be held, wanted to feel loved.

He isn't angry, or belligerent. He strokes her face and kisses her forehead, her nose, her cheeks, her lips. "Will you stay?" he asks, and this time she knows it isn't because he expects them to have sex all night, but because he needs from her exactly the same thing she needs from him: affection, warmth, an embrace.

She texts home to let them know she will be out, and borrows a big, soft, old T-shirt and thick climbing socks from Julian. He gives her a spare toothbrush and they brush their teeth, standing side by side over a tiny sink, Gabby turning to him and talking, her mouth filled with toothpaste foam that spits everywhere. His incredulous expression gives way to laughter, and soon they are having a competition to create the most toothpaste foam, both collapsing with laughter at their childlike behavior, each egging the other on.

Gabby hasn't felt this young, this carefree, in years. In bed, Julian holds out his arms for Gabby to snuggle in, the pair of them falling asleep wrapped up together, sex the very last thing on each of their minds.

Gabby wakes up first. Disoriented for a few seconds, she lies still, letting her eyes adjust to the light, remembering why the bathroom door isn't where she expected it to be. Turning her head, she sees Julian, eyes closed, mouth open, still fast asleep. She smiles to herself, fighting the urge to stroke his cheek and kiss him.

Not that she feels a burning sexual attraction for him. She doesn't fancy him, but she may love him. Not as she loved Elliott, but as a friend. She undoubtedly feels an enormous affection for him, greater now, since he didn't push for anything more than she was able to give.

Could I fall in love with him? she wonders. Why *aren't* I looking at him wanting to rip his clothes off? Objectively, he is gorgeous. He is exactly the sort of man she should be with, and it doesn't make sense that she doesn't want more from him.

Perhaps, she thinks, this is, or could be, a different kind of love. A saner kind of love. There's no question that they fit together. She has had great love with Elliott, and she had, however misguided, great passion with Matt, even though that is increasingly hard for her to believe, now that the rose-colored shades have fallen from her eyes.

Perhaps this third attempt could be a different kind of love. Comfort. Comfort can be love; familiarity can become love. Yes, she tells herself. Comfort is good; comfort is *comfortable*.

And who is she to expect anything more, when she has already experienced more than one woman has a right to? How lucky is she that at this stage in the game, with two children almost grown and a newborn baby, she has met a man with whom she has so much in common, a man with whom she can see herself, a man who isn't phased by all the drama in her life?

Climbing out of bed, she grabs a robe off the back of the bathroom door and goes downstairs to make breakfast. The fridge is almost empty, but there are eggs, and milk, and—oh thank you, God!—PG Tips in the drawer. In the freezer she finds pork sausages, and she is busy cooking when she hears the creak of the stairs.

She turns and grins, no awkwardness, no morning-after-the-night-before gracelessness, for they are both adults. Would it have been different had they had sex? Gabby doubts it. She feels as if she has known him forever.

Julian hugs her, grinning, before helping himself to one of the sausages as she bats his hand out of the way.

"God, this is nice," he says. "I could get used to this."

"Don't get too used to it," Gabby says. "I can't actually believe I left Henry for an entire night. I know he's three months old, but it still feels strange. I'm going to have to run home."

"Are you leaking?"

"No. I carry a small pump and I already took care of it. He has a fridge full of pumped milk, but I miss him. I need to go straight after breakfast."

They sit down and eat, idly chatting and flicking through the papers on the table, before Gabby gets up to leave.

"You realize they'll think I'm a dirty stopout," she says.

"You are."

"Not that dirty." She laughs.

"Not yet. Thank you." He takes her in his arms and kisses her. "This was the most fun I've had in years. I'll call you later."

"Sounds perfect," she says, for it does.

Thirty-eight

Normally Elliott wouldn't drop in to anyone's house, but given that he lived with Claire and Tim for those months after leaving Gabby, he thinks of it as a second home, and knows they won't mind if he drops in.

Tim's car is missing, but Claire is home. Elliott rings the back doorbell, despite knowing the door is open, waiting for Claire to come and answer.

She walks through the kitchen with Isabella on her hip, giving Elliott a big hug.

"What a lovely surprise! I was just dying of boredom upstairs while Isabella played on her mat. God, Elliott. She's completely delicious and wonderful, but I'd forgotten the hours and hours of interminable boredom when you have a small baby."

Elliott laughs. "She's gotten so big!" He doesn't hold out his arms, though, just tickles her chin as she watches him carefully, her big blue eyes fixed on his. "She's just beautiful, Claire."

"I know. I think so too, but I'm ever so slightly biased. It's just me here, I'm afraid, but will you come in?"

Elliott comes in and sits in his usual stool in his usual spot at the kitchen island, while Claire puts Isabella in a bouncy chair where she happily gurgles, grabbing hold of the plastic toys on a rail in front of her.

"So what's up?" Claire asks, pulling up a stool. "Actually, I know what's up. I spoke to Trish the other week and she told me the news. I meant to get in touch to check on you, but . . . you know how it is. I'm sorry."

"How did she sound?"

"I think she's fine. She's sad, but she's clear that you're not ready to be in a serious relationship, and at this point, she doesn't see the point of anything unless it's a serious relationship. She also said you were clearly still in love with Gabby."

There is a silence.

"So . . . do you want to talk about it?"

And Elliott, who has struggled for so long to hold it all in, to keep it together, to present a stoic face to the rest of the world, finally crumbles.

Claire reaches forward and puts her arms around him, holding him as he cries, rubbing his back, letting go only when he has finished, when she gets up for the box of Kleenex on the other side of the kitchen.

"You're still in love with Gabby," Claire says, a statement rather than a question. "And you don't know what to do."

Elliott shrugs, attempting a smile. "I don't want to be in love with her. I've tried my damndest to get over her, but I can't. I thought the baby was this insurmountable wedge between us, that even if we both decided we wanted to be together, that would never happen because there is this baby in the way, this constant reminder of what happened, and I'd never be able to forgive her. I didn't think I could ever forgive her, but it seems that I have. Without wanting to, without thinking about it, I have forgiven her, and I met the baby for the first time this week. Henry. I met him properly, rather than knowing Gabby was holding this bundle in her arms and doing my best not to look at him or even acknowledge his existence. I met him, and held him, and watched my daughters with him, and it broke my heart."

Claire frowns. "I don't understand. What do you mean, it broke your heart?"

"It broke my heart that my family is there and I'm not. And this baby is their brother, and that means he's part of this family, whether I want him or not. I didn't want him, and I didn't think I would ever want him, and I recognize he has a father and I will never have that role, but it doesn't matter anymore. I want my family to be back together and I want to be with Gabby, and this baby is part of my life. Part of *my* family."

Claire takes a deep breath. "I know this might sound harsh, but you're sure these feelings aren't just a result of seeing her with another man? Trish told me about the night you went out for dinner. You're sure it's not just jealousy speaking?"

"I'm sure. Trish is wonderful, but she's so completely different from Gabby. . . ."

Claire barks with laughter before apologizing.

"Well, yes. Exactly. But instead of appreciating Trish, and how beautiful and perfect everything in her life is, it just made me miss Gabby. I missed the chaos, and clutter, and warmth. I found myself constantly comparing the two, and all I wanted to do was run home. Seeing Gabby the other night, with that guy, was really hard, but my feelings and thoughts didn't start after that. They started long before."

"Do you know anything about the guy she's dating? Has it been a long time? Is it serious?"

"I have no idea. The only thing I can tell you is they looked very comfortable together. That's the other thing. When I left, I knew that all I had to do, for weeks afterward, was tell her I'd forgiven her, and my life would be put back together again. I couldn't do it then, I was so angry, but now she's moved on, and I don't have the right to say that anymore." He sighs. "Maybe I never did."

"What about if *I* talk to her?" Claire says slowly.

"You? But you haven't spoken to her for months. The two of you had a falling-out. Why would she want to talk to you?"

"We never fell out," Claire says. "I just couldn't be placed in the middle. I love both of you, but when you moved in here, I couldn't be in the position of looking after you and looking after Gabby, so I had to put all my energies into you. I know Gabby didn't understand, and I know she felt betrayed by me, but I write to her."

Elliott frowns. "You write to her?"

"Yes. She doesn't write back, but I miss her, so I email her telling her about Isabella and attaching photographs. I tell her little bits about our lives. I didn't do it until after you moved out, and I never say anything about you, but I have apologized, and I have told her that I felt I had to make a choice, and it's only now, with hindsight, I realize I didn't have to. She knows I miss her, and I love her."

"She doesn't write back?"

"No. But I just have this feeling that she's softened toward me. If I were to ask her out for tea, maybe for the babies to meet each other, I bet she'd say yes."

"Even if she did, what makes you think she'd listen to you?"

"Because she always listened to me," Claire laughs. "Because I make sense. Or, in this case, you make sense. Look, none of us has any idea what the future holds, but the one thing I'm clear on is that if you don't tell her how you feel, the possibilities for you getting back together are shot. I've seen so many people divorce who shouldn't have, who realized, as the legal proceedings were starting, that they had made a mistake, they didn't want to go through with it, but pride stopped them from telling the other how they really felt, and everyone ended up miserable. Don't let that happen to you. I tell her you're still in love with her and want to get back together, and what's the worst that can happen? That she says no, she's moved on, she's happy with someone else. You'll get over it, and at least you'll know."

"I don't know." Elliott shakes his head. "I'm just not sure she'll open up to you in that way."

"Let me at least try," Claire says. "What do we have to lose? I miss her, Elliott. I miss her desperately and I realize how much I screwed up by abandoning her in the way that I did. I need to see her to apologize if nothing else, and let me use it as an opportunity to finally do the right thing. Please. I need to do this for me."

Thirty-nine

Josephine has become a good friend, but she doesn't have the ability to look at Gabby's life and problem solve, without getting caught in a drama, in the way Claire had always done. There was no one Gabby had wanted more, during this past year, than Claire, and she is stunned that her anger toward her had dissipated, then disappeared.

Perhaps it was made easier by the fact that Claire never asked anything of her. She didn't ask: how are you? Didn't ask about Henry, or how she was getting on, or how the girls were doing through this separation. She said Henry must be getting big, and she saw the girls in school the other day and Alanna's getting so grown up, but she was careful not to ask anything leading, anything that demanded a response.

Until now. When she's asking if they can get together. With the babies. To chat.

. . .

Gabby is first to show up to the Westport Library. She has dressed carefully, anxious to feel in control, confident enough to handle whatever conversation they have, whatever direction it might take. She knows Claire, or at least she *did*. She is certain Claire wants to meet to apologize, and while she is grateful Claire has reached out, she isn't sure how she feels about their future, their friendship; whether indeed their friendship *has* a future.

Henry in his stroller is delicious in tiny jeans and a cabled sweater bought on sale at the Gap for ten dollars. He looks like a tiny little blond banker. Matt regularly sends gifts, toys, or clothes picked out by his girlfriend, Monroe. The outfits are invariably ridiculously cool—tiny leather aviator jackets, exquisite Italian slippers, when he is nowhere near walking yet, T-shirts with hilarious logos that everyone comments on when he wears them out.

Gabby's tastes run a little different. She had no idea how she felt about boys' clothes, having never had to shop for them before. It is not nearly as much fun as shopping for the girls, and guiltily there has been many a time when she has gone to a store for clothes for Henry, and left with a bag full of delicious things for Alanna—she just got pulled in by the pink and couldn't get away.

Claire is likely to have dressed her baby girl in something European and expensive. Her taste was always classic, her clothes from the best stores in New York. Gabby can't afford anything like that, but she has been able to put together something that may not be Ralph Lauren, but is certainly Ralph Lauren-esque for a fraction of the price. She even swept Henry's hair to one side with just a touch of gel. He looks ridiculously handsome, and as nervous as she is to see Claire, she is also proud to show off her beautiful boy.

The library has changed since she was last here, years and years ago when the girls were toddlers. Then, she and Elliott would bring them here for Mother Goose rhymes, sitting cross-legged on the floor with other couples, all of them still in their postbirth haze, while Miss Annie delighted the children with her renditions of "Alligator Pie," as the parents desperately looked around hoping to make friends just like them, for all of them were new to town, most having moved from New York when their children were born.

This was where she and Elliott met so many of the people who were their earliest friends here. Few of them remain—different preschools, different grade schools, meant their lives drifted apart. The only friends that remained from that period in their lives were Claire and Tim.

Henry's birth, the subsequent craziness of looking after a newborn baby as a single mother, at her age, had prevented her from thinking much about Claire and Tim. Until now, when even pulling into the parking of the library, a place that holds so many happy memories from so many years ago, is bittersweet.

There is a café in the library now; a few people dotted around chatting, looking at laptops, reading. Gabby orders a skim cappuccino for herself, and goes to sit down, facing the door, nervous suddenly at seeing a friend she hasn't seen for so long.

Until Claire enters, and a lump appears in Gabby's throat. It's Claire. Only Claire. So familiar it brings tears to her eyes. Claire stops when she sees Gabby, when Gabby sees there are tears in her eyes too, and the two of them envelop each other in a tight hug, unable to stop smiling even as they are wiping the tears from their cheeks.

"God, I've missed you," Claire says. "I'm desperate to see the baby. Let me see Henry." She coos over Henry, how handsome he is, how different from the girls, remembering everything about Olivia and Alanna when they were tiny, as Gabby coos, in turn, over Isabella.

They swap babies, each bouncing and kissing the other's child, both delighted at the other's good fortune in producing such adorable children, before putting the babies back in their strollers and settling in to catch up.

"You look amazing," Claire says. "How on earth did you get your figure back so quickly?"

"Are you joking?" Gabby says, looking down at her belly in horror. "Look!" she grabs a handful to prove her point. "I'm huge. This stomach's staying forever. My bikini days are so long gone it's not even funny."

"Look at mine!" Claire shows off her tiny pot belly. "I don't even care anymore. I haven't thought about Zumba in a year. I haven't thought about much other than this little munchkin. I'm totally obsessed. I think it's because I'm so much older now, I just can't believe that at my age I was able to produce such a perfect little thing."

"So," Gabby grins. "Are you done now?"

"So done, you have no idea. I could never go through the IVF again. But we're complete. This is what I always wanted. How about you?"

"Done," she says.

Claire peers at her. "And are you as happy as you look?"

"I think I am. It's taken a while, but I feel very . . . peaceful. Content. I did always want another baby, but with Elliott, and even though that isn't how it happened, this little boy has just . . . completed my heart. I feel complete."

Claire smiles, then takes a deep breath. "Listen. We need to talk about what happened between us. I've missed you so much, and I want you to know how sorry I am about how I screwed up."

Gabby says nothing, just listens.

"I felt utterly torn. I love you and I love Elliott, and I had no idea what to do. I felt, at the time, that because Elliott came to us, because he was living in our house, I had to choose him, and I know, now, how massive a mistake that was. Not choosing Elliott, but making any choice at all. I was so freaked out and hormonal about being put in the middle, that I took the easiest option and cut you off, because I couldn't cut Elliott off, given he was two rooms down the hall. And I have hated myself for months because of it. It was a disgusting thing to do, and I didn't even know that you'd meet me. I thought you probably would, but I know we can't just jump in to our old friendship because of how I let you down. I'm sorry. I am so, so sorry, Gabby. I would do anything to turn the clock back and change my behavior, but I can't. All I can do is tell you how ashamed I am, and how sorry, and hope you can find a way to forgive me."

Gabby nods, looking her friend in the eye, knowing everything she is saying is genuine, heartfelt. She knew it at the time, which is why she had tried so hard not to judge her. For as wise as Claire had always been at helping other people sort out their lives, when it came to her own, she was never as clear.

"It was a shitty thing to do," Gabby echoes quietly. "I'm the first to admit I fucked up. I was unfaithful to Elliott, one time, and I ended up with, well . . . I can't call Henry a mistake, because he may be the best thing that's ever happened to me, but I ended up destroying my life as a result. I was terrified, and devastated, and my best friend turning her back was one of the cruelest blows of all. I was pregnant, and a single mother, with Olivia hating me, and no one to turn to for help. Claire, I still love you, and it's amazing to see you, but I honestly don't know how I can get over this. I want to. I'd love nothing more than for the two of us to get back to the friendship we had, but I don't know how to do that. It isn't about forgiveness—I forgive you. It's that you're not the person I thought you were. There's a quote I once read, something about people showing you who they are not by what they say, but by what they do." She pauses, for tears of shame are now streaming down Claire's face. "I'm sorry. I didn't mean to upset you. But if there's any chance at all of us having some kind of a friendship again, I have to say these things. I have to tell you what it was like for me. I have to be honest about how I feel."

Claire nods.

"I don't know that I can go back, and I don't know how to go forward with you. Maybe it will get better over time, but I think, right now, I probably need to go." Gabby hadn't expected to feel this. She had hoped that she would be able to move on, to listen to whatever Claire had to say, and to know that whatever had happened was in the past, but she found she had changed over the months they have not spoken, had reprioritized the important people in her life.

People show themselves not by what they say but by what they do. Claire said all the right things; is saying all the right things now, but she abandoned Gabby in her greatest hour of need, and whatever the excuse, however sorry she is now, Gabby cannot feel the same way about her.

"Wait," Claire says, wiping her tears away. "I get it. You're right, and there's nothing I can say other than you're right, and I hope over time things will change. But there's something else. We have to talk about Elliott."

Gabby frowns. "What about Elliott?"

"Do you know he split up with Trish?"

"He did?" Gabby ignores the small thrill that runs through her body. "I didn't know that. Was he not perfect enough for her?"

"I think she was a little too perfect for him. And he realized he's still in love with you."

Gabby's heart stands still as she stares at Claire. "What did you just say?"

"He's still in love with you."

Gabby shakes her head. "Claire, if you're trying to heal the rift between Elliott and me, this isn't the way to do it. We've both moved on, and as lovely as it would be to think there's still something there between us, there just isn't. Even if there was, too much has happened." Her mind is whirling. "Quite apart from the fact that the last thing Elliott wanted at this stage of his life is a baby. I know you think you're trying to help, but you're not. It's just not feasible, even if it were true."

"Gabby, stop," Claire says urgently. "It is true. Elliott knows I'm here. He knows I'm telling you this, and I'm telling you because he can't tell you himself. You're right, he didn't want a baby, and he didn't think he could ever forgive you. Up until a week ago he wanted to pretend that Henry didn't even exist, and then something happened the other day . . . you know what I'm talking about, don't you?"

The lump is back as Gabby reluctantly nods, remembering how tenderly Elliott held Henry, how his eyes softened, filled with incredulous wonder at this perfect little boy. Years ago, before the girls came along, Elliott always said he wanted at least one little boy.

"He didn't think any of you could ever find a way back because the baby would be a permanent reminder of what happened to destroy your marriage, but something happened the other day, and he said seeing you, seeing the girls with Henry, holding Henry, made him realize that you are a family, whether Henry's his blood or not. You're his family, Gabby. Henry, too. Don't let this fall through your fingers because you don't believe me, or because you have too much pride, or because you're dating someone else who may be cute but, I promise you, will never be a patch on

Elliott. Give him a chance, Gabby," she whispers, laying her hand on top of Gabby's as Gabby starts to cry. "Go to him and hear what he has to say."

Gabby can't make sense of what Claire has said. If Elliott did feel that, why didn't he come to her himself? Why use Claire, who Gabby hadn't been in touch with for so long, as the messenger?

And was this his rebound? After things didn't work out with Trish, was he just thinking about her again because she was familiar, the easiest option?

But she saw the look in his eyes the other day. She saw that he was over the pain of the betrayal, wasn't so consumed with hurt he couldn't look at the baby, could barely look at Gabby.

In his eyes she saw, she realizes suddenly, something that looked suspiciously like love.

But it's been so long. So much has happened. And Julian. What about Julian, who is so familiar, and so fun, and so handsome, and so . . . not her husband.

He is not her husband.

He has not known her for twenty years. He has not seen her at her worst, screaming in frustration over some little inconsequential thing, has not seen her red-faced and sweating in labor, has not seen her being selfish, or thoughtless, or unreasonable, but loves her anyway, because he chose her, and he will always honor his commitment to that choice.

I didn't sleep with him, she thinks, with relief. I could have, so easily, and yet it was so easy not to. Julian is a welcome distraction, but if she is honest with herself she knows there is little chemistry between them. He would make a wonderful best friend. Maybe he will become a wonderful best friend, but romance is truly not what she is looking for.

Not with Julian.

Elliott is her husband.

He's still in love with her.

And she is still in love with him.

Gabby pulls up outside the medical offices and takes a deep breath. She isn't sure what to say, how to say it; isn't sure Elliott's office is the best venue in which to repair what she hopes is still repairable, but she can't wait any longer. She's waited long enough.

She walks into the office, chatting briefly with the girls at the desk, all of whom she has known for years, each of whom is as friendly as they have always been, despite knowing they are no longer together.

"He's stepped out for lunch," says Maria. "He should be back in about fifteen minutes."

"The usual place?"

Maria nods, as Gabby smiles a thank-you and heads to the diner across the street. She sees him first, at the counter, hunched over a turkey and Swiss wrap, reading glasses perched on the end of his nose, paper in front of him, so familiar she actually feels an ache.

Walking over, she sits quietly on the stool next to his, saying nothing, waiting until he turns his head to look over at her, his eyes widening when he sees who it is.

So much has happened between them, so many things unspoken, and yet even now, there is nothing to say. Everything is in

Elliott's face, as he looks into the eyes of the woman he loves; the woman he still wants to be with; the woman he wants to grow old with.

"Elliott," Gabby whispers. It is all she needs to say.

Epilogue

"Happy birthday to you, happy birthday to you, happy birthday dear Henry . . . happy birthday to you!"

Matt throws him up in the air, much to Henry's delight, as Alanna and Olivia start, "Are you one . . ." before the room collapses in giggles, as Matt, Gabby, Elliott, and the girls all lean over the one candle to blow it out, before Gabby takes the cake back in the kitchen to cut slices for all the guests.

"Can I help?" Monroe, all endless legs in skinny jeans, messy almond hair, and almost unreal gorgeousness, comes in and swipes a big dollop of icing from the cardboard base and sucks it off her finger as Gabby looks on in approval.

"I thought you models never ate anything. How in the hell do you get to eat dollops of icing and stay the size of a stick?"

Monroe giggles. "I'm a total sugar addict. Don't even talk to me about Reese's Pieces. I've been known to put away a whole bag in a day. But I'm pretty disciplined when I'm working. I'll juice for days to lose weight for a shoot, then celebrate with a chocolate binge. I know, disgusting. I really shouldn't admit to it."

"You really shouldn't. I'm so jealous I could kill you."

"What are you jealous of?" Olivia, who has been following Monroe like a lovesick puppy, appears in the kitchen, pretending to be cool, but Gabby knows she's desperate to become friends with the older girl.

"Your mom thinks I can eat whatever I want and stay thin, so I was just telling her I have to juice to get into shape for shoots. You have an amazing figure; you don't have to worry about it," she says to Olivia, making her blush.

"Ladies? As wonderful as this lovefest is, I need help. Here." Gabby hands each of them two plates with giant slices of cake. "Hand these out then come back for more."

She continues cutting, as Josephine comes in to put the kettle on for more tea.

"This is such a lovely party," Josephine says. "I still can't get over everything that's happened in your life; that everyone's here together. And my God! That Monroe! I can't stand being in the same room as her, but she's so adorable you can't find it in your heart to hate her."

Gabby laughs. "She does seem like a lovely girl. She and Matt look perfect together."

Josephine peers at her. "Doesn't it feel just a little bit weird? That the father of your child is here with his girlfriend, and your husband?"

Gabby pauses in her cutting of the cake to think about it. It should feel weird. It should, by rights, be awkward, uncomfortable, but somehow, aided by the fact that everyone in this family has been open to change, willing to work with circumstances that are unusual, it doesn't feel wrong.

It feels absolutely right.

As a young girl, with a mother who surrounded herself by people, Gabby shut herself away, feeling as if she didn't have a family of her own, or at least, a family who noticed her.

Here she is, as an adult, with not only a family of her own, but with the type of family that surrounded her as a child, the type of family she never knew she wanted, but the type of family she has spent her life looking for.

They are family through choice, hard work, acceptance, and love. They are family because they have found each other, in the unlikeliest of circumstances, and have chosen to stay together, even when it would have been so much easier to walk the other way.

Matt didn't think he wanted children until he was much older, settled down. He and Gabby were a moment in time, a short obsessive spurt for both of them that was never destined to be anything more than it was, shouldn't, in fact, have even been what it was. When Gabby became pregnant, by rights Elliott was supposed to have left her, and Matt was supposed to want nothing to do with the baby.

Gabby was supposed to be a single mother, struggling to raise her children on her own, working all the hours God sends to provide for them all.

Instead, here she is, slicing up a Carvel ice-cream cake, listening to shouts of laughter from the living room, knowing that in her house, right now, are all the people she loves most in the world.

Elliott, who comes in the kitchen to grab another bottle of Scotch, kisses his wife as he passes, tenderly rubbing her back, as if no explosions had happened to dent their happiness, as if, in fact, they were newlyweds, which is how he so often feels, now that he, *they*, have been given a second chance.

Olivia, who at eighteen is a young woman, getting ready to go off to college, and beautiful, naturally beautiful, in a way Gabby never was.

She will go to college, provided, Gabby thinks wryly, she isn't derailed by a potential modeling career. Oh God, please let that not happen. Gabby has had to handle too much in the past two years but *that* might actually derail her. She smiles.

Matt appears, holding Henry up for Gabby to plant a kiss on his cheek. How could she ever have contemplated a life without Henry? No matter how her life was going to turn out, Henry would never have been a mistake. She fell in love with her daughters the moment they were born, but the love she has for Henry, a mother's love for a son, is unlike anything she has ever known. It is all-consuming, and to think she might have missed out on this is inconceivable.

Claire and Tim are in the other room. It is a slow journey back for Gabby. Things are not the same with her and Claire, may never be exactly the same, but they are trying. The four of them have had dinner together once or twice, and those evenings go a long way toward healing the rift. More than anything, Gabby has perhaps learned not to rely on her friends in the way she once did, and that saddens her. In the old days when she had problems, she would turn to Claire. Nowadays, she turns to her mother.

Her mother, who was always so busy sorting out the problems of the world that she never had time for her own daughter, is now the one person Gabby trusts to advise her, listen to her problems, offer a shoulder to cry on if need be.

Gabby carries the last of her plates herself, one for her mother, one for herself. She sits on the sofa next to Natasha and leans her head briefly on her mother's shoulder as her mother smiles and strokes her hair.

It feels natural now, to allow herself to be held in her mother's arms, to have her hair stroked, to be kissed. She wonders if her mother has changed, has softened in her old age, but suspects that it is Gabby herself who has changed. The fiery resistance she used as her armor when she was young has gone. Life is too hard to get through alone, and it was her mother who stepped up when everyone else was gone.

Alanna squeezes up on her other side, the three of them watching Elliott getting glasses out for a toast, Olivia and Monroe chatting as Matt sits cross-legged on the floor, Henry zipping around him in circles, huge smiles on both their faces.

Natasha turned out to be a good mother after all. Gabby watches her son, her elder daughter, as her younger daughter entwines her fingers with her own. I hope, she thinks, watching all the hope and possibility in Henry's smile, I hope I turn out to be a good mother for my children. I hope I can give them everything they need. I hope I can raise them to make good choices, to be good people, to go into the world treating others with kindness and respect.

I hope our year of insanity—for this is how she and Elliott have come to refer to their separation, in terms thinly veiled with humor—I hope our year of insanity hasn't damaged them, or destroyed their hope in the power of a strong relationship.

She looks up then, aware that she is being stared at, and Elliott, standing by the fireplace, gazes at her, his eyes filled with love. He just smiles, and she knows it's all going to be fine.

Somehow, what they least expected—what they least *wanted*—has brought them full circle. A little family. *Her* little family.